Oh God, was he really going to perish in the ocean—just when his career was taking off?

The outcrop when they reached it was ridged like the barnacled hump of a beached whale. Navo felt a shudder against his Reeboks as fountains of foam shot high from crevices along the bar. Melanie stood up ahead, laughing in a rainbow of salted air. When he made his way to her, she grabbed his wrist. He shook his head, truly overwhelmed by the sight of her in the halo of sun and water, her sleek swimsuit blended to her bronze skin.

At this moment the foundation under his right foot collapsed. He lost her hand and attempted a leap to firmer ground. Like jumping over a runner while completing a double play. Next he was in mid-air, wondering how best to avoid jutting fossil and rock. Also thinking *sharks* as he entered the water ass first.

Next came the shocking cold, the deep ultrasound, the building panic as he held his breath. He crawled toward light, finally seeing the surface there above him; breaking it with such fury he felt the force strip away his trunks, that worthless sewed-in jock. He searched water-spackled reflections, not able to locate the strand. Nor could he resist the pull of the solar system.

Lord. He was being dragged—naked—out to the open sea.

His life is about to change...

A utility player for the San Francisco Giants, Navo LeJeune finds himself in the unlikely position of challenging Joe DiMaggio's hallowed hitting streak. And then he meets Melanie...

Her life is about to change.

A prominent art dealer has picked her for international fame and Melanie Blake's days as a barefoot bar artist in Oakland are numbered. And then she meets Navo...

The history of baseball may be about to change...

The world holds its breath as Navo hits his way closer to DiMaggio's record. Will he make it? Or will his dark family secrets destroy his success even as they threaten his life?

Go beyond the batter's box into a world of betrayal, strife, family pride, and a love affair as surprising as the streak itself.

KUDOS for *Streak Hitter*

Streak Hitter by Larry Hill fascinated me from the very first page. It's the kind of book to read on a rainy afternoon with soft music and hot tea. It's a book about life, about what happens when life doesn't go the way you would like it to, and you have to figure out how to survive. In Streak Hitter, Hill has captured the essence of sacrificing for a dream, and the consequences of letting that dream push you in directions you aren't sure you want to go. And it asks—a question we would all do well to answer for ourselves: just how far can you go in pursuit of your dreams and still look yourself in the eye? – *Taylor, Reviewer*

Streak Hitter by Larry Hill is an excellent effort by a debut author. The story combines an in-depth knowledge of baseball, and what it takes to play in the majors, with a complicated, yet surprisingly tender love story of an ordinary and quite realistic couple—a misfit ballplayer and a divorcee with a fourteen-year-old son. It's also a touching story of family dynamics and how they influence our lives. The story focuses mainly on the hero, Navo LeJeune, a pinch-hitter for the San Francisco Giants, who bounces between playing in the majors and getting bumped down to the minors when he isn't needed...Streak Hitter is touching, intriguing, riveting, and realistic. Hill did his homework and it shows in the strength of the plot. – *Regan, Reviewer*

A gripping and passionate story of a man and a woman who find each other while on intersecting paths toward great fame. – *Brandi Hitt, KTLA 5 News*

ACKNOWLEDGMENTS

Many thanks to Lauri Wellington for her keen eye, and to my wife Bonnie Hill for her mentoring and inspiration. To Mark Arax, Steve Yarbrough, and Bill McEwen for their support. To early readers, Pixie Bean and Regina Ashley, for their encouragement. To Hazel Dixon-Cooper and Christopher Allan Poe for their input. And to Rex Hudler, one of the best utility players to ever grace the game, for his knowledge.

STREAK HITTER

By

Larry Hill

A BLACK OPAL BOOKS PUBLICATION

GENRE: DRAMA/ROMANTIC ELEMENTS

PRINT ISBN: 978-1-937329-26-6

First publication: DECEMBER 2011

Published by Black Opal Books **http://www.blackopalbooks.com**

DEDICATION

For Darren

CHAPTER 1

Navo LeJeune showered, gathered his gear, and left AT&T Park without saying goodbye to a soul. At least this time he'd been allotted seventy-two hours to complete his journey. But having a couple of nights free didn't mean freedom. Not when they'd cut out his fucking heart again. The San Francisco Giants had notified him that he was being sent down to the club's Triple-A team, about a four-hour drive away. Players called this trip, "Taking the Bart to Fresno." It wasn't his maiden voyage.

Soon, his aging Pontiac Grand Prix joined the line of traffic on the Bay Bridge's gloomy lower ramp, with Alcatraz hunkering like a ghost station out in the bay. Listening to the post-game wrap on the radio, Navo drove through the Treasure Island Tunnel, reflections spinning off the car's black hood like beaded blood.

When he found an East Bay nightclub he'd heard evil things about, he wheeled the Pontiac into the outer reaches of the loaded parking lot. Feeling numb, but not numb enough, he got out of his car and made sure it was locked. Even in retreat his bats and baseball gloves had to be secured. Then he put his best misdemeanor smile on his face and strode toward the nightclub's entrance.

He had no problem being waved in. Not necessarily because he'd been recognized as a Giants player. More likely the door dude had figured his tailored silk suit put him a step ahead of the milling night crawlers. Or perhaps, his black eyes appeared too menacing to mess with.

He caught a Goose and tonic at the bar downstairs, then shouldered past dancers moving to a deejay's reggaeton beat. Took stairs to a mezzanine, where it seemed the crazies had risen to the top. Up here an excited mob circled a young woman sketching at an aluminum easel, her show card reading "MELANIE." Nothing more. Navo edged his way in for a closer look.

"Marvelous," a gnome-like man wearing a pink turtleneck shouted. He sounded like a shill. "Live art to music. Isn't that a novel approach?"

Navo agreed. The artist's ass bopped under a khaki smock, her bare feet shuffling. Her profile, beneath a backward cap, appeared a tad older than he'd first judged. She worked in frantic gestures, lines trailing her chalk's bold strokes until they formed solid shapes. Fascinated, he studied her composition until she stepped back as if to give the piece her own evaluation. To him the result seemed a mess of human-like forms tangled in sex, or combat—he wasn't sure. In all it had taken her about ten minutes, just long enough to oil her smooth, tan forehead. She waved a spray can in front of her sketch, removed it from the easel, rolled it up and slipped it into a mailing tube. Immediately, she swapped it for a patron's outstretched cash offer. Then she returned to work, readying another effort.

Navo drained his drink. "She has guts," he said to an obvious cross dresser breathing hard next to him. "She ever take a break, talk to anybody?"

When he got no answer, he maneuvered to where he might intercept her should she give it a rest. In a matter of minutes, she finished the piece she was working on, stepped back, and did her bit with the spray and roll. After making a quick sale to a business suit, she put the money away in the breast pocket of her smock. When she turned to leave her spot, Navo managed to block her path. For a moment they stood eye to eye. Then the crowd bumped them along toward the bar.

He touched her elbow with one finger. "Over here."

She drew her arm away and wiped her hands on some tissue she carried. "Over where?"

"There."

"That's my table."

"Unbelievable."

"What's unbelievable?"

"That I picked the right spot."

The way she'd dropped her head, and placed a hand on the back of her neck, it was hard for him to see the grin, but it was there at the corner of her mouth. Tired, but it was there.

಄಄಄

A bartender handed Navo two beers. He passed one to Melanie and they sat across a small table far from her easel.

"A quick break," she told him. "Can't lose my momentum."

"Mo is a must."

She removed her cap, freeing short, damp hair almost as dark as his. Her eyes picked up every reflection in the crowded space. While she momentarily looked away, he searched for what made up such a fine face, beyond her great eyes. Bone structure, he thought, and of course her skin tone. In a tiny head trip he compared her coloring to that of Rudy Cruzamonte, Giants second baseman, a man of such mixed origins his true ethnicity remained unknown.

He took a sip of beer. "I'm en route to Fresno, but I got some time to kill."

"Fresno I know." She said it like it conjured up bad memories.

He remembered the town too—like a preacher remembers he'd left his wallet in a Highway 99 motel room.

"Navo LeJeune," he said, offering "Navo" again with his hand.

"Heard you the first time." Like it was an everyday name. Her hand was cold from the beer bottle. "I'm Melanie."

"Yeah," he said. "Got that off your poster."

"What do you do? Other than drive to and fro late at night?"

"Play baseball."

She dropped her eyes to his waistline, and he knew he'd just had a physical exam, nothing lewd, shit, maybe an artist's appraisal. "How long have you been doing this?"

"Fifteenth year in the game." Truth, nothing, but the truth. "In the majors off and on for half of that."

"Where?"

"Tonight I played in San Francisco."

"Tomorrow it's Fresno?"

"Actually I'm free for a couple of days."

"Sounds like you're going the wrong way."

"Well, I hope to be coming back up," he said, underscoring a sudden promise to himself. He'd give odds she knew little of baseball and those who played it, but she nodded as if giving his claim consideration.

"Well, maybe you will."

"You say that like you care." Not liking the way she'd frowned, he added, "I mean you said it with some feeling. Maybe nothing special, but enough we might talk some more."

"I have to get back to work. And you look like that drive ahead of you has got you trying way too hard."

He almost mentioned the seventy-two hours again, picturing the two of them laughing easy about this allotment of time, like it was to be shared. No, she'd given no signs of being *easy*. He thought of telling her he'd watch her perform again, purchase her next sketch. No, he decided again. She didn't sketch in bars just to be watched. And he'd have no idea what to offer for a completed piece.

In an effort to keep her at the table, he fell into small talk. "You live around here?"

"I'm sharing a studio in Berkeley with a friend. I have an apartment for my son and me." Her shoulders slumped as if she'd surrendered more that she'd wanted to. Her eyes challenged his, not so soft now.

He refused to look away. "You're right about me trying too hard. This is about as hard as I know how."

She shook her head ever so slowly. Not in a stone cold negative way, more like there was a degree of tenderness in the gesture she couldn't hide. "I have to go now."

He reached for her hand, grabbed it. "I don't know if I've ever held the hand of an artist before." Using a bar napkin he risked blotting a bead of sweat coursing the mark near her temple toward a scar that ran just above her left brow.

"One way or another," he whispered, smelling the natural scent of her hair and skin. "I'm going to make my way back to the Giants."

She tipped up her beer, drank, then pulled the bottle free of her plump lips. "You do and I've got an art show in June at the Yerba Buena Center that I'll sell you." A quick smile teased her face, lit up her eyes. "Actually, it's not mine. I'm just having a show there." She hesitated. "Well, I'm part of a group show, so don't expect too much if you happen to drop in."

She stood and spun, filtering through a row of pesky admirers. He imagined x-raying her starched smock, putting the fantasy in context to her paradise eyes, expressive hands, those bare ankles and feet—swift on the dark floor as she scurried away from him.

CHAPTER 2

Navo drove to the Valley that night, still thinking about her. Melanie. From Pago Pago, he'd decided, laughing at himself as he pictured her in a sarong, a white flower in her hair. Then, a real life picture of her came to him. The one he was left with as she shuffled in front of her easel like a boxer, her entire body in concert with what she was desperately trying to create. He conjured up a series of images, his mind's eye putting her at the table with him again. There, he might have told her something more of himself, about how he and his brother moved to this place from Louisiana. Nothing about why they'd moved. Nothing that might turn off that buzz he felt they'd shared.

Dawn tinted the road ahead of him. Northeast of Fresno, the foothills appeared like folded blankets, darker than the backlit Sierra Nevada Range. As if by rote, he slowed the Pontiac and found the drive leading to the weathered, whiteboard house he'd loved so much upon arriving here years before. Two wild boys and their pretty, widowed mother.

The place hadn't changed much since he'd made this drive last winter. Not true of the twenty acres surrounding it. What was once a gentle sweep of vineyard had been flattened. In the breaking light he made out a pyramid of trellis wires, twisted roots, stumps, stakes, and clusters of fruit torn from the fields.

"Hundred years of grapes," his grandfather always said. Now it looked as if it had disappeared in a matter of days.

"Cost of farming has soared beyond the price of raisins," his mother had told him during a conversation in April. "I'm considering sending the Lopez family on their way and dumping the place to the highest bidder."

He recalled the beauty of her face, fixed to appear dynastic.

"Meanwhile, here's the key," she'd added. "For the next time the Giants send you down."

Navo drove past the rust-bleeding tool shed, next to the rancorous hulk of a marooned tractor. After parking, he made for the house through the dry, silky soil. A final glance from the porch showed him the concrete irrigation valves that designated the absent rows like gravestones were still there. But gone was the sweet breeze of fruit and damp soil. In its place, the rising reek of rot.

The key worked, and as the door opened, he reached to his right and raised the window shade. Everything looked in place. Tables, stands, and chairs—all hardwood, except for the stuffed La-Z Boy he'd bought for Mr. Lopez a few years ago. The TV, he noticed, had been upgraded. A few steps took him to the kitchen where scents—Mexican, Armenian, and Cajun—still lingered in the air. He hit the wall switch and started up a fan outside the window, the blades' current warm, but dank with the smell of straw filters.

Back in the foyer he ascended the staircase, his trailing shadow moving along the black metal flue that traveled upward from the familiar wood-burning stove. On the landing, he paused to look down.

"Behold," he said aloud, as if someone, yeah, maybe the artist lady, was standing at his side. And below them a vision of his mother appeared. Gloria LeJeune—daughter of the county's most notorious bookie, Aram "Papa Boo" Paboolian—dancing, drifting, ethereal, and soundless except for the bracelets clinking along her Scheherazade-posed arms. Exotically draped, then naked as her beginning here. Hair and eyes black and cold as the iron stove, moving as she did years ago, daring comparison to the rest of the world.

"What do you think?" he asked the artist lady.

"I'd like to paint her."

"Thought you would," he said, feeling like a damn fool, for Melanie wasn't really here. And down there, of course, his mother wasn't either.

Weary from the drive, he turned into the bedroom he'd once shared with his older brother Clipper. The room was empty of mementos. All that remained were the iron-framed beds with their bare mattresses and the two pine dressers. He stripped, found hangers in the empty closet for his suit, dusted the mattress cover with his T-shirt and stretched out on Clipper's old bed near the window.

ese

When he heard the familiar booming voice from below, he knew that he'd not slept long enough to feel the sun on his belly. Not long enough to escape, even out here where he thought all was forgotten. Blood pulsed in his temples, that constant counterpoint to his and his brother's life rhythms.

Midday sun streamed through the open doorway and windows. Navo's second look at the living room confirmed that Clipper had converted their mother's former quarters into his secret go-to pad. No fear in Clipper as to using

Mom's old bed. Or crashing in the room where the evicted Mr. and Mrs. Lopez had slept for years after working and caring for the vineyard.

Evidence of Clipper seeped through the half open doorway, his aftershave mixed with perfumed scents meeting Navo's nostrils as he faced him now in the kitchen. In just his boxer shorts, Navo backed up to rest his butt against the table, where he had a good view of Clipper's Porsche, framed by the window above the sink. He decided to strike first; making sure Clip noticed how long he'd glanced back across the living room.

"Been bunking out here?" he asked

"You call Mom yet?" Clipper stepped back in that way he had of showing off his ruined right knee, an act subtle, but calculated. Then that inner power he could gather animal quick showed in his wide smile, so much a copy of their father's con man's grin. He fetched two beers from the fridge, twisted off their caps and handed one to him.

Navo raised his bottle. "How are Clair and Heather?" Wife. Daughter, he thought, careful to get their order right.

"Clair's into yoga," Clipper said. "Heather's into abstinence."

"Abstinence? What is she, fifteen?"

"Government-funded program. Guy comes around to all the high schools. Bibles the kids up. Gets them to wear a silver ring signifying they've pledged to remain virgins."

"Jesus Christ."

"Yeah," Clipper said. "Upon His name my daughter's probably into blow jobs and taking it up the ass." Again Clip did his pirouette, looking at the same time vulnerable and majestic. "Now tell me what you're doing here when the San Francisco Giants are playing in about fifteen minutes?"

"I got sent down."

"On waivers?"

"Not yet."

"Plenty of clubs would jump at you." Clipper adjusted his sunglasses, the familiar smolder in his eyes not quite blacked out. "Christ, Navo, you still have your speed."

"Some of it."

"Who'd they call up?"

"Not sure. Maybe someone is coming off the injured reserve." He looked out again at the Porsche. "Where did you come in from?"

"Airport."

"Vegas?"

"Yeah."

He watched his brother drink, wondering when he'd last slept. "Rough trip?"

"Business." He winked. "Working with the tribes on a new casino."

Navo let that go by. Where would another Indian casino fit in these parts? And was Clipper's company in Vegas still involved in that? Likely the son of a bitch got a piece of the government bailout money. Somebody had to help the gaming corporations.

He waved in the direction of Fresno's downtown. "How's your casino here doing? You get rid of all the local competition yet?"

"Yeah, Club Aces is the only show in town."

"Grandpa Boo would be proud." Or turn over in his grave at how much illegal gambling was now lawful. And how the juice was divided up. The old boy would have much to say about that. Navo decided to ask him what was new at the brew pub he'd personally invested in. "How's Dingers doing?"

"I'm thinking of closing the joint."

Two years now with Clip bragging on how great everything was going. Navo pictured the brewing tanks in their glass chambers, the way it looked like a futuristic engine room when you walked in the door. He remembered opening night, how they'd sung and played some Cajun blues, Clip on squeeze box, him on mouth harp. Anger flared up. Navo couldn't put a lid on it. "What the fuck happened?"

"I'm working on things," Clipper had found his hard voice. "Trying to stay ahead of this fucked economy." He finished his beer, placed a firm hand on Navo's shoulder and pushed him toward the stairs. "Get dressed."

"Where we going?"

"The ballpark," Clipper said. "Grizzlies won't be coming in 'til tomorrow night or Monday morning."

Navo relaxed and let his brother's hands push the small of his back. "Christ, Clip, I'm dead tired and hungry. Besides, how will we get in?"

"I'll get us in, bud." On the landing Clipper shoved him hard enough that he had to catch his balance. "And I can still throw batting practice one-legged, yeah."

"Shit, I can hit anything thrown seventy-five miles an hour, yeah."

"Well, I'm going to show you how to hit it where nobody will get it." Clipper was huffing now, his great chest heaving. "We'll get that swing of yours filtered out 'til it's pure as an old Storyville whore's heart, yeah, yeah, yeah."

❧❧❧

On a night in late May, after his hitting and fielding contributed to a Fresno Grizzlies victory, Navo answered a call from the San Francisco Giants bench coach, R. L. Bushmill.

"You're coming back up, LeJeune."

Navo pictured the ancient coach still in the Giants clubhouse, Crown and Seven in a plastic cup, face sun-scorched and twisted from the night's loss.

"Am I coming back to play or sit?" He was fed up ping-ponging from major to minor, when really he'd crawl over broken anthrax vials to play one more inning up there.

"We just pulled Cruzamonte out of the Whirlpool. That give you a hint?"

"Kidney stones again?"

"This time in his dick."

"Ouch."

"You find it funny?"

"Oh, God, no."

"Day game tomorrow."

"I'll take off tonight."

He thought of the artist lady he'd met the night he'd shipped out. How her eyes had lost their light some when she'd said she knew this town. He could've jumped all over that. Or not. The time he'd lived in this tough, wicked Central Valley town wasn't a subject he brought up in casual conversations. He grinned while he packed his gear bag. If the artist lady had lived here in the last ten to fifteen years, she would've reacted to his name. Or not. Who knew anymore?

His brother had watched him play tonight. They'd made plans to meet at Dingers. Should he contact Clip, tell him about being called up? How about his mother? He'd only seen her a couple times this trip.

"No to both," he said aloud. As was his "Navo LeJeune style," he stayed clear of any goodbyes as he departed Chukchansi Park, his Grand Prix cruising out of Fresno's old downtown. Vacated buildings looked on, hunch-shouldered with shame, as he made his get-away.

The night he returned to the big team's twenty-five man roster, Navo was inserted into the line-up to replace the disabled third baseman, Angel Cruzamonte. In a game against the Atlanta Braves, he singled the winning run home in the ninth inning to save his team from being swept in the three game series.

A female beat-writer he didn't recognize caught up with him after the game. "Did you know you have a hitting streak going for yourself?"

That caught him off guard. "Say what?"

"Going back to before they sent you down. Three games in which you pinch hit safely, and those times you went in on double switches and got a hit." She lifted a strand of rust red hair from her right eyebrow with an automatic pencil and flipped a page in her slim notebook. Canting her head, she exaggerated a sympathetic pout. "And the two starts you had against the Rockies where you went one-for-five in each."

Voices rowdy with victory, mix of music, heavy with threats and warnings, smells of flesh, and muscle being tended to with unimaginable amounts of care, all competed with the conversation.

Navo stepped away from his locker. At least the redhead had waited until he'd finished dressing. "So what's the number?"

"I've got you on a streak of ten."

"Forty-six more and I catch DiMaggio." Major League bullshit. Yeah, he took a step toward her, knowing his unshaven face probably looked haggard. "Tell me when you're ready to celebrate."

CHAPTER 3

On pre-game mornings, Navo walked from his apartment on Montgomery over to the Yerba Buena Center, remembering Melanie's restlessness, the way her energy made her hands dance in front of her. The images she'd conveyed with her chalks, free as a kid's, but intense, too, in the manner in which she moved—like taking part in a ritual. He'd liked that, her reverence. When he found that an exhibit was opening at the Center for outstanding women painters, Melanie Blake among them, he thought of what he might say if he were to meet her again. Something like, "You draw these sexy pictures from memory?"

Now, while in front of one of her huge, sensuous paintings, he realized any such opening remark would sound lame. The scope and passion evident in her work had him frozen in awe.

"Hey."

He turned as Melanie had tapped his shoulder and felt his knees go weak. "Hey back at ya."

"I've been watching you since you came in," she said, her breath coming fast. "You went right to my work."

"I could tell." Jesus, that touch of fear, like he was going to fall short, fail to understand something so big only a fool would miss it. "Can you stay with me a minute, make sure I see everything?"

She looked at him, as if measuring his motives. "Sure."

He wavered. "I have no right—"

"Bullshit." She moved close enough that her shoulder rested against his bicep. "I thought at first when I saw you that you could be an artist yourself, maybe a poet." She bumped her hip against his thigh. "Letting your hair grow out, eh?"

He nodded, not mentioning that he hadn't seen a barber since the red-headed reporter informed him about his hitting streak.

Melanie began guiding him from painting to painting, not only hers, but some of the others. Occasionally she stopped to accept praises, once managing to sneak him a wink when a handsome, young man openly gushed over her work.

Navo filed away her mischievous expression along with the others he wanted to remember. There. Another look had taken hold of her features, and he spotted that scar above her eye as it glistened through a dark wisp of hair.

A squad of observers he assumed were artists corralled her. Navo backed off to listen to their hushed voices. "The smell of paint on canvas," said one shadowy figure, looking at Navo as if he might be wearing a wire. "It is pure joy to witness true drawing ability for a change."

"You got that right," Navo agreed.

Melanie took him aside. "Those are other artists who shy away from conceptual art. And all this time you thought I was *avant garde.*"

He grinned until his face hurt. "Not true. I was pretty sure you weren't French."

Suddenly, she drifted away. Not far, but he felt deserted. There she was talking with a man. Her face and mannerisms had changed again. It was her eyes, he thought, not just the color, but something deeper. That dip in his belly hit him again. The man was an older guy, but impressive looking as hell. And so cool in the intense way he'd greeted her. Well, what did he expect? Look at her. So different than the bar artist he'd been keeping in his head since May.

He wondered how he might describe her to someone, and it came to him that he couldn't hold onto a picture of her for himself. The man held her elbows now, his fine features so close to hers they could be plotting a quick escape. No. The man and Melanie began to part, their eyes locked for a moment before each turned away. Then she brushed one of those strands of lustrous hair from her forehead and came back to Navo. He'd bet—in this strange lighting, so targeted on the paintings, so aglow on her simple white gown—she'd never appeared more intriguing, more a mystery.

"Seen enough, Mr. LeJeune?"

∽∾∽

Navo followed Melanie outside. She raised a slim arm and pointed out a bar up on the corner of Market Street.

Tossing her head, she smiled. "Walked by that place this morning. Saw a sign in the window saying they featured chili. My kind of place."

Could be, he thought. So might be the Top of the Mark, the way her white dress fit against her tan skin, the white flower in her dark hair. The fluid way she moved next to him in the warm wind of evening.

They went to the one on Market where, on tipsy barstools they shot tequila, chased it with beer, bit into lime wedges, and her sea island eyes began to soften. She ordered chili, broke soda crackers into it, ate it like a truck driver. He started to order another round when she stopped him with a finger touch.

"I'm going to have to get back," she said.

"Can we sit a minute, get to know one another?"

"That enough for you?"

He looked away from her, at the patrons—blue collar to corporate to city layabout. No one seemed to recognize him, and just last night he'd contributed three hits to a Giants victory.

"I'm actually kind of amazed," he admitted, "that you'd give me any time at all." He could still feel the museum's demand for reverence, the atmosphere of total devotion to what it held. Like how a Major League ballpark's interior could take your breath away at first sight.

She caught the bartender's eye. "Order of chili to go, please."

They finished their beers. She paid for the chili, and they walked out onto the pavement.

"I'm at the Argent." She pointed at the hotel. "My son Joe is waiting in our room for me, soon as I make one more appearance in the gallery." Lights from the street worked on her face. "My son from a marriage that crashed."

He placed his hand in the sway of her spine as they crossed Third Street. "I was married for an inning or two myself."

She turned sharply to face him.

"It was a mistake is what I meant," he said, regretting his flippancy. "We both knew it wasn't working after my first long road trip."

"No children?"

"No," he said as they reached the hotel. "Joe like baseball?"

"He's a surfer but yeah, he likes baseball."

"How about you?"

"Like baseball might interest me—" she said, tilting her face, teeth white as the exotic flower in her hair, "—for an inning or two."

She asked for his cell phone, took it and punched in a number. "Joe," she said looking straight into Navo's eyes. "I'm sending a guy named Navo LeJeune up with some damn good chili for you." Still watching him, she smiled. "Keep him occupied 'til I get there."

❧❧❧

From his chair Navo could see the little park behind the Center. He watched the diminished figures below. What looked to be the man Melanie had been talking with strolled by below, as if he'd left the gallery to scout out something and was returning. Or was that him over there? Seemed the tall man in the pale olive suit had been cloned into a fucking team, all of them gliding along in the darkening day six stories below.

The kid had put the chili away for later. "I hear you're from Fresno."

Navo slumped in his chair. "I moved to Fresno when I was about your age."

"That's where my dad is."

The kid was in-between boy and man, long limbs not fully muscled, facial features untouched by life, eyes so clear and earnest Navo had to stifle a groan as he leaned forward. "Is that right?"

"My mom divorced him."

He'd call Clipper, have him poke around. What kind of man could keep Melanie for at least ten years? "Well, things happen."

"I think, the saying is, 'shit happens.'" Joe said in the deep half of his voice

"Think you might be right."

Joe raked his fingers through a tangle of hair that was either sun-streaked or haphazardly dyed. "You have any brothers or sisters?"

"An older brother, Clipper."

"Clipper?"

"After Joe DiMaggio, the Yankee Clipper."

The kid had his mom's skin, the smoothness and a hint of the color. Same almond-shaped eyes, only less bewildering. He was dressed casually, T-shirt half tucked into calf length pants, some kind of beads and a medallion dangling free as he reached down to rub a bare foot. He looked up. "I have two of your baseball cards."

"Which ones?" Christ. A dozen years. Five different Major League clubs.

"Giants and a rookie card with the Red Sox."

"One from my year in Japan is the one you ought to look for."

"Your Giants card says you're a switch hitter."

"Like Pete Rose."

Joe displayed a toothy, delinquent smile. "Minus a few hundred hits."

Navo couldn't resist dead panning him. "Thought you're a surfer, not much interested in baseball."

"Dad used to buy me cards."

He took a stab at a conclusion. "Not my Giants card."

The kid clamped off his smile. "No. I called my dad to get the info from him."

Leaning back, Navo noticed lights in the nearby buildings, amber now in the growing dark. "Either way it shows me that your mom told you about me."

"Maybe."

"No maybes about it."

Joe opened his phone, checked something and covered it with his hand.

Navo stood. "You want to make a call I can go out in the hall and wait."

Obviously frustrated, Joe tossed the phone on one of the beds. "Nah." He opened the bag from the corner bar. "Excuse me." Like his mother, he broke crackers into the plastic container of chili. "When I first saw your cards, I thought they were Nomar Garciapara's."

"Thanks."

"His hooked nose." Joe slurped his chili, nibbled a cracker. "Not his record."

"Gotcha." Jesus, Navo thought. The kid's cut was deeper than he'd figured him for.

A moment later Melanie opened the door. Navo, at the sight of her, remembered a rule his mother had told him while he was still in high school. "Measure a woman on how she enters a room. If she takes your breath away, plan on having your heart broken."

"Hey," she said. Then to Joe, "You just getting to your chili?"

Navo shelved his mother's rule. "I was thinking. Maybe I could take you both out to dinner."

She smiled a *No* at him. He was sure of this before she said it aloud. Barely hearing what followed, he moved around the beds and found himself searching for words. "Best I get going."

"An opportunity has come up," she said. "A chance to further my career. One that I can't pass up."

He looked at Joe, and was surprised to see him raise a brow behind her back. "Does this mean, Mom, you'll be bringing me something else to eat later on?"

Her pivot was swift in addressing her son. "I won't be late."

Joe spoke again, his words flat. "Mister Gustine again, right?" Then with childish inflection. "Sugar Daddy?"

Melanie cradled her chin in her palm, eyes clamped, long, dark lashes quivering.

Navo started for the door. She followed him out into the corridor. He faced her. "Sugar Daddy, where did he get that?"

Eyes wide open now, teeth barred, her ferociousness cracked the stale air. "If you need to ask that, stay the fuck away from me."

He began to walk backwards, more to give her space than to show her an attitude. Over the pounding of his heart, he said, "I'm easy to get word to. Start with San Francisco Giants." But he doubted she'd heard him. The door to her room had already begun to cut off their view of one another.

CHAPTER 4

God, it had to be three in the morning. Melanie leaned her shoulder against the bark of an ancient avocado tree and peered past her nightshirt at her bare feet. What a picture. I'm an Alphonse Mucha poster, she thought, one of his pale, fair-skinned nymphs turned dark. Right here in the middle of Walker Gustine's rambling Beverly Hills estate. Why was she in such a state of despair? It wasn't her style. The San Francisco exhibit's opening had been better received than she'd hoped for. Walker certainly seemed pleased. Yet she felt lost.

She watched him walk toward her, reflections in the swimming pool's surface illuminating his tall, lean shape.

"Over here, Walker."

She'd known him since winter, and still she felt they were strangers. Or they were wired together in a shared energy circle. He appeared young, old. Sharp sighted, blind. She wanted him—no, she didn't. She had to get out of this. She had to stay to keep painting. She had to paint to stay alive, or quit painting and start dying.

"Over here," she repeated.

"Are you coming back to bed?" He scratched his salt-and-pepper chest hairs, tugged at the waistband of his sweatpants. "Can I get you anything?"

She rubbed her instep over an exposed root at the base of the tree. "A joint would hit the spot."

"I could do that."

She didn't tell him she'd reached back for her request. Back to the beginning of Neil, before Joe, when they'd smoke, drink cheap wine, sing songs of love with monkey-faced grins on their faces.

Walker cupped a palm over her shoulder and escorted her across a lawn that felt cool and damp between her toes. She heard crickets, the far-off bark of a guard dog. Across the pool, shadows of palms and bird of paradise plants swayed against the stucco walls of the guest cottage. She folded her forearms over her chilled nipples and thought of Joe staying with Neil this weekend. How Neil must be grilling him. God, she'd found no way to prepare Joe with any factual story as to how she might keep providing a secure environment for a fourteen-year-old boy.

"This way, Melanie." Walker stepped onto the red brick pathway that led to the pool. "Want to jump in?"

When she'd seen the pool in daylight it looked like a picture from an old movie magazine. A swim normally would tempt her, but she shook her head. "No."

He led her into the back of the main house, through a kitchen styled more for a hacienda than a city home. She followed him deep into the occult dimness of a hallway she'd never been shown. Walker treaded lightly, no doubt thinking about the caretakers she'd seen earlier on this side of the house. He stopped and keyed a code on a wall panel. She half expected a siren blast as heavy doors opened.

He ushered her into a space the size of a ballroom. "This is what I've wanted you to see."

The virulence of art, she thought, while taking the space in. Its potent visual clout buzzed of something unnamable. Certainly alive with history, pieces of his past, of his father's once famous gallery in Santa Monica, of his uncle's in Manhattan. He'd told her about them, gone from the Avenues, but alive in his eyes as he spoke.

"Here," he said. "You are part of this now."

Paintings she recognized covered the walls, modern masterpieces from the New York School's heyday. A massive Henry Moore sculpture reclined in the center of the room's lacquered parquet flooring. She ran her hand over its bronze nudity. Antithesis to flesh, yet the sculpture had the feel of life.

A painting that covered much of the wall ahead halted her. She felt the air go out of her lungs. "God, I've seen this in books."

"Yes."

"Jackson Pollack," she whispered into the closeness of Walker's night smell, his distinctive cologne. The scent from her also. And the rich, musky odor emanating from a hundred years of enamel drips, dashes, and swirls of Pollock's vigor still living on the surface of his huge horizontal canvas. Alive for all time, forever and ever.

Walker's voice broke softly against her ear. "I can pick 'em, can't I, Melanie?"

She shuddered. The vast expanse of the room, a museum actually, overwhelmed her.

"I'm cold." She felt his arms encircle her upper body. "Help me, Walker, I feel so lost."

❧❧❧

Melanie, dizzy from the immensity of the house, thought Walker must have taken her into a library.

They sat side by side on a Mexican bench, the wood warm on her bottom. Bookshelves swirled about her, and the sensation of zooming through a tunnel struck her. God, she was on her surfboard, and it was slicing under the curve of a perfect pipeline of radiant book jackets.

"Is that what you did, Walker," she asked. "Pick me?"

He shifted to face her. "No doubt about it." Then he stood, and his will, or that damned power he could gather seemed to stop the room's spinning. "And you signed up for the chance."

"Shit, Walker, I haven't got enough paintings to satisfy myself, let alone you."

"In your mind, you'll never have sufficient paintings. That's the way it should be."

"And I've got no studio." She hadn't told him yet about Jake losing his lease on the loft in Berkeley. How the two of them had spent the last day getting drunk, drawing each other nude until they ran out of anything to mark on, including the walls. "And if you care about who you pick, why didn't you leave me in the Bay Area?"

"Melanie, you asked me to take you someplace while Joe visited your ex-husband." He pressed his glasses up with his finger. "This isn't a kidnap."

"I didn't ask to be brought here."

"A four-hour drive, including lunch."

"Well, I can't keep this up."

"Keep what up?"

"Being rootless."

He took a step back and swung his palm through the air. "You want to leave? I'll call you a limo, book a flight to San Francisco for you. I'll get you back to your studio quicker than you can blink."

"Jake and I lost the studio."

"I have a question about him."

"Relax," she said. "He's gay."

An easy smile crossed his face. "Good. I mean good for Jake."

Spines of books came into focus. All the great names. Big, fully illustrated art books she'd rarely splurged on during her marriage and certainly not since. She took a deep breath. The thought of giving him a rundown on her problems made her feel dreadful. If she'd been groveling, she'd grovel no more.

"I've got to land somewhere, Walker. I can't take this." A dislodged book behind her head tumbled over her shoulder into her lap.

Walker laughed. "Picasso."

The oversize book with Picasso's signature running across its cover seemed metaphoric. She actually huffed as she got to her feet, gripping the book like she would a slab of iron. "Motherfucker."

Walker laughed. "Me or Pablo?"

One step and she watched the volume fall on his bare feet. For a man of such remarkable control, his wail sounded fierce. She watched him hobble over to the bench. Going after him, she almost tripped.

"Tell me why you picked me." The question roared in her brain. "Why, Walker?"

He rubbed the top of one foot, then the other. "Give me a damned minute." After his breathing smoothed out, he raised a finger. "One, I know exactly what I'm doing."

The walls stopped expanding and receding. She knelt and cradled his feet in her palms, reminding herself how amazed she'd been when he'd asked to represent her a few weeks ago. She wasn't aware such intermediaries still existed.

Now his finger moved side to side. "One, you have the kind of deep, all-seeing talent I'd given up on finding. I really thought such veracious work was lost to my world. Christ, Melanie, I figured I'd run out of time."

She fought back a sob. "That's two," she said, looking up. "You already covered number one."

"Now everything has paid off," he said. "And you can chalk that up as reason number three."

She didn't give a damn about the tears. At least the room had come to a rocking stop. "What did you say?"

He stood above her. "I sold eleven of your paintings an hour ago. Got the message after you'd snuck outside."

"No."

"Midnight, Eastern."

She rose from the floor. Never would he announce such news if it weren't totally true. She was going to pass out. Her heart had failed. Or burst. She was dying. Or being born. She felt his hands grab hers. She'd begun to scream. God, she couldn't stop screaming, every blast lengthened by her son's name. "Joseph!"

Recovery was possible, she thought. Survivors sometime get rescued. Lost wasn't quite lost forever. She broke free of him. With both hands balanced away from her pathetic nightwear, one of Joe's old beach T-shirts, she perched on top of Picasso's brushed signature.

"How much money did we make, partner?"

"Not enough that you can quit." His face, still chiseled for his age, softened. "Your painting, that is. Doesn't apply to anything else."

And that's the way brief lovers can split, she thought. By becoming longtime partners.

CHAPTER 5

During spring training, Coach R. L. Bushmill had taken Navo aside and ordered him to watch over Cyrus Porterhouse, one of the rookies on the pitching staff. "You're both from Louisiana," Bushman had reasoned. "You're the veteran, LeJeune. Porterhouse is the rookie. See if you can watch over the kid, kind of mesh with him."

Yeah, mesh with a two hundred-seventy-pound mix of Haitian and Canal Street black. "I left Louisiana when I was thirteen," Navo said, meaning it aint like he deserved stewardship over everybody from the state.

"You're Cajun."

"And Armenian."

"I'm impressed," Bushmill said. "Links to such tenacious stock can only work to your advantage."

It was almost a threat: Take care of Porterhouse or you're off the twenty-five man roster. Like who needed a thirty-five-in-August utility player?

"I'm not a logical candidate," Navo protested.

Bushmill had agreed. "You're the absolute opposite of what a helpful teammate should act like. This will give you the opportunity to learn, to get better at helping others. You have been around a long time, Navo. Be a teacher. You might stick in the league longer."

"I won't wipe his ass," Navo insisted.

"Goes without saying."

"His unload time from mound to plate is late, but it's not my job to tell him."

"That would be Coach Littlejohn's job, him being our pitching instructor."

"He needs to throw his two-seamer more, and change the grip in his glove so he doesn't advertise it."

"That would be up to Temple or Vitucci, whoever's behind the plate."

"If he's called to lay down a bunt, he's got to lay off pitches above the bat when he puts it out there. Fucker's popped up twice, doubling me off first and it aint April yet."

"See what I'm talking about?" Bushmill slugged his shoulder. "You've been around, absorbed some intelligence about the game."

"Long enough to know some things can't be taught." Damned if he was going to agree with Bushmill so easily.

❧❧❧

On July ninth, the Sunday before the All-Star Game break, Coach Bushmill called Navo early in the morning, and ordered him to collect Cyrus Porterhouse on his five-block walk to the ballpark. Navo found the rookie pacing in front of the ParAgon condos, gasping into an empty McDonald's bag.

"Anxiety?" Navo presumed.

"Hyperventilatin' like a motherfucker."

"We got a game in three hours, Cyrus."

"I'm suffering disturbin' visions again, LeJeune."

Navo glanced halfway up the multi-storied building. "Who's up there?"

No answer, just Cyrus's convex eyes, gothic, the paper bag's logo pulsing in life-death syncopation at his mouth.

"Wait here." Navo dashed into the building and took the elevator to Porterhouse's suite. The door was locked, but he used the key card he'd been in possession of since Coach Bushmill demanded he mentor the younger player.

In the master bedroom, he discovered Maxine the suit lady, her nudity as stark white as the king-sized bed sheets. There was the rattler tattoo between her ass dimples, tousled blond hair, pout on her neon lips as they puffed to a rhythm similar to Porterhouse's bag-breathing three stories below.

Sensing him, she rolled onto her back, sat up and tugged a pillow against her saline-pooched breasts. He thought, *Picture of Blonde Driving Golf Cart*, at every celebrity golf tournament he'd ever played in. On the night table, an ashtray held joints burned to their lipstick. Glasses sat in wet circles. An open carton of Trojan Magnums. Whiff of a party, over and done.

"Navo?" Maxine batted eyebrows drawn to appear forever astonished. "Where's Cyrus?"

"Downstairs, pumping up a McDonald's bag."

"I delivered his Hong Kong suits last night," she said. "He gave me a fashion show." As if to prove this, she pointed to garments folded over chairs, her spray of catalogs and fabric samples.

Navo stepped over the mess to a sliding door that opened to a balcony. He adjusted its blinds to view MoMo's on the corner below, the restaurant's patio empty this early. The sky, he knew, would soon open over the bay. Over the city's slopes, heights and plunging avenues. He flinched as a gull shot past the glass, wings driving hard toward the ballpark. Then he turned to watch Maxine swing her showgirl legs onto the carpet.

"Listen, Maxine, the kid could fail a test on your second-hand smoke." He looked away as she tended to herself. "Christ, he's scheduled to start today."

"I'm sorry." Pretty-golf-cart-girl, to his surprise, began to sob. "I was trying my best to help. He went on and on all night about apparitions, you know how he gets on them phantoms and ghosts, shit like that."

"Anxiety."

"Lot of stuff about you."

"High anxiety."

"Awful things."

He refused to take the bait. "I got to get downstairs, see he doesn't bolt." He bent at the waist in order to meet her eyes. "Meanwhile, pack up your wares and get back to your business wagon."

"Speaking of business, the fog cutter you ordered has been confirmed."

"My private eye trench coat?" He dropped half his anger, picturing a Kowloon tailor working on the garment from a photo of Humphrey Bogart. "When's it coming in?"

"Soon, I hope." The suit lady giggled under her breath. "According to Cyrus's ghosts, you might not be around to pay me the balance."

❧❧❧

Nearing noon the following day, Navo and Cyrus enjoyed the first day of the All-Star break at the rookie's favorite sidewalk café on Market Street. Cyrus seemed unperturbed that he wasn't a managerial All Star pick. Like he was a rookie, and there'd be other days. Navo ordered his favorite vegetarian pasta and shared his sourdough bread with sidewalk birds. Cyrus worked on a plate of grits, sausage and eggs. Yesterday's game had been good to both of them.

Porterhouse raised a loaded fork. "This Andouille tastes like Momma's."

Navo paused. The right-hander's mother, he remembered, was a victim of Katrina, the hurricane always shadowing his words about her.

"Or your daddy's, I'd bet," he said, thinking of how Cyrus had told him about his father dying long before his mother. That he'd met a fate dark and unmentionable, much like his own father had.

Cyrus ate until he finished his plate. "How about your daddy, LeJeune? Did you not say he was a chef in the Quarter?"

"I was just a kid. Mostly I remember his working roadside barbecues, anywhere rowdy Cajuns would pay him to burn meat."

"Did you not tell me he was a musician?"

"What Cajun isn't?"

"I'm not sure you qualify as one."

"The big booty shit you listen to has ruined your chances to be the judge of that." Behind dark glasses, Navo followed the gait of two young women passing by.

"Big booty's all right so long as it's blues." Cyrus wiped his mouth, pushed his bulk clear of the table. "Did you not get a hit yesterday?"

"Did I not get the double that drove in the winning run for you before they had to come and get your ass off the mound in the eighth?"

"What number that put your streak at now?"

"Oh, I don't do that sort of a thing—keep track of my streak." *Thirty-three, his streak was at thirty-three.* "Besides, I told you, that's how you get jinxed, saying the number out loud."

"Just thought if you did know the number, you might want to get it off your chest."

Navo placed a tip under his plate and hauled himself out of a plastic chair. "Look it up in that Old Testament you carry in your hip pocket," he said, "or is that your deck oft tarot cards you been sitting on?"

❧❧❧

Walking Market Street, he marveled at Cyrus's recuperative powers. The big rookie's stride was almost a trot, his dark face set like a prizefighter's doing roadwork. They passed a hamburger joint wedged between a storefront, where mannequins posed in elegant gowns, and a gutted building with Bon Ami-swirled windows.

Navo asked. "Need to pick up a bag for your breathing?"

"Disturbin' visions, they gone now."

"Conveniently," Navo muttered, as they turned onto Third Street. "Seems you see blood only after midnight." Jaywalking, they left behind the Yerba Buena Center. He shared a thought about Melanie with the sight of sun blasting the Moscone Center's turquoise glass. On this side of the street, Navo admired a ray of light illuminating the Museum of Modern Art's atrium.

Cyrus's two-toned mesh tops shot out, cracked the pavement. The air shook with morning-time riffs and rapping. Sidewalk people emerged into their paths. Some called to Cyrus. Navo heard his name in the buzz.

"You ever notice how everybody in this city is from somewhere else?" Cyrus asked as he walked.

"Not everybody."

"Name one."

"Joe DiMaggio," Navo said. "And don't count him out 'cause he's dead."

Peeps and honks of traffic. Smell of the bay on the wind. Daylight brightening with the promise of four days off.

"How you going to spend the break, Cy?"

Cyrus's cheeks resembled ripe plums above his gap-toothed grin. "With Simone," drawing the name out like it contained secret powers, "Banker lady over to the old-timey Wells Fargo Building." He slowed his pace and wind-milled his right arm. "How about you?"

"Artist lady I mentioned."

"The one had those paintings at the gallery last month?"

"That would be the one."

"I thought you said you couldn't get close to her."

Navo grinned. "That don't mean I backed off the idea."

CHAPTER 6

A way from the Avila pier, Melanie swam parallel to the horizon beyond the surfers. Here in the sea, in this force field the old watermen spoke of in their poems, she welcomed what she considered the eternal face of the world. Her entire body became an artful instrument as she slipped soundlessly beyond the first cresting of the waves. Time meant nothing out here, yet she sensed the point coming where the rapture soon would surrender to the abyss one did not challenge. The memory of once going too far invaded her mind and up went the mental barricades. She began to swim toward land.

She chose to bodysurf a wave into shore, the sun warm on her hair. Wading the rest of the way in, she watched her shadow in the shallows as the tide raced back to sea. On the beach, well beyond the tide strip, she slipped her arms into a hooded beach robe. With Houdini-like precision, she escaped from her modified wet suit and tossed the black skin onto the sand.

"You're quite a strong swimmer."

A young man stood directly behind her in that blind spot she'd miss unless he'd made a sound. And he hadn't. Probably got a quick peek of her bottom while he stood there in a casual pose. Lime-colored slacks, bare chest scalloped by a strand of odd shells, face shadowed by a wide-brimmed bush hat.

She smiled at his confident stance. "I give you a nine."

"Say what?"

"Style points." He was no kid, though he appeared in the low sun to be formed from newborn clay. "You get that lid off of Greg Norman?"

"No, he was before my time." His voice sounded mellow, in harmony with the rustle of the gentle breezes. "Up on the pier I picked you out easily. Nobody goes out there that far."

His countenance exposed a cast handed down from a sea tribe. Aware that her own face, fresh from her swim, must contain a similar visage, she asked. "Do I know you?"

"I'm Keyes Haythorne."

Oh, sure. "The New Zealand champion."

"When I was young."

"Listen to you." He couldn't be much past his twenties. "Kiwi lost his wings?" She noted his *Ta Moko* when he turned his shoulder, a warrior's sunburst on his left trap muscle. For a moment she almost told him about her living for a time in New Zealand. Instead, she said, "My son is a surfer."

"Word is that Joe Blake will someday be a champion."

"And where is your information coming from?"

"From Walker Gustine."

Couldn't be. Not Walker. He'd inform her first, before discussing a word of her personal life to anybody. She cinched the sash on her robe. "Bullshit."

He jammed his hands deep in his pockets, rocked back on his bare feet. "I hear a Great White bit a woman in half last summer," he said, ignoring her oath. "Right out where you were swimming."

"Sharks scare you?"

"They scare Mr. Gustine."

The shark attack had occurred two summers ago when she'd been teaching at Cuesta College. She'd swum in tandem with the victim many times, but not on that tragic morning. She gathered her gear, stepped toward Haythorne, and lifted her chin nearly level with his. "I'm a private person. I can only chit-chat so long."

More holiday people had moseyed down from the concrete promenade, their legs wobbling in the soft sand. Obviously, she and the warrior were being ogled.

He looked in their direction, then back at her with a smile, as if they were set apart by certain knowledge. "No time to talk art?"

"I don't talk art. I commit it."

He removed his hands from his pockets, long fingers rising to block his hat over a shiny blast of black curls. "Guess a visit to your new studio is out of the question then."

The way he was sticking to her, she'd had enough. "What would be your motive?"

"I'm a painter."

"Along with your surfing enterprise?"

"Not much of that left." His eyes, as he paused to regard the sea, changed her estimate as to his age. His voice chugged, "Look, Ms. Blake, Mr. Gustine hired me to help his crew fix up the mesa house and studio long before you got here."

She stopped him right there. "What about now?"

"He wants me to keep an eye on Joe." He trailed her as she walked toward Avila's rejuvenated main drag. "And to help you out if you need anything."

Anger lengthened her stride, clipped her words. "And you get what in trade?"

"A place to stay. A place to work."

She swore silently. God, it looked like Walker thought he needn't consult her about much. At her pickup, she squared herself in front of Haythorne. "What happened to your empire?"

"I fucked it all away."

"You clean?"

"Yes."

"Not even alcohol?"

"A beer at sundown." His grin was rugged. "Sometimes about six of 'em."

"Still surf?"

He looked again at the ocean. "Not much. I've lost that too."

She opened the door to her pickup. "I'll get in touch with you after I talk with Gustine. Meanwhile, you come anywhere near my kid with any shit, I'll kill you."

Best she left it like that, she thought. Now that she and Walker were even, this meant he had some explaining to do.

CHAPTER 7

On Wednesday, Navo drove past Pismo Beach, up beyond Black Lake golf course where years ago he'd take a break from college in San Luis Obispo to play a few holes. Melanie had invited him to visit over the All-Star break.

"I'm in a new place," she'd told him on the phone. "New place in many ways."

The home with its adjoining studio sat atop a mesa, the entire layout guarded by trees, except the side offering a peek of the ocean. Impressive, he thought, parking the Pontiac on a coffee-colored brick drive, smell of eucalyptus, faint sigh of the surf far below.

She greeted him in paint-streaked coveralls. After surprising him with a mouth-to-mouth kiss, she shoved him away as if to study him before allowing his entry. All eyes and hot-wired energy, she swept a hand toward a line of undulating dunes that rippled downward at the sea.

"Where Hollywood filmed *Ben Hur*," she said.

"Who's Ben Hur?"

"First version back in the silent days. Not the one with Charlton Heston."

"Who's Charlton Heston?"

She gave him a look that sliced right through him. "Do come in. This should be fun."

He followed her through a great room, open kitchen on right, tiled hallway straight ahead. Sparsely furnished, the visible spaces contained a sort of controlled clutter. A smell of newness suggested much of the place had recently been refurbished.

On the only wall without viewing glass, a large painting heated his groin. On his left, a man-like metal sculpture frowned as if it had read his trashy mind. The chalk-white adobe and warm-toned hardwood all hummed a softer tune that worked to calm him.

At the end of the hallway, she opened a door. "Guest room," she informed him, tough voice, as if she'd led him to his cell.

But the room excited him. It opened to a garden patio. Beyond it more glass enclosed what he figured to be her studio. Jesus, more big paintings. Male nudes brazenly mocking him.

"Wow." He raised his hands, let them drop. "I'm impressed."

She licked her lips. Her face glistened in the sun. "Paid for with my own money." She laughed out loud. "Well, some of it I'll take care of later with my dealer."

"Dealer?"

"Like you signing with an agent."

"I've signed with a few agents," he said. "They all ended up fucking me." Her glare trimmed him. "Though I'm sure art dealers wouldn't think of doing such things."

She uncrossed her arms. "Did you bring your bathing suit, or were you so overjoyed about coming you forgot it?"

"I brought it."

The room swarmed with golden needles of light. The aroma from her and the flowers outside mushed his senses like a narcotic. He resisted the impulse to flop on the queen-sized bed's chromatic spread. Wall graphics teased his eyes. From somewhere music drifted, vague, classical.

"Joe's outside," she said. "I'll get him, and we'll hit the beach."

"Okay."

"Just okay?" Wicked smile. "You look uncomfortable."

Just when he'd begun to mellow. "A little."

"Because you came here thinking you'd find an aging chick who'd never caught a break?"

"Aging?"

"And instead you found she had?"

"Aging?"

"Soothe the struggling artist, get her in the sack?"

"You're getting closer."

"Well, hang in there," she said, not smiling one bit. "Maybe you'll get lucky."

❧❧❧

At Montana De Oro Beach, Navo followed as Melanie picked a spot far from the weekday beachgoers, a lair carved in part of a cliff face securing the cove. Her son Joe looked different here in the open than when Navo had seen him in the hotel room. Taller, more sure of himself, he spread a blanket on the sand and rummaged up rocks heavy enough to hold its corners down.

Wearing a T-shirt and ragged-edged cut-offs, he moved with youthful ease. Navo envied the teen's tan skin, a shade lighter than Melanie's, who'd pulled off her shirt and tossed it aside.

In a colorless one-piece swimsuit she began a twisting trot through ankle-deep sand toward a rock formation that stretched out to green sea. No *kiss my ass*, no *see you later*, the sight of her was thrilling.

Joe had crept to his side. "I hear you're on a streak. Congratulations."

Congratulations? "Don't mention it." He laughed. "I mean, really don't mention it."

"Bad luck?"

"Yeah."

"I got Mom to watch a game."

He met the kid's eyes, crinkled at their corners. "How did I do?"

"Good enough I guess. She answered your e-mail." That line of teeth—he'd have to grow into those. "She has no website yet, how did you get her e-mail?"

"Writer for the Chronicle." Actually it was the red-headed beat writer, Margo what's her name.

"Amazing."

Amazing? Navo dropped his Levi's, exposing white legs spanning up to swim trunks stiff from last summer's brine.

Joe gave him a quick once over, "No tats?"

"Not until I get a Worlds Series ring."

"What are those on your legs?"

"Strawberries from sliding, various bruises."

"I saw you looking for ones on my mom."

He let that go by. "How about you?"

Joe scoped the cove like an old beachcomber. "When I win a major tournament."

He liked the teen's posture and pictured him on a surfboard.

"This isn't a swim beach," Joe said. "Undertow is big time out there."

"Let's try it." Navo leaned toward the lapping surf.

"You'll need to keep your shoes on."

"How about you and your mom?"

"Our feet can take it," Joe said. "Best bring your sunscreen too."

"Shit, Joe, I play baseball under the sun."

"Looks like you been playing lots at night too."

A quick head fake and the kid slipped by him. Navo broke into a run after him. Like trying to beat out a broken bat nubber back to the mound.

∽∾∽

The outcrop when they reached it was ridged like the barnacled hump of a beached whale. Navo felt a shudder against his Reeboks as fountains of foam shot high from crevices along the bar. Melanie stood up ahead, laughing in a rainbow of salted air.

When he made his way to her, she grabbed his wrist. Joe, he noticed had disappeared to the other side of the rocky structure. He shook his head, truly overwhelmed by the sight of her in the halo of sun and water, her sleek swimsuit blended to her bronze skin.

At that moment, the foundation under his right foot collapsed. He lost her hand and attempted a leap to firmer ground. Like jumping over a runner while completing a double play. Next he was in mid-air, wondering how best to avoid jutting fossil and rock. Also thinking *sharks* as he entered the water ass first.

Next came the shocking cold, the deep ultrasound, the building panic as he held his breath. He crawled toward light, finally seeing the surface there above him; breaking it with such fury he felt the force strip away his trunks, that worthless sewed-in jock.

He searched water-spackled reflections, unable to locate the strand. Nor could he resist the pull of the solar system.

Lord. He was being dragged—naked—out to the open sea.

A swirling force struck his throwing arm. Shark. Two sharks, for there was the jarring thunk against his left side, clamping that ring of muscle above his hip. Fear choked him, and he strained to escape, propel upward. Fly into the gravity of the sun.

Then in an instant as swift as the churning frenzy about him, he understood that he wasn't flanked by sharks, but by two sea angels, their hair flowing above calm eyes, blood knowledge of sun and surf in the sureness of their limbs.

CHAPTER 8

Navo sat in a chair Joe described as half African teak, half Hollywood noir. Still embarrassed about panicking in the sea, and being rescued by Joe and Melanie, he admitted, "I'm not your ocean-type swimmer."

"What type are you?" Joe had toted a portable TV into the room and now plopped himself on a floor mat. "I mean like where do you usually swim?"

"I'm not bad in the whirlpool."

He tipped up his bottle of Corona and locked his parched lips on it. He felt dry, languorous, horny, hungry. And as content as he'd been in a long time. No game tomorrow, so he could skip the mental preparation Coach R. L. Bushmill constantly demanded.

"Where's Toby Mayfield?" Joe asked, watching the TV images of National League All Stars take the field. "Isn't he representing the Giants?"

"Mayfield only represents himself," Navo said. "Toby claims he's got a sore toe. Guess when you're the next Barry Bonds, you figure there'll be plenty more opportunities ahead of you."

"Deep." Joe sighed like an old codger. "Your analysis is real deep."

Navo let that go by. He turned to catch sight of Melanie as she moved in front of the kitchen's floor-to-ceiling window, the setting sun outlining her frame. Not the bar artist, not the gallery star, she'd changed again.

The game had no importance in the standings. Joe looked bored. Melanie hadn't glanced at the TV once. There, look at the American League's centerfielder, Ed Longville, making that leaping catch against the fence. She didn't even turn to watch the replay. If she had, she might appreciate the physicality needed to pull it off—maybe begin to understand all the instinctual and schooled choices that contributed to the act. Christ, the mystical ramifications before and after the act.

"More nuances than Shakespeare," Coach Bushmill would tell her. "Millions of games recorded in more detail for history than any of the Bard's great tragedies."

"Navo?"

The kid pointed to the screen. Navo's teammate, Lionel Thoroughgood, had entered the game to play a couple of innings at second base. The Lion, with a hamstring that could unravel at any minute. During a commercial, Navo caught Joe measuring him with a curious frown.

"Mom says you're Cajun."

"My father's side." He stretched, smiled at the kid. "*Lache pas la patate.*"

"Meaning?"

"Don't drop the potato."

"Deep."

"Real fucking deep," Navo said, "'cause it really means don't lose your gonads."

"I'm a half-breed too," Joe said. "One-fourth Polynesian, three-fourths evil white man."

Easy laughter rained on Navo's shoulders. "Soup's on, sport," Melanie announced. "*Caldo de Marisco.* A seafood stew I used to fix when I was a starving artist."

"Smells great," he said, following her crinkled black skirt, her bare legs and feet moving across Mexican tiles in a malted blur.

Back at the TV, Joe turned up the sound. "Lionel Thoroughgood," he shouted.

"Yeah?" Navo felt the stab of guilty joy.

"Hamstring," Joe muted the TV. "They're hauling him off the field."

"Oh, no," Melanie said, and Navo wondered how many times she'd sketched those longest of muscles. "What does that mean for the Giants?"

Navo shrugged. "Not sure about the team, but for me it means steady work for a while."

She teased him with a look. "Thought you were on some kind of tear."

"That's because people are getting hurt, and I've been filling in."

"Seems you're doing okay."

"Long as Cyrus Porterhouse keeps sticking pins in voodoo dolls."

"Should I know what that means?"

"Certainly not." He sniffed the heady aroma of stewed clams, shrimp, oregano, cilantro, and he felt himself pulled back to times with his father, when he'd watch him prepare seafood gumbo.

"Hungry?"

"I could suck the running gears out of a shrimp boat."

"Deep," she said.

"Real fucking deep," Joe added, pushing him toward the prepared table.

∾∾∾

The moonless night was silent but for the barely audible surf and a soft hum of wind sweeping the dunes below. They'd wandered until Melanie's dark skirt had blended with the forest of eucalyptus trees that surrounded them like a cage. All he could see clearly were her gleaming eyes and the occasional flashing of her teeth.

He filled his lungs. "Nice."

"Chumash Indians planted these trees as a blockade against Spanish pirates."

"I heard it was railroad companies, thinking they'd found replacement lumber for their redwood ties." He'd let her know he'd been in these parts a few times himself.

"And I heard smart asses often find themselves walking the woods alone."

The sluggishness he'd felt after eating and drinking had left him. In the deep lavender shadows, he felt her breath warm on his neck. Her hands slid along his biceps as they had this morning in her doorway, only slower.

"Let's stand just like this," she said, facing him.

He stood close enough that he felt her heartbeat against his belly. He pulled his polo shirt over his head. "Close is good."

"Now tell me what's so great about playing baseball."

"What's so great about painting naked people?"

She stood barefooted on top of his shoes. Her words puffed warmly into the V under his Adam's apple. "There's a moment right after I've completed a satisfying piece of work when I feel like I've solved the universe." Her hands met along the divide of his sloping back muscles. "Just me, in a stop frame amid a million years of art."

"How long before you come down?"

"The instant I face another blank canvas." She turned up her face so that her lips brushed his as she spoke. "I've never talked quite like this." She scoffed. "Or, if I have, I've forgotten it."

One quick image of the man she'd returned to see at her art exhibit came and went in his thoughts. Sugar Daddy, that old time expression from her son, and the way she'd dared him to repeat it to her that night outside her room at the Argent.

"So intimate," she said as if to herself. In a fluid movement, she hiked her top over her head, stepped out of her skirt, and dropped the garments to the forest's floor. Then she was close again. "Now tell me about baseball."

His eyesight had grown keener. "Here?"

"This is part of my home," she whispered. "Why not here?"

He stared into her eyes as he stripped clear of all clothing, including his Reeboks. Her fingers helped him, exploring behind his knees, traveling those assailable hamstrings, as he dug his toes into the leafy floor. In return, he flattened his palms against her taut thighs, and ran them across the swells of her flexed ass muscles.

"I've spent almost all my life in the game," he said, not sure of how deep he could dig into his past. "And I've never felt like I've beaten it—you know, got the best of it in any way." She'd lowered her face into his chest hair. He dipped his chin into her fragrant natural crown of hair. "Every second in every game is like no other before it. And every situation that happens on the field, no matter how unique, has to be stored in your mind."

"I do that with the images I keep in my head, almost as if I'm putting dreams away to refer to when I start a new work."

"It's a way to beat the odds."

"To beat the desperation."

He held her waist. "I'm aching."

"I can tell."

He cupped her buttocks again. "You're light as air."

"It's all in the anatomy." She placed her hands on his shoulders and wrapped her slim legs around his waist. Her soft chuckle teased his neck as she worked her bare heels into the small of his back. When he leaned back, she must have read his thought. "Don't worry," she whispered, "I can't conceive."

This statement seemed to embolden her. She made a noise in her throat that he knew he'd never forget. Not ever.

"*Ma jolie Cherie,*" he said, feeling her settle on his stiff cock. The shock of her abandonment, the near fury of her pelvis, staggered him. He widened his bare feet. "I can feel your swimming muscles," he told her, trying to dig his fingers into her flesh without leaving bruises.

"Long distance," she said, breathing evenly now. "I'm a long distance swimmer, LeJeune."

He said nothing. Suddenly everything was ultra-real, their bodies revealing pieces of light in the thick darkness. Their scent was heavy in air stirred by shore breezes. He opened his senses wide, trying to catch every current coursing through the night. Staring upward, he searched for the tops of the trees against a starless black void.

He wanted to tell her this was like being the last man on earth, with the last woman. But he didn't dare push his luck.

CHAPTER 9

Navo awoke the following morning, not moving an eyelid, to the stirring and chirping of birds high in the trees outside. Sounded like a ditty about Indians and Spanish pirates, perhaps from the dunes where movie ghosts raced chariots.

"You didn't tell me you slept nude."

He opened his eyes to see her at the end of his bed sketching. She held up her work—a foreshortened glimpse of him, enormous feet, generous genitals, arm thrown over his eyes in the background. "How did you ever let that man into your house?"

"I wonder." Melanie laid the sketch on her lap. She was nearly nude herself, a cotton robe, untied. "You think I make a habit of this?"

"Here's where I'm smart enough to say no."

She bit her lip and squinted at him, "You know, when you first saw me in that bar working on those quick pieces to music, I was so desperate I'd become reckless. I swear I almost went with you." She looked at her drawing, did something to it with her chalk he couldn't see. "I must've looked tough to you, or maybe lost, crazy. Shit. I don't know."

He pulled the light bedding up. "I kept telling myself that you weren't easy." When she didn't respond, he laughed lightly. "I knew I was on thin ice."

"Why did you try me?"

"I was amazed when I saw you." Again, she waited. "Amazed at you, the way you moved, the chalk or whatever you used."

"Pastels." She held up her drawing stick, "This is a Conte crayon."

"Thanks."

She pulled the sketch into her breasts. "For what?"

"Knowing when I said 'amazed,' that I meant more than I was just horny."

That seemed to relax her. He could tell she was amused, maybe curious as to really why he was after her.

"I have to admit," she said, "I saw more than jock when I first caught you looking at me."

Someone told him once that if a woman started talking about everything you did or said when you'd first met, she was planning to keep you awhile. "Are we connecting, here?"

"I just want you to know how low I was," she said. "I'd just lost a teaching job I thought would go on for a spell. I started painting in bars when I saw the Chronicle had featured a couple of artists who were making money at it." Her hand sketched in the air. "If they were fast." She flung her sketch book at his midsection. "And God knows I'm as fast as they come."

He watched the mirth swirl in her eyes. For a moment he thought she might say something about how she got to this new and improved life. *New place in her career.* "Come here."

"Can't," she said.

"Yeah." He'd learned last night how her rules differed in the house from under the moon and out of sight. "I have to be in Los Angeles tonight. Tomorrow is a day game."

"You told me."

"A rare day game at Dodger Stadium."

"Rare," she mocked.

"Come with me," he said, "Joe, too."

"I've got a job staring at me." She waved slender fingers at the studio's windows.

"Then let me take Joe." Anything to remain connected to her. "I'll see that he stays in my room, has a good seat at the game tomorrow."

"How'll he get back?"

"A service the team uses. I'll put him in a car right after the game."

She stood above him, sketch board as a shield to her exposed abdomen. "I'm driven by forces I can't pick out of a menu, Navo," she said. "But one thing I don't get loose with is my son."

"Trust me." Thinking back quickly, he couldn't remember using this approach with a woman—not ever.

 C/DC/D

Navo had picked Joe up in Pismo, where he'd been surfing. Now the three of them sat at the same table as last evening, in front of them orange juice, trail mix, health nut toast and a selection of Trader Joe's jams. Melanie had slipped on a sleeveless top and stepped into her overalls. Navo wore his first year Levi's and a black golf shirt. Bright sunshine covered the table. Birds sang outside in the rustling trees. Down the hall where it met the studio, a Mexican guy was visible working on what looked like a frame.

"Ernesto," she said. "He and his wife live just down the way. They are a godsend."

With the sun on her face, and wearing a housepainter's cap cocked over one eye, she could be Joe's older sister. He found himself shaking his head.

"What?"

"Nothing." *Last night*, he'd wanted to say to her, *the positions' we were able to conquer together. Those old trees—what must they be thinking about us this morning?*

She smiled as if she'd heard him and nodded at Joe. "LeJeune here wants to take you away from all this." Those graceful hands winged over the table. "For a baseball game in L.A. tomorrow."

No doubt the kid jumped a little in his seat. "When do we leave?"

Navo laughed, but still he wondered if she'd really let him go overnight.

"Who said you're going?" She made a face that mirrored Joe's and laughed, too.

"I figured you'd eventually cut me free."

What had she said about not being loose with her son? Did she know he wouldn't be home until late tomorrow night? Jesus, if she refused to allow him to go, Navo was sure he'd be doomed.

"Yeah," Joe said, "I was pretty sure after Dad let me go to Balboa for a day with Maya you'd eventually give in."

"That does it," she said. "You better start packing."

That broke Joe up. He looked at Navo. "Maya is dad's girlfriend."

"Why did I guess that?"

That seemed to embarrass the kid, surely no easy feat. Navo caught a look from Melanie that shook him. Her vulnerability. It was on her trembling upper lip, in those sun-enhanced eyes. He waited for Joe to turn into the hall.

"Please tell me you want to see me again," he said to her. "I'm dead if you don't."

"You mean your streak?"

"Fuck the streak." Christ, he'd truly forgotten he even had to play tomorrow. "I have to know."

"I'm putting my son in your hands, LeJeune." she said. "There better be a next time."

CHAPTER 10

The ballplayer and the boy sat on a level overlooking the hotel's vast dining room, round table for two, big wicker chairs roomy for their travel-weary butts. Navo peered over a railing of leafy ironwork at the early dinner crowd. "Wonder what the poor people are doing."

He'd put on his thousand-mile sport coat, almost the same tan as Joe's windbreaker. He bumped fists with the kid. "Just tell me what you want to eat," he said. "I'll see that you get it."

"Afraid I can't read a menu?"

"Certainly not."

When he'd driven Melanie's pick up to Pismo this morning, he'd looked for Joe in the water. Once he'd parked and walked onto the beach, he was able to pick him out. Jesus, the way the kid had rushed toward the sea. His gliding silhouette when he rose up on the tallest swell, carved his board to the most brilliant trim of the fastest wave. Long, wet hair flying.

"I was impressed today, seeing you surf." He remembered how carefully Joe had secured the needle-nosed board among the vehicle's elaborate rack system Melanie had installed for her paintings. "Quite a board, you got."

That damn grin. "You think I stole it?"

"Certainly not."

When Joe ordered red meat, he followed suit. The trip had gone well, the kid okay with only one quick pit stop. The steaks arrived and Joe went at his with an energy even Navo couldn't match.

"Not much beef at home?"

"Only when my dad takes me out," Joe said. "Or when Mr. Gustine takes Mom and me to dinner."

"Yeah. I think you sort of covered that."

"Her dealer." The kid chuckled while he chewed. "Art dealer," he added. "Not drug dealer."

The team charter had come in much earlier, and some players had probably spent time at the park since it was gameless today. But a few players, some with their wives, a few with their children, had chosen to make it here on their own. Joe appeared to be mildly impressed when several men, he probably thought were players, acknowledged Navo with a word or a gesture.

Joe polished off his meal. "Isn't that the big pitcher? What's his name?"

Navo spotted the rookie. "Cyrus Porterhouse. Looks like he wants to see us."

He took care of the check. Joe picked up his small duffel bag and followed him through the milling crowd.

Cyrus moved toward them with the grace of a schooner breaking a kelp bed. He could, when free of anxiety, be quite a charmer. Looked like his time with the banker lady had rejuvenated his spirits. But you could never be sure with him. Traditional rivalry against the Dodgers, especially now that the two teams shared the division lead, had intensified the atmosphere. Christ, you could smell it. Even Joe's eyes had widened.

"Joe," he said, "I'd like you to meet—"

"What up?" Cyrus bent at the waist as if greeting royalty. "This must be the artist lady's boy, Joe. Come along." He gathered them both as if he were hitching wayward cubs to his wide hips. "I got you situated."

Navo tried to find a method to match Cyrus's gallop. "Situated?"

Cyrus slowed enough for them to catch up. "We're in the Lanai Building." Did I not tell you I was getting us upgraded a notch?"

There had been a message on his cell phone, but Navo, suffering the effects of the sea and the forest, hadn't replied. Joe stood at his side, bag on his shoulder, breathing easy. Yeah, he was glowing. Cyrus pointed to a double glass doorway. "Follow me."

He'd sung the two words like a call to glory. Navo felt lifted. So this is life, he thought, remembering Melanie's skin, the smell of their night. *Better be a next time*, she'd told him.

Balmy air outside broke sweet with the smell of deep summer. In the dimming sky, the San Gabriel Range appeared soft purple. Thoughts of tomorrow's game sieved into Navo's stride for a moment as they moved inside again. The sensation zinged him once more on the elevator, and his damp palm slid off the handrail behind him.

In the hallway, they paused in front of adjoining rooms. "Night birds aint singing yet, LeJeune," Cyrus said to Navo. Then to Joe, "Buy him a drink out of that little icebox in there. See he watch a movie, get hisself simmered down some."

"Certainly not." Joe pumped the big man's hand as if they had shared a private joke. "Not before playing the Dodgers."

ↅↄↅↄↅↄ

In their room, Navo and Joe crossed to a balcony that overlooked a swimming pool, a bridged garden. Navo thought of his remark at dinner about what the poor people were doing. What a dickhead thing to say. People were dying all over the world while he played a fucking game. Did he really deserve to be in charge of Joe? Jesus, the way Melanie had listened to him last night while he struggled to put a noble spin on his life.

Joe's voice jarred him. "Cyrus Porterhouse is sure different than his baseball card."

"A man like that isn't printed in full on any type of paper." Preachy, but true.

"Speaking of which," Joe said, lifting a brow, "you ever Google yourself?"

Before he could answer, they both started laughing. Joe fooled with his cell phone, tossed it on his bed, just like in San Francisco. "I found out all about you, or at least what I could on Wikipedia. And I got some stuff from my dad." Navo waited. "Your brother is into a lot of different businesses."

"You look up my brother or me?"

"My dad said your mother is going to run for mayor."

"Not true." He opened the goodie fridge and spread a palm in front of it. "Grab anything but alcohol." He stepped back, watched the kid settle for a Perrier. "What does your dad do?"

"Structural engineer."

"That makes sense."

He too chose water, opened it and drank while he thought about his mother. No way could she get the votes for mayor, but then again, look at some the town had suffered through. He'd heard zany stories from Papa Boo about a couple of real crazies.

Joe apprised the room a third time and set his bag on the bed nearest the door.

"Take the one closer to the window," Navo told him. "Better view of the TV."

"Where's your suitcase?" Joe asked.

Navo pointed to the luggage alcove. "Already here." He walked over and kicked it lightly. "Packed for a long road trip."

"Uniforms?"

"They'll be at the ballpark."

"You got an I-Pad? Or a laptop."

"I don't travel with one, but I can hook you up."

"I saw your cell phone." Joe flopped on his bed and sighed like a old trooper. "It's not much better than mine."

"We'll have to see if Cyrus can upgrade us."

"What do you do for music?"

"On a ballclub there's more music than you can stand." He sat on his bed, waited for Joe to do the same. "We've got a mix of cultures, everybody blasting their sounds 'til it becomes one huge sonic war." He smiled. "In fact Nomar Garciapara's entrance music is 'Low Rider' by War."

"Serious?"

"Certainly not." Were they bonding?

"Why do you pronounce his name 'Newmar?'?"

"He likes to rhyme it with moo."

"Serious?" Having some fun now.

"As a bad hop into your nuts."

Joe groaned. "That can happen in the water."

"Call your mother," Navo said. "Tell her to come and get you."

☙☙☙

Sleep was bitch. Navo turned as if dodging razors. They'd watched a film, a good one about a kid on a rogue high school football team in the god-awful winter plains of Wyoming. He'd have to tell Vince Vitucci about it. The catcher was an extreme film fanatic. Visions of Melanie played in Navo's head while in the darkness he heard her DNA in Joe's slow, even breath.

A phone rang. Its faintness told him it was his cell. Joe lay his shape in a youthful sprawl, one arm thrown across the bed for balance.

The cellular voice reached him.

Clipper, his brother.

Here at the hotel.

Down at the bar.

Saying, "Get on down here, bud. I need your help with some assholes."

Joe stirred. Navo shut off his phone. "You awake?"

"Sorta."

He swung his legs, found the floor. "I won't be long."

He hit the hall running. Levis, golf shirt, Reboks laced half way.

⌇⌇

Down in the lounge, it had to be near closing time. There was Clipper in a face-off with a man cut from his same cloth, but heavier and more animated in his madness. A group of fan-type guys had encircled the contenders. Navo was drenched with rancid fear as he measured the scene. Oldest tableau in his history, he reminded himself. A LeJeune against a friend, a stranger, a brother. Then the fucking strays, sniffing a fight between the two main dogs. Meanwhile a trio of dream girls yelled from a nearby table, eve angels agitated by the promise of mayhem. Not many others about this late. Thank god, no coaches or players that he could see.

Here came that brief greeting from his brother's steel-glinting eyes as Navo stepped into the ring of men, his familiar shuffle as he gained his stance.

Navo cut himself loose from reason. He had to get craven or get killed. After the initial fist against bone, the bartender and security came running. By the time they arrived, most of the damage was done. Four dogs had fallen. A fifth staggered off. Blood had spilled. Clipper's voice claimed victory. Navo felt Clip's iron grip on his shoulder as he braced his spent body against the bar and rubbed his hands together as if he were massaging a baseball. Jesus, he pleaded soundlessly, not my hands. Please, no fingers broken, please.

Peace fell over the party.

As it always seemed to do after a melee like this, time slowed down. Navo had experienced it before. A communion had seized the embattled. A common purpose had settled the chaos. The fallen rose to join the two still standing. Woozy gladiators all, they embraced one another like tank-town prizefighters, and sang of how they'd fought with heart.

"Man oh man."

"Holy Christ."

A dream girl called out, "Where's the law when you need 'em?"

"Ah, shit, Janice, let it go."

"Yeah, it's fucking over."

"Where's Andy?" a man on his knees cried. "He's the motherfucker who started this shit."

"He left early."

Everyone laughed, even the two security men.

A tug on Navo's elbow. "Aren't you Navo LeJeune?"

"No."

"I wanna buy you a drink, man." This from a bleeding mouth, the words fuzzy as an old saloon joke.

Over there Clipper had his arm around one of the women, stomping his bad leg as if he'd pirated an ancient vessel. Navo gazed at him for a short count. Or was it the other way around?

He stopped wondering on his dash back to Joe.

CHAPTER 11

The visiting team's locker room throbbed with the beat of a celebratory reunion. Voices, harsh with stored bravado, battled the ever-thumping hip-hop, alternative, punk, and country music that seeped from various headphones. Navo managed to find his locker among the line of spaces. Yeah, there was his gray road uniform and warm-up wear sent along from San Francisco. He tossed it in his personal bag and wheeled a plush, high-backed chair deep into the stall. A tight smile softened his grim face. Cyrus must have arrived. There wailed Corey Harris's National guitar.

He sighed with the tune's harmonica riff. The Dodgers organization applied a strict players-only rule in both of their locker facilities, so he'd left Joe in Clipper's hands. Navo began to change in a hurry. The quicker he found Joe and his brother, the sooner his heart would quit slamming against his rib cage. One space to his left, Vince Vitucci's face appeared in the patterned wire divider. The catcher grimaced and banged the screen like a captured animal.

Navo banged back. "Looks like you enjoyed the break."

Vitucci smiled as if he were on death row. "You remember me telling you about the underwear model I met?"

"Victoria's Secret lady, as I recall."

"We watched movies at my place the entire break."

"Get the fuck out."

"Old *Exterminator* stuff."

"The ex-Governor?"

"This woman has a violent past," Vitucci said. "She's flinching at the heavy action."

Nearly dressed for pre-game, Navo grunted.

Vitucci huffed. "She's okay with the sex scenes."

"Yeah?"

"Grabs my dick whenever Arnold flexes."

In his haste, Navo bumped into Marvin Riggins, the centerfielder, wearing only his precious glove. "Damn, Marvin, you might let me know when you're coming by to see me."

Riggins's fist popped his glove. "Vinnie tell you about his Victoria's Secret lady?"

"Said he was just about to tell you, Marvin."

"Shit, LeJeune, nothin' about her I don't know already." He cocked his head, caught him with those brown eyes that could find a pop up in a hailstorm. "You got your eye black, brother, you better spread it under them peepers of yours."

☙☙☙

Navo checked the red numerals on the scoreboard-type clock just outside the locker room. Had he been rushing things? He stood for a time and waited for the stadium's pulse to match his.

He loved this old ballpark, the way it had been tended to through the years with such care.

"You look lost, LeJeune."

Unnerved, he turned to face sports agent Tamara Bix. "No," he said, "I know exactly where I am."

"Wow, Navo, when are you going to loosen up?"

A pair of players came out of the door, their faces wolfish at the sight of Bix. Their crassness wasn't lost on her.

"Roids," she said to their backs. "Leaves 'em with more balls than cock."

The area had begun to welcome the cast of pre-game characters. Concourse roamers, early birds with the same madness as the players, Tamara Bix included. He tried to break away from her eyes, one drilled on center, the other canted wild. A body fit to command a torture chamber in L.A. She caught hold of the door. "Someone better tell Vitucci in there about the moving-without-a-towel rule. Especially around the food. He's in there dickin' the spread."

"Christ, Bix."

She rocked to a stop in front of his escape attempt. "I'm still waiting for your name on the dotted line."

"Show me the papers."

"I'd bring 'em in right now if I could get away with it." She tossed a dishwater braid that swept her leather-clad rump. "Forgive me for asking if you were lost," she said.

"You're forgiven."

"You're one of the most *aware* men I've ever met inside the game or out," she said. "I've seen you stand out on the field, and I'd bet my bottom dollar you could tell me the type of grass, the brand of dirt—"

"Santa Anna Bermuda," he said. "Base paths and warning track are a mix of crushed red brick and mountain clay." His smile hurt his cheekbones. "Both made for speed."

"See?" Her boot heels cracked flamenco style. "You're a throwback to Pete Rose. I've been researching you, LeJeune. You hit in streaks when the galaxy is in your favor. Over ten games in a row several times. Twenty-three straight one time in the minors."

"Thirty-seven once in Japan." He placed a hand on one of her sculpted shoulders. "Thanks for jinxing me."

She gripped him under his Adam's apple and growled in his ear. "Streak. Streak. Streak. Fucking streak."

He felt his gut start to relax. "Now I won't hit again 'til September."

"It's all in the stars, LeJeune." She let him go. "Learn that and you'll have to whiff a few pitches just to break the boredom." She caught him under the chin again before he fled. "What happened to your face?"

ᘍᘓᘍᘓ

Fresh from the batting cage, Navo began to feel better. His right hand was sore, the knuckles tender, but it would be his bottom hand today against the Dodgers top right-hander, Jose Perdido.

During practice he'd continually lined the ball deep into the power alleys from the left side of the plate. He meandered past the dugout, acknowledging once the hard whammy contained in Manager Domingo Matta's stare. Jangled, he started a sprint. *Look here, Skip, see LeJeune run.*

He took time to watch outfielders, Riggins and Toby Mayfield, discuss the characteristics of the sun fields, Marvin pantomiming various ways to break for long drives that would prove difficult to pick out against the enormous stands behind the plate.

Navo intently watched the veteran Riggins. Today he'd replace the injured second baseman Lionel Thoroughgood. Tomorrow he could be out here with Marvin, inserted into the lineup for the slumping Josiah Swain. He began a sprint back to the dugout. *Look here Toby and Marvin. See LeJeune run.*

About to tunnel his way back into the visitors' clubhouse, he scanned the game level seats he'd secured for

Clipper and Joe. Astonished, he spotted the two of them yards away on the field.

Unable to hold back his anguish, Navo rushed toward them, his throat tight where Bix had strangled him. "How did you get down here?"

Clipper grinned. "Through the dugout."

Joe looked like he was comparing Navo's likeness to Clipper, right down to the nearly identical facial bruises. "What's that goo on your face?"

"For the glare."

"Gotcha."

"Relax, Navo," Clipper said. "The Old Dominican himself let us through."

Maybe, but not to prance all the way out here, Navo was sure. Then he remembered that Matta had played a part in signing Clip with the Yankees, and the Dominican had negotiated for his bonus and insurance after the accident. Long time ago.

Looked like the past had hit Clip, too. That way he had of looking through you for an instant returned. "You in for the Lion?"

"Yeah."

"His hamstring?"

"Listed day-to-day." Navo took in the way Joe had been observing them. "You did tell me you'd never been to a major league park?" When the kid shook his head, he asked him, "You call your mother?"

"I will. Don't worry."

"Well," Clipper drawled, "we better split. Just wanted to wish you luck, yeah."

They all traded handshakes there under the great sprawl of stands. The emerald field, and beyond the fences, of the tree-lined Elysium Park were magnificent, the air tinted with a fragrance Navo reckoned even a surfer needed to smell at least once.

Game time was drawing near when Coach Bushmill, moving with his chronic hitch, took Navo aside. His face looked like it had rusted over the four-day break. His uniform, though only hours off its hanger, hung on his frame. Skipper Matta, everyone knew, traded this fashion sin for Bushmill's scholarship of the game, his ability to deal with the diverse characters that made up this team.

"Listen, LeJeune."

He'd heard that *listen, LeJeune* before. He turned cold. Fuck. He hadn't looked at the posted line-up over near the bat rack.

Bushmill walked him like a doctor would steer a patient to view a bad x-ray. Navo could see his name had been scratched. "McQuarey? He's putting that kid in a game this important?"

"Skipper said you broke his trust, letting you get here on your own."

"No." Loud enough a few heads turned. "No."

"And he got wind of last night's incident."

Incident. The word came out of Bushmill's mouth like he'd suffered an incident or two in his own life.

"That was no big thing." Navo, near rage, tried logic. "I'm hot right now, Coach." He jutted his unshaved chin at home plate. "So fucking hot, I'm like one big trigger finger up there."

"And your brother and your nephew coming out on the field like that."

"What?"

"Serious breach of security."

"I had nothing to do with that."

"You had plenty to do with what happened last night in the lounge."

Navo turned his back to the players and their sizzling energy. "I came down into that bar last night, and five men were all over my brother. What was I supposed to do?"

"Just be glad no charges were filed." Bushmill's eyes darted to the Dodgers pitcher's final warm up delivery. "The way you and your brother left those poor bastards— it's a wonder you're in uniform."

"Christ, Coach."

The once gorgeous field colors blurred. His legs weakened. He couldn't hear the thousands out there in wait. He barely felt the thrush of his own blood.

"Plus," Bushmill went on, "you're going to face kangaroo court. If it weren't for Vitucci getting your luggage aboard the charter yesterday, you'd be here naked."

"I am, Coach," Navo said. "That's me standing here with my dick hanging out."

CHAPTER 12

Melanie backed away from her work. Walker had suggested she cut loose her drawing ability, see where it might take her. So far she'd been using primarily black and white on two six-by-six canvases Ernesto Murrieta had prepared for her.

Going back and forth between the two pieces like they were twin omens of doom, she'd been limiting her silent shouts to the art dealer, but now she let one go.

I'll put these paintings together, Walker, and you'll have my version of Picasso's Guernica. "Either that." she mumbled, "or we better stop sending all our beautiful bodies into war."

She pulled off her latex gloves. *These patients are beyond hope, Walker. I'll bury them later.*

After cleaning up, she located Ernesto on the patio. "Leave the plants for a minute," she told the squat, muscular Latino. "See if you can help me find the game on TV."

"What game you want?"

"Thought you said you'd heard of the guy I invited up here."

"Navo LeJeune."

"She sat in the seat Navo had used while he'd watched the All Star game. "You a Giants fan?"

"Dodgers," he said, "since Fernando Valenzuela."

"Watch it with me," she said. "Explain what the hell it's all about."

He pulled at his gray bandito mustache as he worked the monitor. "It is the top of the fifth. Much of the game is gone."

The first Giants batter flew out to shallow centerfield. "Navo said he'd be batting second."

"That don't mean every inning."

In silence they watched the next two batters strike out. She squirmed in her seat during a commercial. When the game returned, no player in orange-and-black-trimmed uniforms looked like him. "He said his number was sixty." An odd sort of dread turned her hands cold. "He's got to be somewhere." A shot of the stands covered the screen, the announcer commenting on the fifty-six thousand fans in attendance. That many people? "Joe is there somewhere."

Then the name *LeJeune* and Navo's face filled the entire screen. "God," she said.

"There's the guy." Murrieta told her.

A panning shot of the Giants' dugout captured his Paul Gauguin face. In infamy, the way the sportscaster's voice suggested, "Discipline might have LeJeune grabbing some pine."

"Oh," she said, clenching her numb hands. She said, "Oh," again, as if she'd been punched below the belt. "Ernesto, why in the hell isn't he playing?"

"He is a utility man, Melanie." Murrieta raised his palms toward the exposed beams. "You never know with such men. Sometimes yes, they are in the game. Sometimes no, they are not."

"Did you see his eyes?"

"Yes."

"Don't tell me not playing in a ball game can cause that."

She sprang from her chair, stood for a moment rubbing her hands together. Then she placed them low on her belly. "I've got to call Joe," she said. "Where in the hell did I leave my phone?"

૭৩৫৩

Joe scowled at her. "You weren't very nice to him."

"I thanked him for bringing you home safe and sound."

In truth it had been Navo's brother who'd seemed to be in a hurry. She'd barely got a proper look at him, just his shape in the dark, much like Navo, but different, like he'd been sketched in cruder strokes out there near his SUV, everything almost black on black.

"Looked like his leg was bothering him."

"His right knee."

"What about it?"

Joe set his bag on his bed. "He told me he was in an accident. Happened after he'd signed with the Yankees."

Clipper. What sort of man would carry a name like that? Something about him had spiked an uneasy feeling within her, maybe a memory about him, something dark she'd read or heard in Fresno. "Did you do a lot of talking on the way home?"

"Quite a bit."

"What does he do?"

"He's in the gaming business."

"Gaming as in gambling?"

"I guess." Joe looked at the ceiling and puffed air through a pout. "You're grinding me for something?"

"I'd pictured this experience for you differently than it turned out." She still could see Navo's haunted face on TV. "He'd looked so deeply devastated."

"Clipper?"

"Navo, for god's sake."

"You watch the game?" Joe frowned at her and raised a clinched fist. "Navo hit a dinger that won it."

"What?" After asking Ernesto to turn the game off, she'd rested on her bed. She'd run her hands down the insides of her thighs until she'd lost her chill. Then she'd cupped her knees in her palms. Stayed that way for at least two hours. "Dinger?"

"Home run."

"Home run?"

Navo hadn't mentioned that on the phone. He'd just said that his brother would be driving Joe back in a Cadillac Escalade. *Should be home around ten or eleven.* And what had she said? Something about it had better be no later than that. And she had gotten cold again.

"What's wrong, Mom?"

"I thought he wasn't going to play."

"He pinch hit in the ninth." Joe swung an imaginary bat. "Kept his streak alive."

Just last night. It wasn't very cold last night, everything red-blooded, full-tilted and moonlit. She tossed her head and dodged Joe's playful pantomime. "You know what I thought?"

Joe gave her a blank stare. "No idea."

"I thought that LeJeune had grabbed some pine."

"And what?"

She grinned. "Damned if I know."

"Meant he was on the bench, ready when needed."

She hugged her shoulders. That damned chill. "I thought he'd been in an accident, the way he looked. What do you know about that?"

"Eye black," Joe said. "Must have been the eye black he'd smeared under his eyes for the glare."

"That seems theatrical, artsy."

"There is more to the game than you might think."

It struck her that there was an immensity to what this man LeJeune was doing. Apart from her world, he existed in an enormous realm that to her was a mystery. "Don't act like you know so much, kid," she said.

CHAPTER 13

Saturday's game had gone to the Dodgers in a close contest. In for Thoroughgood at second base, Navo had scratched out a meaningless single in the loss. After evading interviews as best he could, he taxied to Newport Beach.

At 21 Ocean Front, he joined a restless Tamara Bix at a table just off the Victorian-style bar, a crimson sunset, the pier out there on shaky stilts above a muffled surf.

Bix shoved a platter of clams casino against his elbow, and he breathed the warm whiff of brine and parmesan cheese.

"Seared black and blue, hitter," she said. "Suck 'em down." She beckoned a server, ordered him a Becks and another chardonnay for herself. "Damn, LeJeune, you look evil. Give me a shot at representing you, and I'll have you in *Vanity Fair,* modeling Prada."

He shaded his eyes against her day-glo, military-cut jumpsuit. "Where's Prada?"

Eating with her fingers, Bix offered a gleeful stare. "You won't regret signing with me, LeJeune. I got all the accoutrements."

"Accoutrements?"

"Motive, means, and opportunity."

"Only three?"

"Don't give me cynical." Bix scanned the bar as if scheming a plan. "You're Cajun and what – Albanian?"

"Armenian."

"Shit, that's even better."

"Some would debate that."

She snagged a pigtail and positioned it between her breasts. "You're hard. You're hard, but it looks good on you."

An Anaheim Angel outfielder he recognized, attractive woman on his arm, pulled alongside their table. The Angel bent to lay a message in his ear. "Way you're going, LeJeune, watch it next time you piss in a jar."

Navo showed his grin. The Angel veered off. From the woman, a wiggle of black-tipped fingers.

"Gabe Albeñez," Bix said. "He's the reason I asked you out here. I wanted him to see you with me."

"You owe me a taxi fee," he said. "Round trip." He stretched his legs where no one could trip over them, the game still alive in his thighs, his hips. "Don't tell me Gabe is without an agent."

"His agent is dead."

"Really?"

"Might as well be." She chomped a shrimp and licked sauce off her lip. "So dead, I pointed out how he deserved to break his contract with the corpse."

"Is that ethical—treating the dead that way?"

A wave of her hand, then those mismatched eyes. "Hard and dark," she said. "What a combination—you put that with thirty-five straight games."

"Could end tomorrow."

"Can't end," Bix said. "It will remain forever, or change to thirty-six."

That stopped him. "That sounded kinda sweet."

She rose with the demeanor of a Black Belt. "Come on, we gotta go."

"Where?"

"Titty bar out past Lake Forrest," She snatched her purse off the floor. "Has chicks with Brazilian wax jobs. They tell me, hitter, it's like dancin' with a porpoise."

"I'm gonna pass."

"You can't." Her voice squealed in mock hysteria. "Vince Vitucci called a few minutes before you got here. He's out there trying to find Cyrus Porterhouse."

Navo felt a stab of dread. They'd juggled Cyrus's turn so he could start earlier. "Cyrus pitches tomorrow."

"Yeah," Bix said. "Vitooch says he's wandered off into the woods, and he can't seem to locate him."

ↂↃↂↃ

Navo signed papers in his lap authorizing Bix to represent him while she controlled her Jaguar's 390, supercharged engine. Soon they approached a district where scattered buildings signified the harm that haphazard zoning and neglect could cause. He spotted the joint. Pink corrugated metal, gray cinderblock, twisted neon blinking a code. Damp-roofed haze of vehicles out front.

"You better wait out here," he said.

She pulled the vehicle into a vacated space near the entrance, released her seatbelt. "Wouldn't miss this for the world."

"A caring agent wouldn't let me go in there."

She wiggled loose of her belt. "How would you know? You've never had one. The entire universe is lined up for you." She dipped her head to stare into the deep evening. "I'll tell you when your luck will crash."

When his eyes adjusted to the pulsing light, Navo lead Bix past a swarmed service bar made of glass brick and Formica. So far, no Vince or Cyrus. Beyond this action, an elevated runway poked through the smog. Three fireman poles supported its glittered roof. Up and down the poles, three women cavorted nude in a hypnotic grace. The smell of sawdust and Lysol fought in the tortured air to conceal the collective smell of heated bodies, beer breaths, sweat-dampened clothing, and nauseating aftershaves. Lights implanted in the suspended ceiling's underside beamed down in variegated colors. The music blared—big-ass hip hop, thunderous and mean.

✑✑✑

A flash of Melanie's nudity blinded Navo. The way she'd popped loose of him and hitched herself higher, so that her thighs held him in a headlock. Then, while he widened his feet even more, she'd arched downward in a twist, perfect to take him into her mouth. There in the deep, shadowed cluster of eucalyptus trees, so intimate, so private, so sacred, he doubted for a spinning moment it had really happened.

Bix yanked his arm. "There's Vitucci."

When they reached the stocky catcher, it took little time for Navo to judge him innocent of ingesting anything too nasty. Or if he had, searching for Cyrus had sobered him.

"Where's the Big'n?" Navo demanded.

"Out back," Vitucci shouted over the crowd noise. "Last I saw him."

"How far out back?"

"Out in the goddamn boondocks."

Navo dropped Bix's hand. "Both of you search inside and out front."

He grabbed Bix by a pigtail as she began to drift, and put a grip on Vitucci's throwing wrist that widened his eyes. "We do not leave without the rookie."

Away from the runway, the club's real sport displayed its true colors. Navo counted six cage-like affairs in the eerie glow where, behind bamboo bars, dancers writhed atop laps of stoned initiates. From what he could tell, Cyrus wasn't a participant.

Behind the building, the night smelled of old fires and rains. Over the sweeping form of a rise in the canyon, stars cluttered the sky. He heard secret voices, a vehicle started up about a pop-up away.

He moseyed toward an inky area, where a gentle wind stirred the trees. Ahead, an arched structure evoked a small bridge. Navo's legs throbbed from today's game. He heard the crystal shifting of slow water.

Slogging in mud over his shoe tops, he tramped forward. Stiff bracken slashed his dress slacks. Wet branches whipped against his blazer. "Cyrus!" The thought that the ditch-creek might seduce someone lost to panic, he yelled, "You out here, Cousin?"

Silence. Mystery and croak of frogs. He plodded, ankle-deep in a level of cool water. A form emerged, distinguishable by its immense outline, not ten feet away. The Big'n, black as the landscape. Blacker. Sitting as a lost king might in an age apocalyptic.

"Cyrus."

"That you, Bossa Navo?"

Cyrus sat Indian fashion in a shallow that beeped of silver slime. He raised a festooned arm and made a quick throw as if attempting to pick a runner off first. Navo heard a *clunk* on the strip joint's flat roof. Cyrus loomed, standing like a movie swamp creature.

"I got those damn runnin' blues again,"

"Let's get you out of there." Navo grabbed the rookie's thumbs. "What brought you out here?"

"Aint this like home?"

"This your Louisiana?"

Cyrus lifted a foot that issued a sucking sound. "Thought it was."

"Maybe Angola."

"Lord. My daddy did time there."

"Mine too."

"My daddy ended up getting shot dead back east."

"Mine got shot dead like Ty Cobb's father." Shit, what brought that up? "Going out the northern window of a southern woman's bedroom." Truth, sometimes it just jumped out.

"Goodness," Cyrus said. "We best head west."

"You ever wonder what kind of species runs the night looking for black water?"

"No." Cyrus stumbled then righted himself. "But when I hear Corey Harris sing 'Fish Ain't Biting,' I feel like somebody cares."

"Listen, man." Navo cupped an ear to demonstrate. "There aint no Louisiana bluesman out here," he said, "Let alone Corey Harris." He had the big man taking a step. "You ready?"

"I need me a McDonalds's bag."

"You reckon to find one sitting with the frogs?"

"Not likely."

"Then follow me," Navo said, not sure where he was going.

CHAPTER 14

Saturday, Clipper had spent most of the morning recovering from his trip to Los Angeles and trying his best to maneuver while under Clair's scrutiny, her consistent questioning.

"I fell down, for Christ's sake, delivering Navo's new girlfriend's kid. She lives up in the forest above Pismo Beach, and it was pitch black." He sighed heavily until he got what could be a sliver of compassion from Clair. "Now, how about we go down to Club Aces and watch Navo extend his streak on the big screen?"

"We all can't work our lives around Navo and his ballgames."

"Then I may as well call off the shindig tomorrow." Give her a little of his indignity to chew on.

"What's tomorrow?"

"The Giants play again in L.A. and I've invited a few of our friends to come by and watch it." Actually he'd left that open, in case Navo went hitless today.

"By our friends, do you mean your family?"

"And yours," he said. "Our daughter Heather is invited."

She'd declined his offer to go to the casino downtown but was waiting for him when he returned home later that night.

"Did you see him get his hit in the seventh inning?" he asked, before she could bitch about the time being too late to eat any kind of dinner. "A double down the line, drove in the Giants only run. Enough the big gorilla, Porterhouse, gets his win."

"Navo looked haggard."

"He's dialed."

She looked at the clothes he'd laid on the bed. "Are you going to Los Angeles?"

"Las Vegas."

"Thought we had friends coming by tomorrow night."

"Change of plans." Which was legitimate. He'd committed over the phone to meetings scheduled for early Tuesday. He left out the stopover in L.A. to catch Sunday's afternoon game and bussing with the team to San Diego on Monday to see the opener against the Padres at Petco Park.

"Great," she replied in that damn way she had of sounding sad and mad at the same time.

∽∾∽

Despite its obsessive transfigurations, Las Vegas always excited Clipper. On the down side, most bare legs in casinos belonged more to men in shorts, and the majority of women wore pastel pants and logo-emblazed tops. And kids ran everywhere. You'd think all the town's busy revamping was aimed to amuse the very young and restless, or the grayheads too old to play.

He'd arrived last night, met with the key people who'd helped him set up Carousel, a Sacramento-based company doing much of their work here.

After all, if the tribes needed assistance in building their massive gaming industries throughout Central California, where better to find the knowhow than Las Vegas?

Besides, Clipper had done some individual investing in off shore gambling enterprises, rampant now on the internet. Maybe illegal, but no one had found a standard to control it. His grandpa would laugh at that. He always believed that was how Vegas got its start.

Clipper began his listing amble toward the Mirage. He'd managed to free up a healthy sum of "marginal" cash from Carousel. His scheme to negotiate the Fresno foothill stand-off involving a new casino and its sub-contractors had begun to reap rewards. Because of his inventive factoring, the tribe had gained extra time to open, and the subs were getting paid.

His mother hadn't tried to interfere. "Papa Boo would call that playing the middle," she'd told him.

"Little juice from both ends," he'd agreed.

The interior of the Mirage Sports Book this evening could double as a Star Wars control room. Last night's hangover and this morning's haggling with tribal reps began to recede and he felt that old ache under his belt. The kaleidoscopic display of posted odds caught him like a rip tide. Damn. It could sweep away the smartest chance-takers. Last year in rooms like this, more than one hundred billion was lawfully bet on team sports alone. Clipper knew the figures and could give an educated guess as to the amount wagered on the fringe or beyond the law. Economic down-turn? He remembered Papa Boo telling him, "People do two things in hard times. They go to the movies to dream. And they gamble to have nightmares."

On the move, he beamed his best grin at Angelo Capagni, the Sports Book director. "Hey, Angie, been a spell, man."

At the line of betting windows, Capagni offered a hand, limp for such a big man. "Nice to see you, Clipper. Clair and Heather along this trip?"

"Not this trip."

"We're all pulling for your brother." Capagni flicked a hand at the action behind him. "We got him favored today."

Clipper had bet on Navo stretching his streak soon as he landed on Monday. He tipped his head toward the baseball scores. "Game's in progress," he said, "Navo just hit one into that little mezzanine in Petco's right field." He looked into Capagni's Sinatra blue eyes. "I just beat you out of seven grand." He let that sit. "Less the vigorish, of course."

Capagni offered a so-be-it flip of his palm. "How's your downtown casino in Fresno?" he asked. "You and your mother having any trouble?"

"Club Aces is holding its own," Clipper said. "And my mother is still giving 'em hell."

Deep smoker's chuckle. "No fucking Geronimos involved in that gaming parlor?"

"Not even a squaw."

It seemed like the betting line's gravity had pulled the big man away. "Nice. You're ahead and it aint dark yet," Capagni said. "Maybe you can take care of your bottom number."

He mentally figured what it would take to square his balance. "I said I'd get it paid."

The huge room was rolling now. Clipper felt better as he watched the bulky Capagni drift away. He'd have the man's dick pounded in the sand by cocktail hour.

കൈകൈ

Clipper's tossing about woke Alice Jang. "Holy cow, Clipper. Stay in one place."

She'd offered her home in the master-planned community of Summerlin, but he opted to stay here at the Mirage, high in the desert sky. The night outside the window displayed that supernatural glow he enjoyed from all the neon along the strip. If Alice got to snoring, he could throw on pants and a Tommy Bahama shirt, drop downstairs, and toss some dice.

Trying to excite himself, he lapsed into hallucinations of women he'd underscored in the past, some from illusion alone. He landed on the artsy squeeze his brother was involved with, her skin the color of a bayou mullatta. The way she'd greeted him like ice after he'd driven her kid home from the Dodger game Friday night.

The bitch standing there in coveralls, big porno painting on the wall behind her. He envisioned her at her easel asking Navo to pose.

Clipper nudged Alice Jang. "Wanna talk?"

Alice sat up alongside him. In the half-light, he noticed she'd put on weight the last couple of times he'd come over here—breasts drooping more, deep crease across her belly. She resembled that nasty-talking Korean comedienne. The one Clair caught Heather watching on HBO.

Clipper swayed over to lay his wad against her. Christ, Clair's body would put hers to shame. Except Clair's boobs were pumped. He couldn't stand the way they just sat there like discarded volleyballs.

Alice asked in a dry voice, "How'd you come out today?"

"Lost my ass." He liked being able to confess the truth to her. She'd been around, wasn't afraid of life's gambles. She'd told him once she was a target girl for an impalement artist in a Reno act ten years ago.

"A what?" he'd asked.

"I was on the wrong end of a knife-throwing gig," she'd said. "It finally worked my last nerve."

That told you a lot about Alice Jang. Also, she'd been a rhythmic gymnast.

"A what?"

"Contortionist."

That had been good for a few laughs over the years. You break it down, he was quite fond of her.

"You should get to sleep," she scolded him. "Aren't you meeting those City guys in the morning?"

"I canceled."

"Why?"

"They're pussies. All that green lumber, solar power bullshit."

"What then?"

"Going northeast."

"What's there?"

"Fifty-member tribe of Paiute Indians."

"Bring me back some mushrooms."

"They're too busy trying to lease out a half million acres up on Snow Mountain."

She sat up. "Fifty Indians own all that?"

"Sovereign land." He tossed the bed sheet aside. "Something I know a little about."

Never one to over-talk anything, Alice changed the subject. "If you bet on your brother tomorrow, bet a hundred on him for me."

"I can do that."

"Don't book it yourself."

"And bet against my brother? What's wrong with you? He made it to thirty-nine today."

"Didn't you bet on him?"

"I did."

She reached for the sheet, yanked it up to her chin. Still not a bad face. "You said you lost your ass."

"Don't mean I got shut out."

☙❧

Angled away from Alice Jang's soft snoring, Clipper watched the electric daybreak of Vegas beyond the glass. Below you could actually feel the action. The city hummed like a giant blender, handicapping factors before pouring out the morning line. A brew to start the action was the only thing that helped him forget what could have been. The game of baseball had been lost to him now for a long time. Betting took him to the game's edges and moved him among men again. An athlete in his every manner, despite his fucking knee.

He considered waking Alice. Telling her about how, after his freshman year at USC, he'd signed with the Yankees. But no, that story had lost its value long ago.

"Alice."

"What?"

"Nothing."

He stole out of bed and gimped over to the window. His mind lingered at that junction where the past overwhelmed him with woe. Where it spilled over the rim and even gambling wasn't enough.

He used to face these moments with wrath. Now he'd learned to go back to when Navo would follow his shadow as it sped across the fields, the blacktops, the damp grasses. Infields and outfields of playground ballparks. Clipper's speed had been uncatchable, even by the younger Navo, who could fly.

In private thoughts, Clipper had led his brother now for years. Through three bush league summers, where Navo choked down hot dogs, put on dirty uniforms, and played in ballparks surrounded by dusty cars and rusted pickups.

Navo was nothing then, not even a face on a bubblegum card. Winter ball, where Navo was the gringo kid, competing at shortstop with boys from Venezuela bred for the job. Muggy and spiced Japan nights. Clipper had flown across the Pacific to watch, as excited fans spilled onto the field after the game to praise Navo with words he couldn't understand.

How many years now in the Big Show? More than a decade. Mostly considered utility, not valuable enough to play every day, but too versatile to get rid of.

Clipper stood naked before the enormous pulsing sky. In slow motion, as if demonstrating to an arrested audience, he took a full cut, his phantom baseball bat sweeping the spellbound air, controlled and balanced by his every cell.

"Like that, Navo," he said. "Just like that."

CHAPTER 15

Snoring, laughter, curses, boasts of past accomplishments, promises of future glory—all this in the hollow drone, the cologne-tinted air flow. More time away from home meant time to re-invent yourself. Slumping? That's way back in history. Now, sit back and digest your dinner entree. Pick your brand of drink. Need more to stop the pain? You're on your own there, Jack. Three with the Chicago Cubs coming up on Friday. Good time baseball.

Across the aisle from Navo, outfielders Marvin Riggins and Josiah Swain, both wearing headsets, battled at a chess board while bopping to their own choices of music. Sportscasters Fred Hickman and Brian McDuff, retired veterans of all this craziness, traded barbs with Vince Vitucci until he squealed.

First baseman, Suzuki Ogata, slept next to Riggins, an open book on his face. Navo smiled. Man called Su, with only book on board, its title in Japanese graffiti. Clouds passed in a near audible pace through Navo's window as he studied the sky. Next to him, Cyrus muttered words about cabbage greens, his voice folksy.

Navo nudged him. "I've heard of collards and mustard greens, but never cabbage greens."

Lionel Thoroughgood passed by and shook his head. Navo winked, knowing the man thought anything he and Cyrus had in common should be shot and buried, especially the blues. "That includes Keb Mo," he'd made clear. "Music to shuffle, step, and fetch to." Navo watched him pick out his seat. Landing would demand seat belts soon.

Cyrus, still on his subject, said to Navo, "Never heard of jelly roll grass?"

"Not unless I smoked it by mistake."

"Then you never drove Highway 10, where the Bonnet Clair comes at you like a picture card."

"Lived close enough to it." And a couple of other hard-time spots in Louisiana as a youngster, Clipper keeping his head straight more than once. Aware suddenly of difference in his and Cyrus's ages, he added, "Smack dab in the floodway, long before Katrina."

"Then you should know cabbage greens."

"They got a tune?"

"Just some chug-chug blues."

"Thought your fingers went dead after Sunday's game?" Navo asked as Cyrus often complained of this after his starts. "Did you not tell me that?"

"What's that got to do with cabbage greens?"

"You were snapping them. Your fingers that is."

The plane hit a bump. Cyrus gave him a long look. "Tamara Bix fixed 'em."

"How'd she do that?"

"Pressed her thumb between my toes."

"No."

"I say she did."

"Then pull out your harpoon and play the damn thing."

Cyrus brought up a harmonica, silver-glinting in the dome lights. "You play it."

"Can't."

"I say you can."

Navo took the instrument, cupped it to his mouth and ran a breathy pattern across its comb. Chicago bloomed below like a million candles.

Navo felt the drag of loneliness, wishing he could juggle time and place, so Melanie would be waiting below, a moon, lapping surf and just her coming toward him, that sureness in the way she moved. A sigh escaped him, a low moan against the mouth harp, pushing and pulling at a tune his father had taught him.

"Cabbage greens," Cyrus said. He rummaged loose a pocket recorder and sang his song into it.

> *"Eat 'em for breakfast*
> *"Jelly drippin' from they head*
> *"Eat 'em in the evenin'*
> *"When they soakin' up my bed*
> *"Eat 'em round midnight*
> *"When my baby turns red*
> *"Believe by Jesus*
> *"I'll eat 'em 'til I'm dead."*

"That aint bad, Big'n." Navo wiped his mouth on the back of his hand. "Not bad at all."

With panache, Cyrus shook open a McDonald's bag he'd been sitting on. "I love to fly," he said. "It's the coming down that can bother a man."

Navo got game number forty-one on Friday. First inning. A triple. No, it would be recorded as a double, for he was thrown out at third, trying to stretch a sure two into a maybe three.

Domingo Matta thought making the third out at third base was worse than killing your parents and their dog. Navo couldn't remember much after that. Except watching the Cubs celebrating their victory in the heat squiggles. In the dugout, he sat as if stoned. Someone had mercifully placed a towel soaked in a mix of ammonia and ice water over his head. When he peeked out, he could make out Coach Bushmill blocking the team's escape to the showers. "Give it a minute, men, before you hit the AC," the old mentor said, apparently knowing how dehydrated they were.

Navo spun dizzily in the aura of a heatstroke. He smelled the threat of rain on the air and prayed for its success. Beyond the park's ivy walls and above the multi-storied old apartment buildings in right field, lightning snapped white in the grape-colored sky. The team's keystone combo of Canderas and Cruzamonte shuffled past him. Rudy Canderas clipped him lightly on the chin. "C'mon, man, we'll cut a vein tonight, bleed all over Rush Street."

Navo got to his feet and walked up the ramp between the dugout and tunnel. Figures criss-crossed beneath him. On the field, a bullet-proofed security team formed a lane to stave the fans off. Jesus, they were after *him*.

Coach Bushmill stood in his path like a singed rat on a burning ship. "That's right," he said, as if he'd read Navo's face. "How you taking all this attention?"

"You're lookin' at it."

"I've seen worse," Bushmill said. "Though I can't think where." From Wrigley Field's underbelly rose the cries of madness. "You will do a bit with Hick and Huff. They're set up in the locker room."

"I will do that."

"After?"

"They'll eat me."

"If I give you some help, might you take it?"

"I might," Navo said, slipping past him. "Tonight, I just might try anything you can come up with."

e⁙⁙

The secluded candlelit booth was perfect. Across from Navo, Bushmill added a gnawed rib to the platter of bones between them. "Man should not ask for more than this."

It was the first time Navo had seen him chew anything other than tobacco and cocktail ice. "Not 'less he's greedy." He tidied his mouth with a wet nap. Recalling their cab ride, he'd guess they were outside the South Loop, just short of Chinatown.

He basked in anonymity. The ribs had gone down easy. And now the beer slid after it. Bushmill, who'd been keeping one eye on the street entrance, suddenly scooted out of his padded seat. Navo, surprised to see a smile crack his face, stood with him. A stout black woman had entered the joint from the rear entrance and was rocking her way toward their booth. Patrons, clearly in awe of her, parted. Bushmill accepted her hug, and pecked at her face like he'd found cake crumbs.

"Lil," he said.

"You old dog," she said with a scowl on her broad face. "Why didn't you call earlier?" Big smile for Navo. "You must be Mr. LeJeune."

"Navo." Her palm felt soft, fingers strong. "Call me Navo."

"I'm Lil Alston." She knocked Bushmill into the booth with her hip and heaved her buttocks in after him. "Did you all enjoy the barbecue?"

Before Navo could answer, an old man, same flare of orange on his brown face as Ms. Alston's, cleared the table with quick hands and set up a round of fresh drinks.

Ms. Alston squirmed, found her spot, and smiled. "Thank you, Hadley." Her jacket reminded Navo of a hunting slicker that Clipper used to wear. Beneath that, a silky tangerine dress stretched across her voluminous bosom. She poured beer into a chilled pilsner and lifted it, pinkie extended. "Cheers."

Navo guessed her age at seventy. Eyes of a pool shark, scrapper's nose, soft pillowy lips. Hair much too perfect to be real under a floppy pink sailor's cap.

"Hadley burns some mean ribs." She tilted a look at Bushmill. "You remember, baby, the first place over on Wabash?"

"Near Comiskey Park."

She looked at Navo. "Brother Hadley originated this business over sixty years ago, Mr. LeJeune." She waited for him to nod. "All of us coming here on the Silver Streak, just before the war. Daddy for the stockyards, Mama for nothing but raising Hadley and me."

Bushmill sucked a tooth. "Which was plenty, I'd imagine."

She launched a merry laugh. "Red dust still on our little feet from Coahoma County, Mississippi."

Navo noticed that past the bar a trio of musicians had mounted a small stage. The place had been filling up. He could sense the crowd's anticipation as they glanced Lil Alston's way.

She gave no sign of being watched. "I heard you beat Ty Cobb's record today, Mr. LeJeune."

"Navo."

"For hitting safely in forty-one consecutive games."

Stood to reason, her knowing baseball if she'd ever hung with the Coach. "Yes."

"And you don't talk much." She began moving her way out of the booth. "Well, Navo, from what I gather, you can be mighty proud." She was up now, collecting a string of white beads that had snagged her breast. She turned a quaint smile to Bushmill who'd stood with her. "Remember this necklace, R.L.?"

"Yes, I do."

"It's a piece of fairground jewelry you gave me when you were a young man playing at Comiskey Park."

"I remember."

"Well, if you two will excuse me—"

Bushmill followed her midway into the crowd where others made a path for her to gain access to the stage. Their heads met. Navo guessed a memory or two passed between them.

When Bushmill returned to their booth, he settled with a facial grimace, like he was fighting off a hurt, or giving in to worry. "I've known Lil for some years." He finished off his drink, motioned to Mr. Hadley for another. "Thought you might enjoy hearing her sing."

"Thanks, Coach. I bet you're right."

"I met her when times were different." Bushmill squinted through people of all colors, ages, and persuasions. A spotlight flooded Lil Alston. Her fire red outfit shimmered and shot flames at the room.

Bushmill leaned across the table as applause greeted the singer. "We've gone our separate ways time and again. Two different worlds is how you'd describe us."

"I understand."

"Like you and your artist lady."

This coach—the way he absorbed so much and managed to keep his distance was a mystery. Navo lowered his head. "Just a fling," he said. "My artist lady has evidently backed off."

"Then go after her."

He looked up. "Think so? I can't get a read on it."

"Yes, and there's no book on it." Bushmill's voice laid reed thin above the trio's meandering intro, the appreciative applause. "No permanent philosophy," he said. "Each answer cancels the rest." His eyes, in the candlelight appeared, blistered with emotion. "No matter which way you fall, the trip is foredoomed."

Lil Alston's voice roughed its way through the haze like an ancient bell's tolling.

The coach leaned forward and whispered, "That's not to say that the fall aint worth the drop."

CHAPTER 16

Awakened by the weight of someone joining her in bed, Melanie was merely confused at first. Then she raised her head from the pillow, her cropped hair damp at her temples. It took a second for her to adjust to the shadowy room. The rectangle of blinds became an op-art painting, casting noir stripes across the room.

Fear swished through her body like an ocean swell. An intruder had slipped into her bed. Not Joe. A man. The smell of him brought something familiar. So did the way his bare flesh slipped against her own nudity—a *déjà vu* of sorts.

She screeched, "No."

His hands found her balance points. One hooked its way into her armpit. The other clamped her crotch. For a moment he rested behind her, spoon position. An iron hard erection rammed into the crack of her ass.

"No." One waking breath and the knowledge came to her. "No."

His cologne, the feel of his nearly hairless chest and arms. The way his hands worked on her now—gentler, like he'd gained enough control. She knew from now on his every move would be directed by his past performances.

She *knew*. But still panic rose in her blood as she arched her back, tried to push herself up from the bed with her hands, elbows, the heels of her feet. The superior physical power of the man bound her. God. She remembered how deceptively strong he was. Not a big man, his strength had often surprised her.

"Neil." Using all her strength she attempted to turn her shoulders in order to see his face, to plead into his eyes. "Please, Neil, I've got to catch my breath."

He relaxed the hand under her arm. She gasped into the crook of his elbow. Panic streaked her vision like rain on a window. *Think*, she ordered herself. Put together the day's events.

It was Saturday. Her work had zapped her. She'd crashed after painting for hours. The earth odor of her studio clung to her flesh, her hair. Thoughts whirred in her brain. Where was Joe? Was the house empty? She felt the man's muscles move to offer her a few inches of space, as if he'd risen higher, and his face appeared over her shoulder for a moment.

"Neil," she said.

"Mel."

"For God's sake Neil, let me go."

Somehow he'd managed to keep her pinned while he switched the position of his arms. A hand grabbed her throat. Another must have flung the light bed covering onto the floor.

"Let me in, Melanie."

A hand clamped her jaw and she felt her neck being jerked. She wanted to cry out, but no sound escaped her mouth. Now a hand passed over her belly, worked into the nest between her thighs, fingers rote and expert.

"Goddamn you, Mel, let me in."

She was suffocating. How was this happening? She bared her teeth, growled her son's—their son's—name into his hair.

He pushed her head back, stuck his fist in her mouth. "Goddammit, relax."

His voice sounded dark and far away. She tried to find him in the streaked and clouded room. Her room. "Get the fuck off me." God, she was passing out.

"Joe is fine, Melanie." Was that what he said, that Joe was *fine*? "Now open up for me, and I'll let you breathe."

She opened for him then froze like when she was a child, waiting out a nightmare.

"It'll be good," he said. "Remember, sweetheart? How it was always good between you and me?"

જ્જ

"When did you tell Joe you'd pick him up?" She had to string together events. Had to, in order to regain her strength. Every little bit of information brought her back to now. *Find the now,* she warned herself, *before you try to kill him.* She picked up the sheet he'd thrown from the bed and made an oversized sarong. Then she slumped against the wall. "Tell me, Neil. It's Joe I want to know about."

Neil raised his pale eyes then looked down while he answered. His face had remained flushed since the bed, since the raping, since his final yelp as he'd climaxed.

"I told him I'd call him at Keyes Haythorne's place in Shell Beach." He cleared his throat, an old stalling device he used when challenged. "Where I dropped them off."

"That was okay with him?" She knew Joe had been surfing with Haythorne. She'd even set it up after Walker had verified the young man's aspirations. But Joe had never been to his place. "I don't let him get that tight with anybody unless I okay it."

"I'm his father, remember?" He walked past her, stepped into briefs he'd stacked with his other clothes outside her room. "I gave him permission."

"Didn't he ask what you were going to do? After all, you'd said that you'd be coming for him tomorrow."

"I told him I was coming back to see you."

"Did you give him a reason?"

"Not really." He squared his shoulders, picked up his cell phone. "I should call him, let him know that I'm coming to get him."

"I'll be the one doing that." She exhaled slowly to disguise her fury. Should she attempt to dash past him, grab a kitchen knife, and cut his throat? God, she couldn't even hold a brush right now.

Neil tried a softer voice. "I told him I'd bring you back with me, that we'd all go to dinner at McClintocks."

"Eat some red meat after an afternooner with your ex?"

"My intentions were innocent."

She unwrapped her makeshift sheath and threw it onto her bed. Purposely facing him, she dressed in jeans and a long-sleeved flannel shirt. "Look at me like I'm a whore, and I'll hire a hit man the minute you leave."

"We made love," he said, as if correcting her.

"The fuck we did." Her hands began to shake. God, was she going into shock? "You sneaked into my bed like a night stalker."

"Please tell me it was a little like old times." He looked out to her studio. "Looks like you're still painting my dick on lots of your subjects."

Dressed now, he could pass for the man she'd found real passion with—what, a thousand times? No. Many times it had fallen short of any real truth. And she'd never blamed him.

She'd just finally called it quits. To her, the good old days were over. She reached for an iron chair and it skittered down the hall tiles.

"You raped me, Neil."

There. It had to be said. She watched his face wince. His hands turned to fists. He'd never hit her. But minutes ago those hands had violated her.

"Call Joe," she demanded. "Call and tell him that I'll be picking him up."

"Come on, Mel. Get real with this. You know I'd never do anything to hurt you or our son."

"I've always held that thought." *Shit, don't give him the satisfaction of seeing you break.* "Now, I haven't even got that."

He stepped toward her, impeccable in his summer slacks and sport coat. "Let's go together."

For a dizzy moment, she was puzzled as to what he meant.

He added, almost casually, "To your surfer friend's pad."

"No." She studied his reaction and took a step back. He must have called Joe this morning, maybe met with him. He *knew* she'd be alone. Probably had checked out whether Ernesto would be here.

"This surfer friend," he said, smiling easily. "Has he replaced your ballplayer?"

Surfer friend? Ballplayer? What had Joe told him? "Your time is up, Neil. The party is over." She felt her mouth twist. Was she snarling? Sobbing? "And you're not getting Joe, today or tomorrow. You can drive back alone."

She began to move toward the front door. She glanced back once to see if he was following.

He was. "We're not through talking this out, Melanie."

"We certainly are for now."

"Where does this leave me? My son is waiting for me."

"You can go back to Fresno." She swung the heavy front door open wide. "Back to your girlfriend."

"We've split."

"No shit."

"It has nothing to do with this." He frowned into the slanting sun like a younger man, a good-looking boy, the world outside the house too harsh for his sensibilities.

⌘⌘⌘

Melanie drove her pickup toward Shell Beach, her hands locked on the wheel. She checked on Neil's silver Audi, saw it pass as she exited the highway. Memories roared through her mind. Little episodes surfaced containing degrees of cruelty they both were guilty of, although nothing forewarned of the perverse way in which he'd stalked and raped her today. It was Neil. But it wasn't. He was a stranger.

Angry now, she rolled her window down and stared out at the ocean, the low sun over the bristling green water. A curl of air struck her face. *Breathe*, she commanded herself.

Should she consider telling Joe? No. Not telling him would leave her with bargaining power. Something that might hold Neil to his promises. But would that be enough? She'd never trust him again.

East of the highway, she found the metal buildings Keyes Haythorne had mentioned earlier in the week. At the end of the strip she stopped her pick up. A roll-up door to Keyes's work place ground its way up, exposing a forest of lithe and youthful legs.

She could discern Joe's, then Keyes's. More legs helped form a quartet of girls who looked to be well into their teens. Haythorne, she noticed, had gathered the girls into a huddle. Bitches—the way they shot her delinquent glances while breaking away toward a car that held surfboards on its roof.

"Later," one said.

"Ciao," said another.

Walker might have "picked" Haythorne as he had her, but she had her reservations. Right now any advice from Gustine or any other male dissolved as she stuck her head out the window. "Joe. Get in the pickup."

Joe threw his arms up in that way he had of exaggerating a point. "What's up? I thought Dad was picking me up."

"Change of plans."

She pulled her head in. Fuck. No telling what she looked like. Then the thought of calling Navo LeJeune hit her as the perfect thing to do. His face came into focus. Those Old World eyes, the way his smile could flash and fade in an instant. Yeah, she could call Navo.

But what would she say? *You look like a hit man, Navo. In fact that is what I've heard you called—The Hit Man. Well, I want you to kill someone for me.*

"The Giants won today in Chicago,"

What had Joe said? "What?" The way he slammed the door shut made her cringe. "What did you say?"

"I said the Giants beat the Cubs. It was on TV."

She waited, eyes closed.

Joe struggled with his seat belt, his eyes fiery. "Navo got a hit."

"Forty-two games now." She guided the pickup through standing water, over bumps on the inroad. It wasn't until the vehicle had smoothed out on the highway, that she sneaked a look at her son.

"Yes," she said. It was something she could hang on to. "I've been keeping count."

CHAPTER 17

They'd been able to get yesterday's game in before it rained. Navo—in for right fielder, Josiah Swain—had helped keep the game's only rally alive in the eighth inning. He'd singled in Vitucci with the go-ahead run that proved the difference in their three to two win. Cyrus, pulled in the seventh, didn't get the decision.

He laughed at Navo's comments about the inequity of pitching so heroically and getting nothing for it. "I'm like you, Bossa Navo, I don't keep my stats."

"Like why bother?" Navo agreed.

"It would be like you having to think about how many fucking games you hit in a row."

"Forty-two," Navo said. "Only reason I know was they announced it on the P.A."

"Otherwise you draw a blank."

"Not a clue."

༺༻

Sunday's game was halted after five innings because of rain. Giants led two to one. Navo knew if the weather didn't clear in the next hour, the game would be recorded in the books as it stood.

Marvin Riggins watched the Cubs grounds crew cover the infield. "Had an uncle that was struck by lightning," he said, eyes closed mournfully. "He's been funny-turned to this day."

"Played in Atlanta once," Lionel Thoroughgood said. "We went to rubber cleats, took off our belts 'cause of the buckles. Put gum on our cap buttons, and still our catcher caught a bolt on his mask."

Cyrus scanned the menacing horizon. Navo could almost hear his silent prayer for clear weather later tonight on their flight back to San Francisco.

"Go ice that arm," Domingo Matta ordered Giants' starter, Mirabal Pacal. "No matter what happens, you're not going back in." He appraised Navo in an up-down glance. "You too, LeJeune."

"I'll be ready."

Matta checked his scorecard, played as if its many scribbled remarks influenced him. "You were hit by a pitch in the first, and you hit that sacrifice fly in the fourth," he told Navo. "Way I see it, you're zero for zero."

"True."

"Well," Matta said, "it's your call." Plainly meaning: *If you come out now, your streak remains alive.* "You don't have to go back in."

"I said I'll be ready."

One last look out through the slanting rain, showed Navo that most of the fans had hunkered under umbrellas or were creeping up the aisles for drier ground. Media equipment seemed to be everywhere, draped but loaded.

"No cameras," Matta told the TV crew next to the dugout. "No interviews, no nothing 'til this game is decided. Send that word up to the media boxes." The skipper evoked his ramrod stance. "My clubhouse is off limits to anybody not wearing a Giants uniform."

෭෨෬

Each player had his own way of handling long waits like this. The veterans managed to take these situations better than the younger players. Navo admired Matta's decision to allow Cyrus to call it a day. Pitching arms were not made for rain delays.

For that matter, no anatomical component was. Ask his knees, elbows, that slight tremor in both hands now when he held them straight out.

"You okay?" Vince Vitucci had crept up on him.

Navo sat on his restless hands. "Just checking my nails."

"I've always preferred clear polish myself," Vince said, with one eyebrow raised.

Toby Mayfield and a clubhouse attendant had hooked up a game station on one of the large plasmas. Weird Al Fletcher, the Giants' closer, brushed his teeth to head-set Sonics only he could interpret. Pitcher Pacal Mirabal, undulating to a rhythm in his ear, winked as Navo passed him. *"Fijacion Oral,"* he stage whispered.

Navo raised a fist. "Viva Shakira." He too had hot flashes listening to the Columbian goddess.

Josiah Swain, pocket bible in his lap, tapped a foot to what Navo reckoned was a Toby Keith ode to freedom. Swain had been sullenly holding a Bible and moving his lips since Navo had replaced him in yesterday's lineup.

Near Swain, mid-reliever, Will Campion, waved an open copy of *Rolling Stone* under Swain's pious expression. "Nissan Z," Campion barked, holding the magazine now so Navo could appreciate the two-page layout. "That's my next ride." He dropped one hand away from the pages, made a jacking motion aimed from his groin to Swain's little bible.

Swain swatted Campion's attempt at lewdness away with zeal. His eyes moved to Navo, nailing him with an angry squint. "What you staring at, LeJeune?"

Navo had seen this look on swamp preachers who used rattlesnakes in their sermons. "Who, me?"

"Who the fuck you think I mean?"

"I'm just passing by, Josey." Was this the stress of a rain delay, or what? The fucker hadn't played an inning in two days.

Swain stood. With precision, he placed a golden silk bookmark where he'd stopped reading and slammed his book shut.

Navo, in an otherworldly funk, questioned its gilded title out loud: "American Revised Edition?"

Swain yanked loose his earplug. "Don't think for one minute, LeJeune, you're going to Wally Pipp this soldier."

This got attention down the line.

Navo looked left, right, and couldn't resist a grin. "Who's Wally Pipp?"

The nose.

Right on the Paboolian honker.

A white-hot ka-pow. Brain slamming its anterior pan. Molecules spraying out the corners of his eyes. That sickening lull of consciousness, before everything came back into view, distorted as in a bad hangover.

Don't go down. This from his LeJeune strain. You don't show hurt, son. God dammit, you don't fall.

∽∽∽

The rain stopped.

Nobody tried to interfere when he made ready himself in a fresh uniform. Neither Bushmill nor Matta raised a hand to prohibit him from trotting out to his position after the Giants went down one, two, three in the top of the sixth.

He went forward on wobbly pins, head held high, seemingly oblivious to the wads of cotton stuffed in his nostrils. Then sometime later—they told him it was in the top of the eleventh inning—in the darkened day or the lightning-filled dusk, Navo LeJeune, utility infielder/ outfielder, San Francisco Giants, sighted past those cotton-plugged nostrils, and in a slitted quadrant of one swollen eye, found a white sphere, fuzzy in its horrific speed, tiny in its comparison to all else, and he unleashed upon it an awkward swing.

Four-three speed to first, and his right toe clipped the inside corner of the first base bag, his whole being slanted now for second. Whoa. The Cubs' second baseman gave him an arms-up gesture and said in his ear as he passed, "Slow it down, LeJeune, you hit the motherfucker into the rooftop seats."

It was as if he were watching himself from the deep purple sky, his pewter gray image moving on bright-lit sienna. His jerky movie-frame steps mimicked Babe Ruth's so he wouldn't stumble, his shadow a paradigm to all who spoke of struggle, of desperation.

Of being in the grasp of wanting something so bad that the desire belittled the present glory. And his trip around the bases would be this game's final splendor. Weird Al Fletcher retired the Cubs in order in their bottom half of the frame. Navo, a solitary figure out there, watched the game's final strike as if he'd set anchor in the drenched green of Wrigley's hallowed right field.

❧❦❧

Vicodin and ice. Lime Gatorade and tequila. Navo was in the sky again—saying to Cyrus, "I never showed you Rush Street."

"Vitooch and Pacal took care of that," Cyrus said, his huge left hand holding a small ice pack he'd composed.

Navo decided not to ask why he chose to keep the chilled pack in his non-pitching paw. "Coach Bushmill took me to a barbecue joint."

"Say he did."

"His girl, Lil Alston—you should've heard her sing the old jazz standards. So sweet it made my teeth itch."

"Say she did."

Must be a Tamara Bix method of getting back the feeling in his fingers, this thing with the ice. "We should've checked out the architecture." Navo thought of Luke Kaminski the architect back in Fresno, the passion in his voice when he spoke of Sullivan's Gage Building, Adler's skyscrapers. "Frank Lloyd Wright's houses in Oak Park."

Cyrus nodded at Wright's name as if he knew of his great work. Nodding again, he placed the ice bag on the bridge of Navo's nose.

"Hold this on that beak," he said. "We'll catch all the temples and theatres next time, man." He stared out at the endless darkness. "We are going home right now."

Navo snorted into the ice mask. "I got old Josiah, didn't I, Cy?"

"You got him."

"I mean on that Wally Pipp thing."

"Say?"

"I *really* know who Wally Pipp was."

Cyrus, with that all-knowing nod. "He's the cat let a young guy named Lou Gehrig take his place for one game and never got it back."

Navo propped a pillow behind his head and leaned back. "I'm thinking about going home tomorrow."

"We're halfway there."

"I mean Fresno."

"Go there and you might end up playing Triple A ball."

Navo snorted. "Not with a forty-three game hit streak."

"I thought you don't keep track of shit like that."

CHAPTER 18

Navo watched his brother challenge the road out to The Fort Country Club, his Porsche smooth around the very bend that stole his knee, the route much improved from twenty years ago. Navo wondered what had made him hop in a cab, soon as they landed in San Francisco last night. It sure as hell wasn't to play golf in Fresno. Had the ten-day road trip torched his brain cells?

"Far as the brew pub goes," Clipper said as he drove, "I'll cut the losses, no big thing." He winked at himself in the mirror. "Mom considered it a vanity venture, and Clair called it a meat market." He'd impersonated their expressions with a skill Navo couldn't help but grin at.

They reached the road to the clubhouse. "By the way," Clipper said, "I sold your Grand Prix."

"You what?" Here we go, he thought. The asshole had thrown a brick into his life again.

"It was in my company's name, remember?"

He did recall a transaction, but he'd reimbursed Clip long ago. "I was going to drive it back to San Francisco tomorrow."

"How did I know that?" Clipper slowed for a pair of golfers crossing the road to play the eighteenth hole. "I come back from delivering Joey Boy and your car is sitting in my driveway."

"That's a problem with you?" He gave it a count of ten. "You got four fucking garages. Plus a space at your company."

"I'll drive you tomorrow. I was planning to anyway." He turned, displayed his older brother squint. "This artist you been staying with—"

"She put me up one night in her guest room."

"Whatever."

"Yeah," Navo said. "Leave it at whatever."

"Get that tight-jawed about it and I will." Clipper dipped his head to eye a hawk glide over the course's ancient trees. "I bought you a Jap minivan," he said, as if it were a consolation prize. "I know how you hate the monsters."

"Jesus, Clip."

"Called a *Mere*." He laughed their Daddy's savage laugh. "I told the dealer that meant 'motherfucker' in Cajun."

"Why the generosity?"

"Vigorish on your Dinger investment."

"It was a half million," Navo said. "That's like pissing in a lake and looking for it to rise."

"Or thinking a whore's gonna gag when she takes all you got."

He decided to drop the auto deal. What was he doing here? Christ, he had to play tomorrow night. He could be hiding out in his pad on Montgomery. Or out at the farm house sleeping. That's what worried him. Where had sleep gone? He'd caught a couple hours on the plane, another couple on the cab drive here. No real sleep since when? Shit, he'd lost count.

Clipper parked near the practice fairway, where a clubhouse attendant waited with his golf cart. "I got one of those huge band aids in my golf bag for your nose. Ought to be worth a stroke on the first tee."

The clubhouse had been completely re-built since Navo last played here. Members, guests, and a few strays greeted him, extending their hands, using body language that suggested they knew of fame themselves, true or dreamed. Clipper's bullshit acted as a buffer while he acknowledged men he'd never met or had forgotten. At a bar table overlooking the natural swales, so green in the summer heat they calmed Navo, the two of them were served pita burgers, the patties formed from a mix of lamb and beef swathed in Cajun mayo. Navo smiled, knowing the menu item was in honor of Clipper, who'd damn near established himself as the perennial Club Champion. Not a soul asked about his nose. Why would they? The way the media was all over him now, he was public domain.

Twelve o'clock sharp, Clipper negotiated their match on the first tee. "My partner today is my brother, Navo," he announced. "And as you know he hits baseballs, not Titlelists."

Marty Fishman, Clipper's personal attorney, and Marty's pickup partner, Timmy Bellringer, grinned as they stepped forward. Navo had met Fishman a couple of times and heard of his teammate, Bellringer, his musical name a misrepresentation of the way he played.

Coming back to Navo, Clipper muffled his words with a gloved hand. "This Bellringer I know from other clubs. He'll fold first time you hit one past him."

Navo took a few practice swings that felt like a bad anxiety dream. He held the driver's metal head against the wide sky. "What's with the right-handed clubs?"

"Oh." Clipper mocked great sorrow. "You hitting lefty this week?"

"I don't know." The curse of being a switch hitter.

"Shit, bud, a man can only carry so many clubs."

Well after three o'clock, sun slanting a bit now, worse because it was striking contaminated atmosphere. Christ, not like the Bay Area where you could breathe. Navo decided to have his second beer, gain some liquid. Clipper parked their cart alongside the seventeenth green's teeing mound.

From their opponents' cart across the way, Marty Fishman marched up to Navo. "For a guy who hasn't been playing any golf, you hit the shit out of the ball."

Navo knew Fishman to be a very convincing guy. "Long don't mean straight."

Fishman pressed his face into a small towel he'd brought out of his ice chest and gazed northward toward the mountains. "The new Indian casino is going up right over that first batch of foothills."

Navo was aware of Clip's involvement with the project in some way. "That right?"

"Subcontractors up there are claiming Clipper juked them, told them they needn't pre-lien, that the project sits on Federal Trust land."

Clipper threw his good leg out of the cart. "Wasn't my place to tell 'em shit, counselor. It was the tribe claiming that."

"General contractor is Carousel Entertainment." Fishman grinned at Navo. "Last I looked, Clipper, it reads Carousel on one of your business cards."

Clipper stepped closer. "Cute."

It was clear the attorney was trying to break Clip's competiveness. Good luck, Navo thought.

"And," Fishman went on, "Carousel is Vegas-based."

"Sacramento-based."

"And I'm Mark Geragos."

"Wish you were," Clipper said. "He's Armenian, and it takes nine Jews to skin one Armo with some Bayou blood." Clipper withdrew an iron from his bag. "Now get back to your golf partner and tell him we'll accept a push to get even."

Fishman stood silent. Then when Clipper was out of ear range he said to Navo. "Pardon my unprofessional comments, but they were meant to enlighten you." A fierce glance at Clipper, then back to him again. "Your money is involved here."

When Fishman walked away, Clipper motioned for Navo to join him on the seventeenth tee. "I'm playing the middle up there." He jerked a shoulder toward the hills, and Navo realized he wasn't talking golf. "Like Papa Boo," he said, "little factoring here, little over there." He grinned. "The Tribe buys some time. Subs pay a fraction of what lawyers would cost them if they were to wait and file suit."

Navo pictured it. His brother grabbing ten or fifteen percent off what? Probably close to twelve million. "Am I on a dotted line I don't know about?"

"Fishman is looking for ways to shake me up." Clip's game face returned. "Hit your eight iron here, partner. Pin's in back."

Hell with it, Navo thought. Forget anything bothersome, drink a couple more beers, and go sleep in your mother's old bed. "Should I go for it?"

"Go for the fat of the green," Clipper said. "I'm the one going for the fucking pin."

"Yeah, Clip," Navo said under his breath. "Keep up your impression of Jack Abramoff until you reach the Trail of Tears. I've given up on you."

ᥱᴔᥱᴔ

Dingers Brew Pub was packed for a Monday night. Navo found himself captured by what he and Clipper called the Armenian Mafia, some of whom were relatives; others mostly longtime friends of Gloria LeJeune.

Navo looked for his mother. So far she was a no-show. No surprise there. He did sit down with his uncle, Haig

Varakian, and his third wife, Roxie. Marty Fishman, though he'd lost big time at golf today, smoothly joined the high-spirited group. Luke Kaminski wished him luck and offered to drive him to San Francisco tomorrow.

Kaminski, always cool under pressure, had been his mother's main man for years. Navo owed him. Clipper owed him, too. But no one owed him more than Gloria.

The restaurant's executive chef, Chad Van Arsdale's, huge hands landed on Navo's shoulders. "Give us a song, man."

Everybody loved Chad, his rusty hair and his puffy mustache. Except Navo. To him the guy was loose-lipped about his sport betting. "Easy, Chef."

The pub's hostess, Tatum Dearborn, skinned Navo with a glance that wiped the grin off his face. The good times they'd shared might have ended too soon for her, he thought, feeling the gnaw of guilt.

Clipper shouted over his squeeze box and motioned for Navo to join him. "Let's sing that old Guy Clark song you like."

Navo felt several sets of hands urge him along the Spanish Oak bar, patrons off their stools glad-handing him toward the music as Clipper called out, "South Coast of Texas."

A mix of patrons began an alcohol-infused dance. Navo ran a riff across his harmonica and led his brother into the song.

On the small stage, they broke into song about the Mexican Bay of Campeche, the shrimpers singing goodbye to their ladies. Navo's friends, enemies, and fifteen minute fans danced and gyrated next to the small riser.

But not one supple-limbed sea angel could he count among the crowd. *She would, if she were here with us, set up her easel and sketch things so secret about our bodies we'd never see ourselves the same way again.*

The song soared. He bent low to find a note. His legs, in his tightest of jeans, belied his age, yeah. Up tall again, he leaned into his brother's bulk.

They turned to work back-to-back, just as they'd teamed up in a Pasadena Hotel's lounge, when he should have been with Joe.

"*Adios, Jole Blon,*" he sang.

***

With things dying down, Navo sought out Tatum Dearborn and followed her netted stockings out onto the patio.

The night air smelled of torched asphalt. Tatum's perfume drifted behind her, something she wore or something else, maybe the fragrance of her mahogany hair pulled into a knot high on her head tonight.

When she stopped and turned to him, it was as if the night had stopped, just the heat still stirring, a few cars starting on their way home.

"What happened to your nose?"

"Hit a fence in Chicago."

She shook her head. "No one can say you don't play hard." she said. "Your picture is on the front of a couple of magazines."

"Really?"

That head shake again. "Really."

"Listen, Tatum, about this shake up, we'll take care of you," he said. It sounded phony and he wished he could pull it back. "We'll take care of getting you something else after we shut this place down."

"We?" He didn't like the way she looked at him—older, harder.

"I'll see to it."

"Clipper already did," she said. "I start at Club Aces tomorrow night."

"Similar job?"

"Here I was your floor manager. There I'm a hostess."

"Great."

"Yeah, great. Like you'd know."

He looked away, lost as what to say.

She looked down to watch her right foot swing back and forth on a high heel. "I really thought you'd call me."

"I told you the season was coming up."

She began to brush past him, her face prideful in the eerie light. He caught her fingers, squeezed her hard nails. Tatum Dearborn, see-through peasant blouse, smooth shoulder, pumped black bra—she wasn't much older at all.

"Tatum," he said. "I'm not involved with the business part of this."

"Well, you better start realizing that you *are* part of your brother's dealings, like it or not." She spun from his hand and swished through the patio's wrought-iron gate, her figure perfect in the glow of the parking area.

Turning back to face him, she added, "He's made you his shadow in a way. Or maybe it's the other way around. And that's not a good thing, Navo. You mark my words, it's going to bite you both in the ass when you least expect it."

Her stance dared him to count the years he'd been Clipper's patsy.

Jesus, he thought, you'd have to go back to before his brother had lost his chance at playing for the Yankees— before his dreams had been ripped away.

Navo shuddered as Tatum's warning sent chills down his back.

Oh, man, now he was getting paranoid, afraid of what Clipper's dark dealings might include. Marty Fishman's words of warning on the golf course earlier today, and now Tatum's, resonated in his mind.

He'd better grab some shut eye, get his ass back to San Francisco, where his own history could be easier forgotten.

CHAPTER 19

Melanie wandered through Keyes's studio. The warm air contained fragrances of beach girls, and odors of paint that had been squeezed onto wooden pallets, art-school style. Sketches were pinned to the walls.

The dozen or so paintings here and there proved to be more precise than Melanie had expected. And better. Fantastic images of men, women, and animals found themselves suspended in a wonder world between past and present.

Keyes followed her around, his bare feet swishing when he moved. "Too much Conan the Barbarian?"

"Maybe."

"Too cartoony?"

"Not if it's your choice, and you have an I-have-to-or-I'll-die vision for taking that direction."

"Walker says I'm no Frank Frazetta."

"That might work in your favor. Admiring someone's work is one thing. Copying him is another."

She'd found a stand-out piece wherein a triangle of naked warriors praising the super anatomy of a goddess, formed a pyramid to a celestial heaven.

"Gorgeous," she said, remembering the value of youth, their innocent homage to eternity. She heard his feet move closer, but kept appraising the painting. "How do you compare yourself now to when you ruled the surf?"

Both in jeans, they were thigh to thigh. He took his time turning then shrugged. There. She felt the hard mound behind his fly pressing against her right hip.

"You don't feel the confidence on land you felt in water." She smiled when he retreated a step. Her thoughts shuttled back in time. Was she ever as green as this ex-champ? "And you'd do anything to get your land legs."

He smiled, too, and pulled his T-shirt over his head then shook out his dark curls. "You really come here to see my work?"

"Not exactly."

"What then?"

"Your work is a complete surprise."

"In what way?"

She imagined how his heart must be pounding, could see its beat against his brown chest. Stepping past him, she gave his studio a final, sweeping glance. "It's so damn good. Good enough, I can understand where you're at."

That you'd do anything to find a foothold, a step up, she started to say, but held it back.

"I wish you'd think of me as a man, not just a friend of Joe's."

"Let's say I think of you as a friend to both Joe and me." She studied him, watching for more than practiced charm. "Seeing your work, I think you might do some of that yourself."

"Do what, exactly?"

"See people as friends, not as opportunities to advance your art. Your art is strong enough on its own."

"You've got Walker Gustine."

She cut her smile off abruptly. "He's an art dealer. Dealers and collectors are open season." A lie but so what?

He smiled as he put his shirt back on, his face darkly handsome, eyes young and playful. Many lessons that he needed hearing crossed her mind, things she'd learned the hard way. "Keep working, Keyes. Let all that talent come up to the surface on its own."

"Thanks."

Surprised that he still had a hard on, she didn't look away.

His quick fingers found the stretcher bars of a canvas, and he pulled the piece up to his waist. "Sorry."

"If that's some kind of apology, I'll take it." God, she'd damn near thrown her arms around him. Not lust. Or was it? I'll draw you, and you can draw me? Well, fuck you, Neil, I'm still alive. "Remember what I said about being a friend, especially when one looks up to you."

She left him standing alone in the space, skylight making him a Frazetta mega hero, a veritable ton of the finest art supplies courtesy of Walker Gustine. Left him there to ponder how far he'd go to please his benefactor before saying no to anything but honest work. And maybe she needed to ask herself that same question.

಄ಌ಄

Determined to follow up her call to a friend for help, Melanie drove away from Keyes's metal digs. All the false bravado she'd stored up to confront the youth had now evaporated. The drive out Los Osos Valley Road to Cuesta College went amazingly fast, and Valerie Del Toro was waiting for her. Val had changed little since Melanie had last talked with her in person—still the same hungry stare; hair trimmed an inch from her skull.

Melanie sensed her entire upper skeletal structure when they hugged.

"The models I sent you told me everything went well," Valerie said.

Melanie managed a smile. "Until they had to take their clothes off."

"Oh, no. What's the matter with these kids today?" Valarie finally broke from their embrace. "Next time I'll try to do better."

A bit of silence slipped by. "Long time since I taught summer courses out here." She felt more student than associate as she accepted Val's offered chair. "I appreciate your time." Across the huge desk Valerie sat and here came her patented gaze.

Melanie remembered the Del Toro approach to STD and student health, her irrepressible lectures. "I feel like I'm keeping you from getting out of here."

Valerie ran dark nails through darker hair. "We'll worry about that when I start seeing bugs on the wall at martini time. You know how I feel about this, Melanie."

The room felt suddenly claustrophobic. "Yes."

"Your blood test will tell us only how clean *you* are." She leaned closer, dark circles under her great eyes. "We'd have to test you in a few days to know anything if your ex-husband was clean when he raped you."

"Yes." Claustrophobic, yet the windows were open to campus buildings that stretched toward the gentle hills beyond. On the phone, this shit was tough. Face-to-face it was unbearable.

"I advised you to request test results from Neil."

Still shaken, Melanie shuddered. "This just happened last Saturday."

"What are you waiting for?" Valerie opened a drawer, pulled out a fistful of dark chocolate chips, and tossed a few in her mouth. She dropped the rest in front of Melanie. "Will he comply?"

"If he wants to see his son again, he will."

"What do you know about his present sex life?"

"Not much." She felt stupid, inadequate. "Am I supposed to?"

"You said he takes Joe every other week?"

Shame burned her throat. "More like once a month." Swallow, swallow. "I've quizzed Joe some. From what he's told me, I know Neil's been seeing someone regularly. But he told me that the affair had ended."

"When did he tell you that?"

"After he jumped me. Before I ran him out of my house."

"You've still not reported the attack? Tried for a restraining order?"

"No."

"The man broke into your home, forced you to have sex." Valerie shrugged at her silence. "That's what rape does. Makes you go mute."

"You said, 'how clean *I* am.'"

"You spoke of current partners."

Current partners? "You knew about Walker."

"I've met Gustine." Valerie went for a chocolate chip and placed it on her tongue. "You mentioned a professional athlete."

"Navo LeJeune. Plays for the San Francisco Giants."

Valerie cut loose a resigned rasp. "The guy on the streak? I've seen the papers and the tabloids. We can check the internet."

"Like that is where we'll find the real Navo LeJeune?"

"Oh, shit." Valerie leaned back as if astonished. "The way you said his name."

"You think I should say it differently? How did you think I'd say it?" Melanie was hot now with anger, and it felt good. "I made love to the man, Val."

Valerie reached out and grabbed her hand off the table. "My bad," she said. "And I'm sorry. Okay?"

"Okay."

Outside there was a sound, as if the wind had picked up. "You ever hear of paygirls?" Valerie asked.

"Playgirls?"

"*Pay*girls," Valerie said. "As in, I'll pay you, girl, to have your ass ready for me when and where I want it."

"I'm not sure whom you're categorizing here." Did she actually throw bait out like that to Valerie?

"I'm referring to certain women and the multi-millionaire jocks who keep them on the burner for immediate pleasure, not any serious relationship they might incur. The fucking N.B.A. is known for this practice."

"NBA.?"

"Professional basketball players."

"Navo plays baseball."

"Oh, excuse me." That Del Toro stare-down. "They make millions too."

Did the palms along the walkways outside the window suddenly sway? Had she heard voices out there tinkle to a chiming in her brain? Was that an object in the room crashing to the floor? She rose off her chair as it began to skitter out from under her. She nearly fell, grabbed the desk. Valerie was standing, holding onto the desk's opposing corner. They faced each other like drunken saloon squabblers.

A word bared Val's teeth. "Earthquake."

Three words seemed more appropriate to Melanie. "A fucking earthquake."

Rustle of feet outside and inside the building. That tintinnabulation—had she actually borrowed Poe's word?—that weird warning tinkle had turned into the sound of cascading bells. Someone cursed. Someone horse-laughed. Someone screamed and the earth moved again.

"File out of the building," Valerie shouted to an unseen audience. "And don't panic."

Melanie joined Valerie's deliberate pace. "I've got to leave," she said, noticing a tattoo above Val's slim ankle she'd forgotten—an eye, an arched brow, black on ivory.

"Things will be all right, you'll see," Valerie whispered, so as not to disturb any wrathful gods. She hugged her. "Stay here, Mel. Don't drive on the road."

Melanie didn't reply. She hustled away from the scene of evacuating students.

She had to find Joe. Call the streak-hitting ballplayer. Tell him she was in an earthquake, and was scared to death.

CHAPTER 20

After Bushmill told him he'd been benched—just a night off to rest a bit more after the Chicago trip—Navo watched his teammates win the home series opener against the Houston Astros and later accepted a ride to his apartment from Luke Kaminski.

"I could have walked, Luke."

"You would have been mobbed," Luke said. "And I wanted time to tell you not to be worried about signing with Tamara Bix. "I only helped with your contract because you wanted me to. It was Marty Fishman who did all the negotiating."

Navo thought about that, about how Marty had helped him on many things without receiving due credit. It was just so hard to trust a lawyer who seemed to be in bed with Clipper. "I kinda looked for Clip to drive me here this morning. I wished I'd known they were going to rest me."

"Maybe it will prove good strategy."

"I imagine my brother is going nuts, wondering if something happened to me during pre-game practice."

Luke glanced at him. "He called almost every inning, then said he might not make it tomorrow, citing a family crisis."

"Should I know about it?" Now what the fuck was the matter? "Is this about Gloria?"

Luke laughed. "It's *always* about Gloria. Looks like I'll have to miss the game tomorrow, too. Are you sure I can't take you out to dinner? His eyes were quick to take in the passing neighborhood. "There used to be a French restaurant on this corner. I took Gloria here before she ran off to New Orleans. Strange how people run to places they know nothing about."

"I think she knew where she was running when she ran back to you," Navo said. Husband murdered, he didn't say. Two kids with no father, he also left out.

Luke turned on Montgomery. "My senior year at USF, I had a string of forty-three straight free throws."

"Made or missed?"

"Made." Luke chuckled. "And I tossed them all underhand."

"Old school." Navo thought of how, after the accident, Luke had gotten him to play football his final year in high school when he'd refused to play baseball. Got him playing baseball at Cal Poly, when it was clear he wouldn't become an architect like Luke. "Hitting is easier than shooting baskets."

"Like hell it is."

Navo thought he'd be just fine without that heavy burden of *family* watching from the stands. "Well, it's easier than shooting free throws underhand."

Luke pulled his Cadillac over and stopped in front of the apartment. "Good luck," he said, a tremor in his voice. "I'll be pulling for you."

Navo said the first thing that wouldn't catch in his throat. "This old Caddie..."

"Twelve years old."

"Why don't you stay in my apartment? I got plenty of room."

"Got my usual spot. Little hotel your mom and I have used in those heights west of China Basin."

"Old school."
"Old school."

ᏋᏉᏋᏉ

Navo's apartment building's foyer was cold and gray as a penitentiary, the metal-faced elevator stark as a food locker. Nobody down here either, not even Manheim the place's security guard, after six o'clock. On the elevator, Navo breathed the still air and celebrated his decision to call it a night. And he would have the place to himself. Or maybe he wouldn't. The door was ajar. Probably meant the player named Macon, called up until Cyrus's hand improved, was still packing for the trip back to Fresno. Man, he felt for the young pitcher. He hadn't had time to prove himself.

Two steps in the door he discovered he'd misread the situation.

From the kitchen's service bar, three strangers stared at him with evil in their eyes. Two men and one woman, all in store-bought grunge, camouflaged for little else than malice. Navo was certain of his impression as he mentally registered the three intruders—Leader. His enforcer. And most likely his bitch. The trio was apparently not too busy to smoke, have a cold one out of the fridge, and lounge on barstools he'd bought at Crate and Barrel.

Navo stood before them on weary legs, one ear turned to the other rooms for friendly sounds. Nothing.

"What's up?" he said.

"You Clevus Macon?" Leader halved a Heineken in one draw and set it next to empties on the bar. Slightly built, his skin contained a dark olive cast, and his slitted eyes were stone cold.

"Macon's gone," Navo said. "He won't be back for a while." That must be it. They were after the rookie.

"Maybe someone shot him."

"Shot him?"

"Like right now, man, it would be good-paying work."

Enforcer said, "Give it a name." Like, for sure this guy Macon fell into a category. Navo noticed how the squat, muscular punk looked cut out for chaos. Tattoos danced on his pasty white biceps and calves. His hands were wrapped in half gloves. "Shit, Jim, this dude don't look Yokum 'nuff to be a Macon."

"Macon with the bacon." Their bitch exhibited a row of yellow teeth against cinnamon cheeks. She flipped a mass of tribal strands off her face and leaned back on her stool, leather pants straining to fit her extended legs and crotch.

Enforcer asked Navo, "Who are you, man? What's yo bidness, coming in here like this is your real estate?"

"I'm the guy who bought the beer you're drinking."

"Cope with it."

Navo felt a reverberation, his muscles reacting to fear, anger, and a rush of panic. "My name's Navo LeJeune."

"The dude on the streak." Jim the leader smiled like he'd cornered a zoo animal. He held his hand out as if to display Navo to his students. "This man is one streak hitting motherfucker."

"Caucasian invasion." Enforcer stroked his chest in a gesture Navo took to mean there was an association by skin between them. "We the white Supremes."

"They was three of them, wonder boy," the bitch reminded him.

Jim stepped forward. "You'd cover for your buddy?" He shook his head as if the very thought of it would solve everything right now. "Aint nothing but six large, LeJeune. Pay and we'll be gone as Michael."

Navo squared himself. "I aint near that kind of cash." He picked his wallet clean of bills, placed them on top of the counter. Removed his one priggish valuable. "Louis Vuitton," he said, adding his wristwatch to the mix.

Leader Jim sorted the payoff, face turning viscid, then tragic. "This don't cut it, swinger."

Roughneck baller hunched his back, ignored the bounty. "Not even close."

She-devil said, "I draw that much, they throw you on the floor and I do yo dick."

Enforcer turned to Leader Jim. "Give it a name."

Right then, from the apartment's entrance, the distinct gait of Cyrus broke the loaded air, causing the three invaders to tighten their stances. Navo watched them flinch at Cyrus's rumbling impersonation of Samuel Jackson doing Isaac Hayes.

"What's going down?" Cyrus showed that look he had when an umpire missed the call on his slider. "We serving beer now to anyone walks in off the street?" Then he smiled that crazy smile that even Navo feared.

The oddmented trio, mute and stupefied at such a set of choppers, became a line-up of shot-and-killed desperadoes propped up for public display.

"Now then," Cyrus warned as he patted them down one by one. "Break bad someplace else, or I'm gonna start snappin' me some pencil necks."

☙❧☙

"Thanks, man," Navo said as they walked down to the street level.

"I like your apartment." Cyrus was ahead of him, that way he had of walking like his purpose was to outrun a demon. "But your security need some work."

"Manheim said he thought they went up with Macon." Navo wondered if the leader, Jim, had paid his way up.

"Macon left most his stuff there, so I don't know what to think."

"You was going to let 'em take your Louie V?"

"All I could think was they'd kill me while I'm hot with the bat." Navo took the lead, and they headed up Powell. For some reason he wanted a good look at the Saints Peter and Paul Church, how it looked in the late, soft summer night, maybe work on thanking someone.

He and Cyrus stood like mournful saints staring at the church. Around them, breezes hummed off North Beach. "What brought you to my place this late?" Navo asked.

"That earthquake."

"What earthquake?

"One yesterday, didn't you feel it?"

"I've been feeling nothing but quakes for days."

"Me, too." The big man gazed at the sky, apparently looking for a moon. "Made me think of Haiti."

"So you were coming over to snuggle up with me?"

"If you'd have me."

"Any time." Navo began to head back, streets empty, a few cars. "Those guys – they weren't carrying?"

"They were, we'd be dead."

Navo could tell Cyrus was picturing it.

"Don't want never to die for a man's drug debt," Cyrus said. "That motherfucker Macon ever come back up, point him out to me."

From a cab cutting by, Tha Carter rapped about KY Jelly and female basketball players with cornrows.

"Slippin' and a-risin'." Cyrus bent double, like he'd been punched in the belly. "Least we aint taking the BART like that fool kid."

"How do you smoke up six grand?"

"Depend on how long they give you."

Navo laughed at that. "Clevus keeps it up, he'll be pitching with a LoJac on his ankle."

"Say he will."

"Lord, I could walk all night."

"Hell yes," Cyrus said. "Walk 'til we hit water." And his strong laughter cracked rim shots into the night. *Bam Bam-bam, de-bam.*

CHAPTER 21

Melanie breathed a sigh of relief. Walker had acquired gallery space for her in Bergamot Station, a historical railway junction transposed into an art complex in Santa Monica. Yesterday, he'd enlisted the help of Ernesto and Keyes to transport some of her work from her studio. Other work of hers that he'd planned to photograph for prints also were loaded in the rented van.

Joe had asked if he could go along. She'd refused. "No telling how much time they'll need to unload and set up things."

"So," Joe said. "I sit on my butt and watch you paint?"

"We can find some surf," she said. "Maybe a tsunami from the quake."

"That's fucked up."

He had her there. She abhorred treating tragedy lightly, something Neil had done with such ease. They were in her studio. She'd completed little work since Neil's attack. "We can have fun," she said. "We always do."

"Isn't Valerie coming by?"

"Not today." She was glad about that. Valerie was relentless about documenting the rape, and forcing Neil's hand. Neil hadn't called. By now he must be scared to death, or lying to his divorce lawyer, or an attorney more ignorant of her. Anybody knowing her at all would be suspicious of his account of what happened. Or would they? She was the woman fucking around with a billionaire art dealer and a ballplayer currently brawling and streaking his way from game to game.

She followed Joe out to the patio and sat across from him. "You know something is going on between your dad and me, something not good, don't you?"

His eyes chipped a piece of her heart away. "I can tell something is wrong with you," he said. "What's Dad doing that's so bad? Did you have a fight when he was here? Why didn't we go to dinner together?"

She'd lost track of the day. Where had it gone? She felt sick. Loosing time made her want to upchuck. If she'd eaten anything today she would have.

Where was her opening here with her son? She had to find words to keep him close, not drive him away. "Can I ask you to give me a few days, just to gather myself? Like the times when I've given you some space, occasions where I've let you slide."

"Like never."

So she was the bad guy. "I know your dad isn't as strict as I am, but he sees you when there is no pressure. Takes you out for some fun, brings you back to me, and drops you off. I wake you from sleep the next morning to make sure you go to the dentist."

He looked at her, confused. "So?"

So? Wasn't that the deal? It struck her, the pattern of it, how it worked against her. Sure, she was the bad detective. Now all she could think of was getting him to smile. "At least now I can afford it."

"What?" His innocence, it could drive her to tears.

"The dentist."

"I only have to go to the dentist for checkups, remember?"

She laughed with him. "Sure."

Everything went silent and she felt for a moment on the edge of an earth splitting chasm, then a lone bird's song brought her out of it. When she looked at her son, it seemed he'd paused as if afraid of something.

"I don't think Dad is with Maya anymore," he said.

"No?"

"He has some other girlfriends, though."

"Tell me about them."

Joe slowly raised himself out of his chair. God, he looked taller today. A breeze had caught his hair, teased it to exhibit its beauty. She got up and wrapped her arms around his shoulder muscles, firmer, more developed than ever before.

"I've never asked you to take sides." When he remained silent, she said. "That might change. I hate it, but that might change. So be ready for it."

ღღღ

A sound awakened her. She'd fallen asleep on the bed in the guest room. Had she been painting? Yes, ever since puttering around with Joe earlier and letting him drive a few back roads east of Arroyo Grande, his skill at the wheel relaxing her. After they'd returned, she'd left him to deal with a pizza they'd picked up. God, she must have fallen asleep.

She turned on a lamp to read the time on her cell. Three hours. She'd painted three hours. Now, Joe's familiar knock sounded again.

"You caught me dozing," she said. "What's up?"

Joe entered the room with that anxious look that made him look older. "Navo is coming to bat again against the Astros."

She wasn't awake enough to stop the adrenalin. "He is?"

"Probably will be his last chance to keep his streak going." He stayed in the doorway. "If he gets a hit, he ties Pet Rose's record."

Rose. Didn't he have to go to prison? What was it about these streaks that got these guys in such trouble? Or were the headlines skewered for publicity? She'd watched Navo once on TV, could still see it in her mind. Did she dare go back for more? An aching lump throbbed in her windpipe as she followed Joe into his room.

A close up of Navo's face nearly dropped her. Those eyes of his, black as an old movie villain's, his face at once Messiah-like and hellish.

Strike one, swinging and missing badly.

Strike two, looked like a replay of strike one.

Strike three, in a trance, not a full swing.

She watched him toss his helmet aside, his face a frozen scream, lips mouthing the word *fuck*.

"Will he bat again?"

"Not likely, Mom."

Overpowered with a mood of self-denunciation for outing him from her life, she cleared a sob from her throat. "Good. He's had enough."

❧❧❧

Answering Joe's call, she returned to his room.

"No," she said, eyes on the TV screen.

"You'll never believe the rally."

"He's up again?"

He was. In the hanging hush, there on the screen in her son's room, Navo stood, bat in hand, eyes steady on the opposing pitcher as he moved forward. A voice claimed millions were watching. To see what? Their own glory on earth. That must be it, she'd decided, and wondered if that made the spectacle art.

He swung and missed. "God, he keeps missing the ball!"

Next pitch almost hit him. Thousands booed. Joe yelled, "Shit."

She felt her heart drop.

Seemed forever, but his swing again hit nothing but air. She couldn't breathe.

Navo stepped out of the lye-drawn box. Then back in. Ambidextrous, he was batting right-handed. Those Halloween-colored gloves choked the red bat's neck. Then, holding it in his left hand only, he pointed it at the pitcher, brought it back slowly. Now both hands held it upright above his right shoulder, the barrel sketching a lazy circle up there in the San Francisco night.

Then the furious speed of his swing and a click.

She heard it that way, his bat so quick, then, *Click!*

The pitcher lifted one leg, swiped at the blur of white with his black glove. Two infielders behind him collided as the ball shot between their extended gloves, bounded across a band of sienna, and out onto the immaculate green of the outfield.

Navo became a sprinter to Melanie's eye. Running away, high-assed, legs pistons, turning at first base, and then returning. No smile as the camera closed in. Challenge in his eyes as if he welcomed the storm he'd wrought with the crowd's mortal thunder.

"Look at him." God, he could be a madhouse sketch of Gauguin by Van Gogh.

"That tied Pete Rose's record," Joe shouted, punching the air.

"God, Joe. Look at him."

She had sunk beside his bed, hands spread on the tile floor, one knee up against her chin, her other leg stretched out to her side.

"Mom."

"What?"

"You're crying."

She was. Bawling so hard her stomach was contracting as she fought for a breath. The game had continued, but it was as if the sound had been snuffed. Navo moved now in slow motion. Another camera showed him in a replay. His face again.

"Oh, God, Joe," she cried out. "I can't get up. See him? Do you see him?"

CHAPTER 22

Thursday the Giants lost the final game in their series with the Astros. But any grief seemed lost in the post-game frenzy over Navo's breaking Pete Rose's National League record of hitting safely in forty-four consecutive games. Tamara Bix managed to break him away from interviews, sneaking him to a Jaguar she'd moved in behind paramedic vehicles outside the emergency doors. Now, way over the speed limit, she headed for 80 and the Bay Bridge.

"It's early, LeJeune." She offered Navo a crazed smile, long-nailed fingers choking the wheel. "We got the whole night to celebrate."

She was right about the time. It had been a one o'clock start today. "Easy, Bix." He straight-armed the dash for balance." I aint spending the night in Oakland."

"Listen to the Libra in you. Logical and detached, always fighting one another. You absolutely have to apply your Venus influence tonight."

"My what?"

"You need to get laid." She activated a mechanical voice that startled him. "Audio navigation. I told it where to take us. Can't do anything about it now."

"What did you tell it?" Actually he was glad to get away from Clipper and the crowd from Fresno here on a surprise visit. He did give them an hour or two after the game, all of it while pinned to the wall. Man, he couldn't breathe. But now what? "It's getting dark, Bix. Tell me what's up."

Batshit smile again. "Told it to take us to someplace where you might loosen up."

Was that what he wanted? He'd not looked for the wild side much. Not in these last few years. Maybe that night he'd met Melanie; he'd been hunting for a place to let it all go, release fifteen years of suiting up, running out in the yard. Alone. Man, you talk about feeling all alone out there on the field. The bigger the roar, the more *separate* you felt.

He thought Melanie had understood. She couldn't have been so intimate without feeling it. It was in that intimacy they'd understood one another, joined one another. Fuck, he'd given her his essence.

"You okay, hitter?"

౿ৎ౿ৎ

The place was named Blue Sugar, an old gutted theatre in Oakland Navo had heard about, but had until now managed to avoid. Bix couldn't hide her motives any more than she could hide the breasts spilling from her scalloped tank top as she raised her henna-tattooed arms to praise the teeming venue.

Voltage snapped in the air, as members of the crowd clustered at large round tables, gripping various vessels of drink and pressing stage-ward, where Judi Gillespie had swaggered out from the wings to join a band of zoned grenadiers who'd been warming up the masses with music mean and grungy.

"Judi's a true cult figure," Bix whispered.

Navo couldn't find a common thread to these people, other than they obviously were in search of a life away from the office, the home—or just away—until they got caught. He yearned for a night like he had last year, when he and Luke Kaminski had watched the Avett Brothers perform at the Fox Theatre, not far from here.

At the mic, no more than twenty feet away, Gillespie swung her guitar off her back, posed in a petrified pelvic thrust, fist in an upshot salute to her screeching fans. No doubt about it, the young woman was a stone beauty. Tie-dyed t-shirt, wrist bands, short leather skirt, black stockings, platform boots, she presented a naughty image under the spots, colors blinking in her pale green eyes and chestnut hair.

Lips kissing the mic, she began a stream of barely intelligible words aimed at plugging her new film, gibberish about the sordid life a female rock star faced and the bastards who ran the business. "Such a worthy experience," Gillespie exclaimed, "I decided to take it on the road."

On this cue, the band kicked off on a confused excursion into metal-chinking, amp-burning, bass-slamming rock. Strumming her guitar with a spastic wrist, Gillespie, it was plain, knew little about music.

Navo dropped his head to sneak a pull on his beer. Shuddering at her vocal licks, he was amazed at her gall. Jesus. Gillespie doing Joplin doing Big Mama Thornton—his daddy would have laughed at that stretch. Besides, wasn't there a classic on this same theme, Bette Midler in *The Rose*? He must have uttered this as Bix had just whacked his thigh.

He tried to space out, work on a memory of his father taking him and Clip to see Bonnie Raitt, saying to them while they watched her, "Aint nothing like a woman who can play the blues, boys."

Navo looked up to focus on Gillespie. Her face did show the beauty of paying a few dues. That's what had drawn him to Melanie, the way life could be a fine craftsman and make a face more intriguing.

Time had its way of killing, too, he'd come to realize. Of killing something you didn't know. Something weren't ever meant to know. Otherwise, how could you keep going? He thought about glory days, how long you were given before they flamed out.

He glanced left and right. Was thirty-four too old for this shit? Thirty-five next month? Thirty-five and thirty -six next season? *Christ, I'm Methuselah sitting here.*

Most of the crowd seemed to be digging the show. Yeah, it must be a cult thing all right. Lesbian, gay, ambisextrous. And women hostile up-to-here in men's bullshit. He could feel that.

Bix jabbed an elbow into his ribs. "What's Judi doing now?"

"Playing a Jew's harp." He let a grin slip loose. Gillespie was indeed whacking on a wire mouth harp. "Looks like she's on to something she's trained for."

Gillespie's repertoire grew slimmer as she ground down. Obviously drained, she returned to riffs again and again. Finally breathless and spent, she thanked her band. To the last wail of guitars and crashing cymbals, she swan dived into a hammock of welcoming arms. Desperately finding a foothold, she vamped her way among the privileged tables. In time she found Bix. Tamara greeted her with enormous animation, as an asylum of fans swarmed, shoved, and clawed their way around the tables and chairs to get a touch, a feel of their beloved Judi.

Tangled with Navo, the film star rocked to the raucous tempo of the crowd. Navo felt her teeth against his neck.

"God damn," she snapped in his ear, "I've been wanting to check you out."

"Everybody wants to meet the hitter." Bix was hawking him to the lunatic fringe, shaping them into a kind of circle with her coaxing hands and wild-eyed glances. "Someone," she invited those with cameras, "get a picture of these two."

"You better hold on to me, man," Gillespie shouted as she turned him toward a gauntlet formed by what looked to be a contingency of hired hands. "Grab on tight, slugger, before the dykes reach for their razors."

☙❧❧

Navo followed as the party moved from Judi Gillespie's dressing room to Tamara Bix's flat, a gutted level centered in a revamped building in Berkeley. Pine flooring, brick walls, floor-to-ceiling windows overlooking the city. The space contained furniture she called late Omega Salvage.

A kitchen occupied the dimness at one end, bed and bath the other. A row of wooden casks topped by an aluminum painter's plank made up a bar that held Jack Daniels, Evian water, plastic cups, a tub of ice, and jars of Trader Joe's blistered peanuts. Also clay ashtrays for your choice of smoke. Someone told him there was a bong in the kitchen.

He caught up with Bix. "I gotta get out of here."

Bix gave him a tender look that surprised him. "Why not try for once to relax? Hide from all the pressure."

"I can't hide here."

She kissed his forehead. "Wind down with Judi. I'll kick everyone out soon, and you'll have the place to yourselves."

He could have called a cab and left the party. Instead he stayed to himself, thinking about today's game.

☙❧❧

His first time at bat, with nobody on the bases before him, he popped up the first pitch to the Astros catcher. Matta froze him with a look. Shit, he should have worked the count.

e/ɔe/ɔ

The bedroom was divided from the rest of the space by suspended screens. The bathroom, except for a toilet closet, was decked out in stainless steel and zebra-patterned tile. Navo watched Judi Gillespie shower.

The jet sprays transformed her slow moving body from painted vixen to undefiled waif. He stripped as she toweled herself dry. She whipped her head wildly in a fog of scent, lotioned her limbs and belly with quick hands.

Feeling apish on the oversized bed, he lifted the sheer cover as she slipped in beside him. Across the wide room he could make out the shape of a Harley Davidson motorcycle, Bix's idea of sculpture.

In the dimness Judi's face looked almost girlish, except for her lips, bruised from that damned Jews harp.

She said, "Bix told me you guys get tested regularly."

"Yeah, how about you?"

The cult star made a soundless gasp. *"Touché."*

She talked, cussed her film's distributor like a sailor, her tour manager for missing a jazz festival at the Greek Theatre.

"If it weren't for Bix, I wouldn't have had the Blue Sugar gig and all those lesbos." She leaned across the bed and kissed his eyes, his damaged nose, his mouth, down his chest. Murmured against his sex how she knew shit about rock, less about the blues. "I'm an actor from Menomonee, Wisconsin, for Christ's sake."

She looked up at him through the chestnut hair that had fallen over her face. "Home of Billie Frechette, the girlfriend of John Dillinger. You know who he was?"

"Saw Johnny Depp play him in the movie."
"Are we talking too much?"
"Yes."

⌘⌘

In the fourth, with Thoroughgood on first, two away, he had worked the count to three and two. The next pitch came in too close to let go by. He got enough wood on it to foul it off. Did the same thing again. It happened then. He felt the crowd in his pulse, in his head. He could sense Clipper in his DNA and lined the next pitch into center, where it was caught knee-high by a charging centerfielder named Chuck Atwood, a man he might hate forever.

⌘⌘

Navo smiled as Gillespie worked her way out from under him, stretched, and switched on a bed lamp that sculpted her with eerie light. Thirty some years of conditioned bone and flesh, eyes in deepened sockets, she had her face bent to thoughts he couldn't catch in his wildest dreams.

"Bet I can find us a cold Pepsi," she said.

He watched her stride past the Harley's visible chrome, its ghostly pin-striping. The erotic art on its tank was tame compared to Melanie Blake's paintings.

As if she knew the place well in the dark, Judi soon sat next to him holding cold cans of soda. "When you went down on me, you must've noticed."

"What?"

"I don't really have a piercing there. The one that shows up in that video that's all over the net."

"What?"

"That ring on my clit with Malcolm in the film? It was a clamp on."

"Malcolm?"

"Lead singer with Deep Thrombosis."

∾∾∾

With the Giants trailing six to one, he led off the sixth. On a three-ball, one-strike count, he laid down a bunt. Batting left-handed, he broke from the box fast. Everything was so fucking silent, he thought. The entire world had stopped except him. Scorching his lungs for one more gasp of oxygen, he crossed the first base bag ahead of the throw. Then the roar broke. Cracked like holy thunder, the kind that destroyed sacred barriers.

∾∾∾

Navo lay in a state of obliqueness. "I broke Pete Rose's record of forty-four straight hits today."

"That's kind of a crude way to put it, but you know what?" Judi said and nestled close to him. "I'm glad it was with me."

∾∾∾

Navo was in the first stage of a dream, when the noise woke him. *Motorcycle,* he thought, as he swung his feet out to find the wood flooring. Right before the machine and the cult star riding it slammed him back across the bed. Lucky for him, he managed, by instinct or chance, to turn his body sideways. Sure, there would be damage, he knew, but somehow he'd not offered the Harley's spinning wheels an avenue between his legs.

Yeah, today had been divine.

It was tomorrow he feared.

CHAPTER 23

Gloria LeJeune walked ahead of Luke Kaminski, thinking, how can a man so proficient in the sack take so long getting out of a roomy Lexus?

"You okay, Luke?"

He caught up with her and escorted her through a fenced courtyard. "You bring me back from the Bay Area on a Sunday for this? Christ, both of us should be in San Francisco."

That stopped her. "I thought Navo has been in a motorcycle accident, and will not be playing for a couple days." When Luke seemed to fluff her off with a half-hidden grin, she punched his shoulder. "Don't think for a minute I won't find out the truth, Luke."

"Wouldn't try it."

"I heard some bimbo riding a Harley tried to run him down."

"It was an accident," Luke said. "She mounted it and managed to get it started, but it got away from her."

"Navo is quick as lightning," she said. "He couldn't get out of the way?"

"Not under the circumstances."

"And that's all you know?"

"Just that the bimbo, as you call her, jumped aboard a hog that was actually a piece of sculpture and—well, I guess the tabloids will soon be reporting the details."

"I don't read those rags."

"There's a good chance he'll start today," Luke said. "They lost both Friday and last night to the Pirates." He made a scoffing sound. "The fans today will tear the park down if they don't get a chance to see Navo before the Giants leave again."

Enough, she thought. Enough about how they should drop everything for Navo. Clipper hadn't tended to his work-related problems in weeks.

This morning he called from Sacramento, saying he was off to see a baseball game. At least he'd told her the truth. If only he'd be truthful about more things with Clair, his marriage might work, and he'd be a better father to Heather.

Gloria would have liked to discuss this with Luke, but his cavalier attitude about everything simply made it impossible. They stepped onto a walkway that tunneled through what she remembered was once a depository warehouse.

She glanced overhead. "Like walking through a tomb."

He'd chosen a door near the end of the passage, keyed it open, then swung it wide for her to enter. *"Voila."*

She centered herself in the space, spun a full turn that flared the bottom of her sheer broomstick skirt. "No walls?" she asked. Actually she was pleased with the open feeling. She loved the iron staircase and the tiled service bar. And the windows. Much more light than she'd thought possible from his drawings. "God, it's suffocating in here." Why reveal enthusiasm that might give him the upper hand?

"The only interior wall is up in the loft," he said.

Her hair, stiff from yesterday's touch-up, felt like it was splitting into pieces. She fingered its shards up off the nape of her neck, struck a pose she knew was suggestive. "I want to do this same thing with those buildings over on R Street."

He'd spread his long arms. "Christ, Gloria. Build it and they will come?"

"Don't pull me into one of your non-productive arguments." She crossed to the iron staircase, banged the meat of her palm against the railing to test its stability. "When are the appliances coming in?"

"I'm on it."

"You better be. We've got a waiting list." She figured a white lie now and then was harmless, and it might motivate him to get off his ass.

Luke loitered near the door. Outside, light traffic echoed against buildings whose identities were lost to time. "I'm going to mosey over to the stadium," he said, with a jerk of his thumb. "Want to join me?"

That damned park named after an Indian tribe, here in a town full of Mexicans. "I'd hoped we could go somewhere cool and have a salad."

"We'll have a beer; watch the game up in the 600 Club, and pull for Navo's streak."

Pure Kaminski, she thought, always a hidden motive. "Streaks are just that," she said. "Runs of luck that run out."

She shifted her weight to balance her fury. She'd like to hit him with the past and wake him up. She'd allowed him to influence her sons after the accident. Look at how that had played out. Only Clipper, the one who'd lost the most, had remained anywhere close to being loyal.

"Runs are for gamblers like you, Luke."

His laugh was exaggerated by the emptiness of the space. "What do you know about my gambling?"

"My father told me plenty."

"Papa Boo was too true a bookie to rat on his clients. If you want to make a point, Gloria, don't blame it on him." He ran a hand over his thin hair, down the back of his neck. "And it's not *my* name on any gaming licenses."

"That side of it isn't a gamble." Or was it? Marty Fishman had Clipper under control, and the accountants agreed Carousel was making money. For now that was good enough for her.

"Papa Boo would beg to differ," Luke said.

"You'd have Clipper a crippled coach, hanging around playgrounds. Lucky to take in a living wage."

"Where's that coming from?"

She beat a fist into her hip. "You helped Navo into Cal Poly, only to have him quit architecture for fifty-dollar-a-day baseball, three thousand miles away. He sends me a note two years later, picture of some blond bimbo, saying he's married. Next year another note, saying he's divorced."

"Well, he's in San Francisco today. And half of Fresno is there hoping he'll play today, along with half the nation. You might say he's kind of busy."

"Too busy to call?"

"Some P.R. people are helping him with his messages."

"I thought *you* handled his P.R. Aren't you his agent?"

"I've helped him now and then. He's gone through two or three agents."

"Clipper has helped him."

"Right now, Gloria, he might need less of what he's had and more of what he needs."

"I don't need you telling me what my son needs."

"You coming with me, or not?"

"I wouldn't be seen dead in that money-draining stadium." She noticed that he'd put on a white dress shirt and wore his slacks today. "How will you get home?"

His long legs had taken him away. The slight hitch in his knee reminded her how awful and cruel the world could be.

ᔆᔆᔆ

The leather burned hot against Gloria's back as Luke shut the car door after her. He gave her a two-finger salute and walked toward Tulare Street. Bastard. His loose gallop reminded her of how he'd taken the court to beat her high school's team two years running.

She'd asked him to come across town for her senior prom. They'd had fun for a while. Until restlessness—wildness maybe—had driven her to break up with him. She'd quit her job downtown, clerking at Gottschalk's. Just twenty years old when she hopped that Greyhound.

"Why New Orleans?" Papa Boo had asked her.

"The colors in a book I saw."

He'd given her money and said, "Go look at the colors."

ᔆᔆᔆ

The Lexus idled. Maybe she should have walked with Luke, gotten out of this mood that had bothered her so much lately. The car's air conditioning finally cooled her brow. Then, in a time frame more dream than memory, François LeJeune tried one of his sneak attacks—the touch of his custody.

She'd been serving a life sentence, she reminded herself, for one youthful mistake. Frank LeJeune. That son of a bitch. She'd given so much to him and got nothing back. Why couldn't she bury him? Some said there was sweetness in regret, but evidently not for her.

She revved the engine. She was hungry. Hungry enough to charge across the street and choke down a sandwich at the hofbrau that had replaced the old Coney Island eatery. "Red hots," she'd called them when Papa Boo used to walk her in. All in white cotton. Brushed black hair. Huge and spectral Armenian eyes.

Someone rapped on her window. Was it Luke coming back to apologize for deserting her? She put on her sunglasses, faced the glare and lowered the glass. A man far younger than Luke stood there. More fastidious in dress and manner. Formal, the way he bent at the waist to look in at her.

"Ms. LeJeune, I hope I didn't startle you."

She backed off the engine. She knew him peripherally enough to attempt a smile.

"I'm Neil Blake," he said. Nice haircut, good teeth, dress shirt and tie in this heat. "I'm the structural engineer on this job." He tilted his head toward the building. "Is Clipper around?"

"No," she said. "You might find Luke Kaminski at the stadium. He's the architect."

"Guess you'll have your eyes glued to the game today, rooting for Navo."

She experienced a sensation at once foreboding and thrilling. "If I'm near a TV."

"I've never met Navo."

"He doesn't spend much time in town."

"We're connected, oddly enough."

"Connected? With Navo?"

"In a way we *were*." Blake's pale eyes slanted away, then back. "He's been seeing my ex-wife."

Her mind raced, slammed to a halt. Contrary to Luke's opinion, she knew when to listen. "Oh?"

"My wife and I are experiencing a rediscovery of each other."

"Your ex-wife." She couldn't stop herself from making that clear. "You said she was your ex-wife."

"Right," he said. "A chance to get back together." He swiped the back of his hand at the beads of sweat under his nose. "We have a teen-aged son who needs us both."

"Not if your marriage didn't work." Ask me, she thought, I'm an expert.

He backed off then came back with a grin working on his tanned face. "Have you been following him in the blogs?"

"I don't follow blogs," she said. She was going to quip something about remembering when *Twitter* was a cheap version of *Playboy* magazine, but didn't want to date herself.

"Loads of stuff lately, pictures of him and Judi Gillespie."

"Who?"

"Film star," he said. "Big cult following."

Surely he was talking about the bimbo with the Harley. "She's in porno?"

"I wouldn't go so far as to say that."

Now he'd completely turned away. Not a gesture of goodbye, only a glance over his shoulder that caught her off guard. She'd wanted more information from him about Navo.

No telling what his life was like, all the crazy women out there. Jeez, didn't Frank used to sing a song about that?

It wasn't until she'd driven free of the alley, settled the car on its northern route that it struck her.

Her spine was up.

Old World style, Luke would say.

That intuitive rush to protect what was hers.

It might have been veiled, but that man had just threatened her youngest.

She turned on the car's radio. Must be the station Luke had dialed in. She turned the volume down to just a dreamlike patter, some talk about Navo LeJeune back today, after being out for two games. How the lay-off might hurt his chances to keep his streak going. She knew enough about the broadcasts to know one of the sportscasters, either Hick or Huff, was talking about Navo coming to bat in the bottom of the first inning.

She found herself paralyzed, as the voice on the radio became secretive. The crowd added a strange silence. The sound of mid-breath, she thought, how heavy it felt, how it was as if her life had stopped.

Then she heard it. The sound of it. It could be nothing else. The impact of her son's swing finding the target. In the storm of noise, she couldn't breathe, couldn't see through her tears, couldn't stop her trembling fingers from raking trails through her thick, damp hair.

"Forty-six," she whispered.

CHAPTER 24

Navo reminded himself that the team was in Arizona, had been for a couple of hours. In the secrecy of his coved elbow, his voice resonated like blue rushing air.

"Nice voice." Tamara Bix said. "I thought you were asleep."

He rolled over in bed to find her at the hotel's window table with Cyrus. "John Mayer," he said. "One of his old ones. *Gravity.*"

She shut down her laptop and reached for a magazine. "See this bit in *Someone.*" She held up the copy. "You'll notice my name's in the credits."

"That right?"

"So you can blame me if you don't like it."

"I do," he said, "blame you, I mean."

She howled in apparent frustration. "Blame me for networking you while you're at it."

Navo wished for the elusive narcotic of sleep. "We take care of everything, Bix?"

"Almost," Bix said. "Except that message at the desk—those precious words of support from your ex-wife." She pulled her top off, cast it aside. "You even remember her name?" She stepped out of her slacks, kicked them away and stood, magnificent in black bra and panties. "Roll over."

"Bix," he pleaded. And yes, he did remember. Her name was Tess, a yellow-haired girl from a town near St. Louis, who'd thought she liked baseball.

"Now," Bix shouted.

"Do what she say, Bossa Navo."

Hearing Cyrus, harrumphing about his giving in, he complied with her order. Face in a pillow, he felt her straddle his lower legs. When her fingers began to work along his back, he began to relax. Damn, he hadn't slept a wink on the flight.

"Bix." She'd pulled down his briefs, her thumbs digging near his balls. He felt her grip and release his ass cheeks, his hamstrings and calves. Up and down his legs in a continued pattern.

"Turn over and show me your shins," she said.

He complied. "Careful, they're still smarting." He thought of the night in Bix's loft with Judi. "Whatever possessed her," he asked Bix, "to mount that fucking Harley?"

"Wasn't that wild?"

"Say it was," Cyrus said.

"That's Judi for you," Bix said. "Always looking for some excitement." Her eyes found Navo. "Jesus, the play it got us. That little bit you and Cyrus did on Saturday for the barbeque chain?" She placed her palms on Navo's knees, and leaned over him. "Five minutes, and you both netted fifty grand." She laughed. "And you get to keep the Harleys." When both men remained silent, she laughed again. "Jesus, the video of you two riding those hogs into the restaurant, demanding ribs. Pure genius, you gotta admit."

Navo felt her hands go from his knees to his feet. "Ouch."

"Got my hands from working four years as a plumber's helper in my uncle's shop."

"Say you did," Cyrus chimed in, like a curious old squire.

"It got me away from my mother and her hard-dick boyfriends." Her hands warmed his toes. "Wasn't sixteen and I'm threading, fitting pipe like it's a metaphor—if you'll excuse the comparison."

"Mercy," Cyrus uttered.

Navo raised a hand, attempted to work his mouth around a reminder to Cyrus that he was scheduled to pitch tomorrow. "The heat on that field tomorrow—you can't get a full breath."

"Shush," Bix told him. "Field will be covered tomorrow, and it's a night game."

He slipped toward slumber, all the while listening to Bix and Cyrus conversing in low voices about how tomorrow was already here,

"I think he's out, Bix."

Her hands left him, and he regretted her dismount, the sheet floating down over him. He dared a peek to see her sucking in her abdomen to snap her pants. Cyrus at the window was tinted blue from lights below.

"Look at him, Cyrus," Bix was saying. "Broke Rose's mark and he's Rip Van Winkle over there, sleeping through the cyber age. Jesus, if he ever knew what I'm dealing with here and what's going on with my staff in California…" Her voice trailed off.

"Nothin' but him on the TV, too." Cyrus, the ever faithful.

"Look at this stuff." Navo heard her collecting her papers.

"He aint doing too bad."

"Resurrection."

"Say?"

"He's finally playing for himself," Bix said. Navo peeked again to see them at the door. "For himself," Bix repeated. "It's a lot like what I do, Cyrus. You kill your mother, kill your brother, and kill a few lovers. Then you start page two." Silence, then, "You coming?"

"Say?"

"Your room, rookie, we got to work on *you* now."

"I got this pounding in my head."

"What's it sound like, honey?"

"Like someone."

"Someone approaching or following?"

"Both."

"Well let's go. Sounds like we got a lot of work to do."

Then she said something about Navo's moon being in just the right celestial position for him to rule the universe.

Right before the door clicked shut.

❧❧❧

Navo's heart dove when he heard his phone. Few people knew his new number and he'd just got off the phone with Clipper. Then he remembered calling a number Joe had given him not that long ago.

"Navo?"

"Melanie."

"Forgive me calling. You must be swamped with messages."

"New phone, just for certain numbers." He waited, hoping her voice would soften, creep into his ear like it had that night in the tall trees. "I wondered if I'd ever hear your voice again."

"I saw you on TV the last couple of days."

"Yeah?"

"You damn near broke my heart." Her words sounded constricted, clipped with emotion. "I'm ashamed about not calling you back."

"Forget it." The one quality that had drawn him to her was her blunt honesty. Now she sounded guarded. "You're different."

"No."

"Is Joe okay?"

"Yes."

"Your work?"

"I've run into some shit I need to sort out."

"Can I help?" Could he? Probably not. This hit him like a cold wind. That she and her realm were beyond his involvement. "Talk to me, Melanie." He counted the seconds. "Christ, I haven't been able to get you out of my mind."

"I need some time."

"That's a movie I saw once."

"I know it."

"What about us, Melanie?"

"I felt close to you, your image on television. I've never wanted to have someone as much as I did watching you."

He almost said, *to fuck?* "To have?"

"To be close to."

He said it. "To fuck?"

Right back at him. "To fuck." She sounded like she was in trouble. She sounded like him. "And to be close."

"Close," he repeated. He heard voices in the hall, knuckles rapping on his door.

She said, "Good luck later."

"Later is here. The wolves have found me." Beyond the window glass, the Arizona sky developed like a Polaroid photograph in the afternoon sun. A tremor of heat raced along his legs as if someone had applied a secret balm. "I'm coming," he shouted at the door. "God dammit, I'm on my way." Then into the phone, "Melanie?"

"Yes."

"I gotta see you again."

"Me, too." Her words had yearning, mourning, pieces of everything he'd heard in his own voice. "I mean it's *you* I gotta see again."

CHAPTER 25

Outside the retractable ceiling, the blazing sun was finally out of the sky when Navo's broken bat flare dropped inches beyond the Diamondback shortstop's extended glove and shallow of the left-fielder's desperate dive. Insignificant little blooper, born of splintered wood.

Still, it made forty-seven games now.

Bank One Park roared as he rounded first base, danced back to the bag, stood under the raining noise. A flood of relief fed his depleted muscles and nerve circuits. It was getting late in the game. This might have been his last chance to garner a base hit.

Arizona's first baseman, Bill Bruce, planted an encouraging slap on his rear and grinned.

Everybody loved a streak.

***

Surviving this long in the big leagues had stirred Navo into many a teammate's domestic life. Not for any extended time, though. It's not the game's inclination to keep players tight. Fellowship comes in doses determined by club owners' heartless trading, their constant efforts to field winning combinations.

"Your best friend today, might be your hated enemy tomorrow," Navo had been told early on by wary veterans.

He tended to edit his teammates' histories, carve them into stereotypes. Especially those who were married. It was easier than knowing them in full. Tonight after the game, Lionel Thoroughgood approached him when the media finally cut him loose.

"You're coming with me," the Lion ordered him. "You and your blues brother over there."

Navo glanced at Cyrus, still at his locker, looking lost. He waved a limp hand as if to break up a bothersome fog. Pitching coach Tex Littlejohn had told him he wouldn't start until the Colorado series this coming weekend.

Navo could tell Thoroughgood was on a mission to offer salvation and wanted to take him and Cyrus home for some time away from baseball.

"Don't worry, LeJeune," the Lion said. "We got air conditioning and an extra bed or two."

It became clear on the drive that Thoroughgood's methods were admirable, taking two mates away from the world of hitting streaks and weird arm ailments.

"We're a bit oddball, the three of us," Thoroughgood said. "Not tied to an army of agents, accountants, lawyers, personal trainers, physicians, church leaders, gurus and other such types, one hand patting your back, other in your wallet."

"Not tied to them," Cyrus agreed from the undistinguished minivan's back seat, "Or does the company store own you yet, Navo?"

"Tamara Bix claims I'll be signing endorsements and agreements faster than I can write."

The Lion laughed as he drove. "She'll have you part of the pudding."

Closer to Tempe than Phoenix, the drive took thirty minutes. Thoroughgood talked about how he'd purchased the land six years ago when he was a member of the Arizona organization.

"Got lucky as loaded dice when I met Emma," he said. "Built her a house out here. Started a family." He slowed the van. "Here we are." In the darkness the building's lines rose in soft monotone against the sky. "You like the style, Navo?"

"Jesus."

"Amen," said the Lion. "Beats the hell out of living in Watts."

What set Thoroughgood apart and made him so righteous in an old school way? Maybe the way he grabbed up his children and held them to his chest. The expression he exchanged with his wife, Emma, that glint in their eyes.

"You've met Emma," Thoroughgood said. "These two scandals are Wallace and Norah."

Wallace raised a hand to control the scene. "We got us a secret."

"Oh, oh," Cyrus mugged. "What's the scoop?"

The boy's grin lacked a few teeth. "Daddy struck out today."

Easing his kids to the floor, Thoroughgood turned to kiss his wife. "Put these two back in bed where you got them."

Wallace swung a plastic bat. His sister Norah, obviously younger than he, dropped to all fours. "Strike three," Wallace shouted.

Emma smiled at the teammates. "I've cooked a brisket in case anybody's hungry."

❧❧❧

After dinner, they sat in a den, all the seating plush, yet short of the Southwestern craze for hugeness. Navo liked the colors in the decor, which ranged from white to rich sienna. Thoroughgood brought them drinks. Emma crossed the room to punch up dark jazz from a display of cutting-edge console equipment.

She frowned as Thoroughgood handed her a drink. "It's after midnight," she said "What am I drinking?"

"Jack Daniels and a fistful of ice," he said. "What else?"

"Maybe Navo and Cyrus would prefer something else."

The Lion rumbled from deep in his chest. Navo knew the sound well, had witnessed it settle many a clubhouse squabble.

Navo held his tumbler forth in wordless salute. "Suits us fine."

"Fine," Cyrus repeated taking a dainty sip.

"Quick story," Thoroughgood said in a voice that found an orator's sonority. "Ten years ago, I left a boat in an L.A. marina, Rolls Royce in a dealer's service department, said so long to five thousand square feet of pool and hot tub I'd never tried sober." He drank, smacked his lips. "Gave my chopper to some fool who cycled off to where no man's heard from him since."

"Wasn't a friend of Tamara Bix was it?" said Cyrus, chancing an interjection.

Thoroughgood sloughed him off. "Shit, I left a pool table and a *snooker* table with a first wife who thought they were for dancing."

"Spare us the details." Emma could be a salon portrait, relaxed with her long, brown legs tucked under her. Exotic eyes behind upheld glass.

"Point is, finding a groove in life cost me more than anybody should pay a man to play a game simple as baseball." In a moment of oceanic silence, he leveled Navo with a look suggesting paragraphs of thought. "What I'm saying is a man has got to be careful."

"Aint but a game," Cyrus put in.

"Damn kids' game," Navo agreed.

Emma hummed to a horn that rallied in the background.

"Who we trying to kid?" said the Lion. "The last ballgame played will be God's final edict." He stood to collect glasses. "Can we handle one more?"

Tension in Navo's neck eased. He blocked out all but the soft turn of time here among friends. How generous the Thoroughgoods, how genuine the Lion's qualms about quick fame when measured against a child's secret, against the taste and smell of slow-roasted brisket, against a lover's chiding, against the sound of John Coltrane and Miles Davis in your own home.

When all conversation began to stall, Emma eased herself from her lounge chair and motioned to Navo to follow her.

"Lionel's messages," she whispered, "are earnest if not eloquent."

"He gets his points across."

Navo glanced about as she showed him the home. Everywhere signs of her hand and her man's histories presented themselves. But missing were glossy superstar portraits, magazine covers of Thoroughgood. Absent too, the obligatory trophy case.

"What subject do you teach?" Navo asked in front of photographs showing Emma in situations suggesting academic reward.

"Social studies, high school."

He pictured her in front of teen-aged savages. "That can't be easy."

She grinned. "It's the pay that keeps me going." She opened a door to a large, windowed bath facility. "Cyrus's room is next door. It really pleases Lionel when he can bring pals home."

"Pleases us."

"He's choosey. Tell you the truth, him picking you surprised me a bit." There was a teasing dimple at the corner of her mouth.

"Yeah?"

"You must be in trouble."

"The streak."

"And something else."

"That it can end on my next swing?"

"No." She crossed her arms over strong breastwork. "He tells me you've met someone." She shook her hand in the air between them. A gesture he bet she used in class to indicate her student had gone after a wrong answer. "Someone apart from the women riding the streak with you."

"An artist who has her own world." He wanted to say more, but nothing seemed to fit Melanie. Nothing fine enough. Jesus, he felt lame.

She gave him a long look. "Time for one of *my* quick stories?"

"Shoot."

"I'm married to Lionel less than a year. I follow him to New York for a series against the Mets."

"Yeah."

"Has to be separate flights of course, but I get to stay in the hotel room with him."

"Of course."

"We go down for a pre-dinner drink." She watched Navo's eyes. "Some guy saying he's a coach for the team comes up to me, hands me three hundred dollars, says it's for our dinner."

"Yeah."

"As long as I get my ass out of the bar and take Lionel with me."

"Wives aren't allowed." Navo said, thinking, no surprise there.

"Right," she said. "I can't have a drink with my husband in the team's hotel, for fear I'll see other married players screwing around on their wives."

Navo waited. Finally that lively dimple tugged Emma's mouth again. "This friend of yours, can she deal with shit like that?"

"I haven't known her long, but I'd bet a few bucks if a coach or anybody else tried that with her, he'd wish to hell he hadn't."

"You'd bet on her with your bottom dollar?"

"Yeah, like that."

Emma turned, obviously preparing to leave him alone in front of his room for the night. "Then you better try entering a piece of *her* world.

"And while you are filing that away in your mind, you might remember what this season means to your lion of a teammate." She hesitated with a slight smile, as if anticipating a roar to rise from the other wing of the house. "Mr. Thoroughgood might fool you into thinking baseball is just a game, but he would kill to get into a World Series. He was a year short when he played here, and a year late going to the Giants."

"I have the feeling you're telling me to stay away from motorcycles."

"I knew you would understand." She began to walk away, but turned back as if remembering something. "You won't find much stuff in the house building up his image, Mr. LeJeune, but Lionel wants a World Series ring."

Navo chose to merely nod.

"And that isn't all," she said.

"Hall of Fame," he offered. "The Lion wants to make the Hall of Fame."

"Lionel *expects* to make it," she said softly, almost to herself, as she walked away.

CHAPTER 26

It was the first day of August and over ninety degrees even this close to the beach. Melanie turned left on Spyglass Drive and found a spot near the delicatessen she often patronized. She parked and thought about what she needed.

Her workshop began in about an hour, the same time Navo's game would start on TV. Couldn't sacrifice her scheduled life, couldn't put off art for a lover's game, right?

Hell, she couldn't watch all his games, any more than she could watch Joe every time he surfed. Nice level way to put it. When in reality she hadn't been able to shake the gripping image of Navo's face, his natural grace on the field. God, she'd never survive if she kept *feeling* him, feeling this ballplayer who'd talked about desperation with such trustfulness that he made it sound honorable. Like their mutual recklessness that night was a sign of hope.

After picking out cold meats and cheeses, she found a package of sliced pumpernickel bread and a loaf of San Luis sourdough. To her regular purchase of two gallons of cider, she added two chilled bottles of red wine from a Paso Robles winery. After they finished tonight she'd have a taste with the group. Valerie Del Toro too, if she stayed until everything ended,

At the counter, she heard Navo's name being tossed around between two couples. By the amount of sunscreen on their noses and their seaside sweatshirts, they appeared to be vacationers. A woman in the foursome made a sour face. "The idea of this guy trying to be Joe DiMaggio—"

"Give some guy enough steroids and look what happens," her male partner said. "No one's even heard of the guy before this."

"Give him a gun and he could be a poster for Al-Qaeda," the second female said.

The second male held up a tabloid and pointed at the cover photo. "That aint a gun, Eleanor, and I don't think that's a bat in his pants here either."

Melanie stopped and looked. *The Enquirer.* Navo. Holding in his arms a young woman dressed for rock, or roll, or torture. Fuck, she couldn't be sure.

"Excuse me." She used her basket as a scraper, moving the group out of her way. She halted when they'd formed a half circle, not an arm's length away. "That's nine inches of cock in his pants," she said, smiling like Miss Hawaii. "And you can tell, if you look close, it's not even hard." There, she'd just given Navo a couple of inches he didn't deserve.

In her pickup, she unwrapped food items with trembling hands. Blindly, she shoved stuff into her mouth and chewed it much like a starved and abandoned animal would.

eﾗ⊃eﾗ⊃

Melanie knew Walker had leased this building south of San Louis Obispo two months ago. Little more than a vacant shell with an office and a restroom, it served its purpose. He had equipped the space with settings and adequate lighting for the models. He'd even thrown in a few aluminum easels and drawing boards. When Valerie

Del Toro informed Melanie she could provide models with dancing experience this time, Melanie had e-mailed a few young artists who'd been attending her workshops. Though it was Tuesday, all eight of the students she'd invited showed up.

"You know the drill," she said, feeling stronger now that she was in what her father used to call her *element*. "This is a workshop. That means I get to work too. We start with quick poses. Valerie will guide the models. We're lucky to have three dancers tonight, so let's take advantage of their physicality. Two and three-minute poses."

She turned and addressed the dancers." Stay on the move until the mood hits you to freeze. Don't be reluctant to come together at times. If the notion hits you, *intertwine."* She laughed. "But not for long. The idea is to *flow."*

When Valerie started the music, two females and one male came from behind the partition. All three wore robes they began shedding once they were inspired by the music. Melanie could feel the excitement in the room. This trio of models was a good age, into their thirties, with well-defined muscularity.

The real test would be their ability to stay energized. A quick glance at her workshop artists told her they'd need to keep their approaches fresh and vital. She remembered each student's stalling points. While she hoped to get in a round of sketching herself, she'd act as their mentor, never insisting on anything but the *life* in life drawing.

She moved with the music, stopping for a minute or two when she'd found the pose she wanted to use as inspiration. She had her own unique way of holding an eighteen-by-twenty-four sketch pad in the bend of her left arm—the way she'd hold a drunken buddy—then drawing upon it with a lithograph pencil held between her thumb and forefinger.

"Look for the attitude," she said, as she drew blindly on her pad. "Draw what you feel the model is suggesting. Draw the model's ethos. Define the *stance* of the model." She wanted to take her smock off. She wanted to be naked. She wanted to be free. She wanted to live forever. And she wanted to make love.

Someone blew a whistle.

She fell on her ass. "What was that?"

"You told me to let you know when twenty minutes were up." Valerie grinned from across the room. "Thought I better end this debauchery."

Melanie sat cross-legged on the floor and assessed the damage. The models—two fillies and a colt, lathered and wild eyed—were breathing hard, but remained upright. Her workshop members had carried their drawing boards away from their easels. Assessing sketches scattered about them on the floor, they stood hunched, hands on knees, abdomens contracting. It looked like every one of them had taken off at least one garment with each sketch.

"Watch out for the drawings," Melanie shouted. "Collect them, and let's take a break while we tape them up for praise."

"What's next?" Valerie asked.

"Longer poses, more detailed studies." Her voice rang above in the exposed ceiling structure of the building. "Let's put DiVinci on the run."

❧❧❧

Melanie matched Val's evil smile and shook her head.

Valerie swigged straight from the wine bottle. "I'm sorry about Lashawn's dick sock. He makes those things himself." She grinned. "He and two other black guys do private parties."

"I just asked that he wear a jock during the quick stuff. Tell him next time to knit one any color but pink."

It was late. Delbert, one of her most promising students, a truck driver by trade, had brought in an ice chest full of Fosters. Along with deli items, the ever-living pot of coffee, the cider, and Val's batch of hemp-laced brownies, everyone had managed to fill their mouths. A necessary function, she'd learned.

Draw naked people, and you had to eat. She'd heard that was true of gamblers. Bet money, and you had to put something in your mouth.

She would have to ask Navo to check with his brother Clipper on that.

"Great session." Valerie, poured her more wine. "Very generous of you to give everyone one of your quick sketches before they left. How much are they worth now?"

God, if Walker knew she'd given any work away, he'd die. "I really don't know."

"Take a guess just for me."

"A thousand, maybe, if you had a buyer." She remembered sketching in that East Bay bar, trading her rhythm-induced drawings for whatever bill was offered her. Navo's voice, '*She ever take a break, talk with anybody?*'

She looked at the two pieces she'd done from the ten minute studies. "Gustine should be pleased with those."

"How much for them?"

"Hell, I'm not sure, Val." She was irritated now, another emotion that came with the territory. *Her element.* "What was all that about the cell phones?" Valerie had ordered them to be turned in at the door.

"I made them check 'em with me," Valarie said, appearing to be on edge herself. "Not because they might go off, Melanie." She paused, went on even more upset. "If someone wanted to, this session of yours could be working its way throughout the net right now."

She pointed a finger at an imaginary monitor. "There you are Ms. Blake, splayed on the floor, nothing on under your smock." She gave her a look that said, yeah, I peeked. "And all around you, nothing but naked and half naked people."

Melanie felt a flutter of panic. "I have to be more careful." Val's dark eyes wouldn't let her go. "God, Val what is it?"

"The stuff being put out there..."

"Yes?"

"Stuff about you is fairly tame. Suggestive but tame."

"Me?"

"Everything about Navo LeJeune is getting crazier by the minute. So we have to watch out. You don't want to hand Neil Blake and his attorney anything on a platter."

"I gotta go home," she said, collecting her work. Here she was again, dealing with the panic. "Gotta get back to Joe."

ભઃઃ

Outside, Melanie accepted Valerie's help to arrange everything in her pickup.

"When Delbert went out to get his ice chest?" Valerie stepped back and placed her hands on her narrow hips, as if demanding attention.

"What?"

"I told him to find out how your ballplayer did."

A truck passed in the night, bringing in its wake the smell of a flower farm across Tank Road.

"They give scores on phones?"

"Some guy named LeJeune went wild. Delbert said he would've hit for the cycle, but was robbed by a great catch in center, right up against the fence."

"Cycle?"

"Yeah. Let me help you in your truck, girl. You going to be okay?"

"I'll be fine, thank you."

"I'm not sure how many games that makes," Valarie said. "But I think it's forty-seven."

"Forty-eight," said Melanie, "That's forty-eight."

CHAPTER 27

The thing that brought Jim Caruba to the San Joaquin Valley heat on Wednesday was the fact that Junior Shavers had called and said he had a plan that involved the streak hitter who'd made it forty-eight in a row yesterday in Arizona.

Now, if Jim could remember Junior's directions, it shouldn't be long before he reconnected with Shavers, an old prison buddy from his days in Lompoc.

His enforcer, sitting next to him, tossed corn chips at his mouth. "We there yet? Or are we lost?"

Jim wheeled the sputtering Bronco onto another two-lane blacktop through patchy farmland. "Cope with it," he said, fed up with the journey and the constant gripes from his crew.

"Give it a name, Jim."

They passed crossroads where small trailer parks sat catty-cornered from crops. Here and there were abandoned farm-looking stuff, a beaner taco wagon, the beginnings or endings of a neighborhood.

The bitch in the back seat snapped awake. "Explain to me how we always end up without any fucking ice or a place to go to the bathroom like normal humans?"

Jim wondered if all this was worth the drive. Just to drop by, pay a visit to a pal he hadn't seen since prison.

"What's this guy's name again?" the enforcer asked.

"Junior Shavers," Caruba said. "Claims he knows the ballplayer."

"Guy on the streak?"

"Yeah."

"Guy who gives you the Louie V, then takes it back?"

Tired of verifying, Jim watched the scenery crawl past. He decided to stop alongside a pickup in distress, three black dudes studying what lay under its rusty hood. From the window, he asked them, "Don't Junior Shavers live around here?"

Youngest man in the group smiled at the bitch in the back of the van. "Junior's on up the road 'til you see the white house," he said. "Dog out front you got to watch."

Jim waved adios to the shade-tree mechanics. "We in the right area," he told his enforcer. Up the road, he spotted an old, white Victorian style house. "This must be it."

"The house from *Psycho*," the bitch said.

Jim chuckled. Shit, you had to laugh at the bitch now and then, else she turned cold. He wheeled the Bronco onto a rutted drive with citrus trees either side, and stopped the van, and put it in park. A girl/woman stepped from behind the trees, canting her face as she walked toward them.

She pointed to the house's porch. "Who you after? Nobody up there but a mean bastard and a champeen fighting dog."

A figure came lumbering off the porch. Looked like crazy Junior.

"Tell that ugly fuck that Jimmy Caruba come to see him."

Yeah, that was Junior, wild eyes, Jerry Garcia beard. He'd talk to him; give him a chance to air out his scheme.

The girl was on the driver's side, nipple smudges on her Lady Gaga t-shirt, meth-ravaged smile on her chapped lips. "I'm Charlene."

Junior Shavers seemed to be picking up the pace on the route from the house downhill. "God dammit, Charlene, where's Pig?"

Jim opened his door, stood outside on stiff legs. His roughneck enforcer was easing out of his side over there, and the bitch—well, she'd jumped out from the back seat and was clutching her purse to her short leather skirt.

"I got to pee like a racehorse," she said.

Down the slope came Junior, screeching, "Pig!"

And it occurred to Jim, *Pig must be the champeen fighting dog.*

"Pig!" screamed Charlene, terror in her voice.

Right then, his roughneck baller went down in a fury of dust as a madman's rendition of a yellow cur attached himself to the tattoo above his hi-top Zappos.

"Yeow!"

"Pig!"

"Holy fucking Christ!"

And a shot rang out.

Answered by an almost human yelp.

Another shot.

"That's enough!" Jim yelled at the bitch. The ho stood there, piss splattering the dirt between her widespread feet. "I'd say you got the motherfucker."

Two bullets gone from her five-shot .32 with dog fur fluttering down on the now-silent scene like godless snow.

☙☙☙

Jim and Junior watched the farmhouse from the Bronco as the merciless sun finally arched over their heads.

"Tell me again how it works," Jim said.

"He's got different ones he brings out here. Did I mention that?"

"You did." Fucking Junior, the way he told his stories, emphasizing the juicy parts. "You ever like, peek in the windows?"

Junior shot him a loopy grin. "Who me?"

"So then what?"

"I mentioned it's always two cars?"

"You did."

"Him first, then the chick."

"She has to knock on the door?"

"Like yoo-hoo, anyone home?" Junior grinned again. "They go at it an hour, hour and half tops. Then the chick comes out, drives off. He stays, listens to fucking Cajun shit, and sometimes dozes off. Then bic, bic, bic." Junior walked his fingers through the van's heavy air. "He's back in his Porsche heading home to his old lady."

"Bic, bic, bic?"

"Just like that."

"You got to hand it to the guy." Jim looked away from the silent farmhouse, the ravaged land. "I told you I seen his brother in San Fran. I tried to hit him up for Cleavus Macon's debt, the two of them being roommates and all."

"See how it's a small world?"

"His brother, the guy on the streak," Jim said, making it sound as if he'd contributed great weight to their discussion.

"See how it's tied in?" Junior said. "Like it's fucking ordained."

"How often does this Clipper come out here?"

"Every few nights."

"Like I said, you got to hand it to the guy." Jim looked eastward at a smear of mountain peaks. Heat in the van was intense. Using his leader's voice, he said, "All in all, I'm thinking, pass."

"Jim, this comes to me as something you can handle." Junior pulled on his beard, his eyes rheumy and crazed. "I aint physical enough to handle it alone."

"Sounds to me like it's an old score you want to settle."

"Maybe, but the money is there in that farmhouse." Junior's black eyes surveyed the scene before them. "There's so much money involved here…"

"Junior, you been smokin' your home cookin'."

"Fifty years of a bookie's action. And Clipper LeJeune knows where it's buried."

Jim chuckled. "After the Yankee Clipper?"

"One bro named after him, the other bro chasing his record."

"It's all kinda ironic."

"Like I say, it's ordained."

"I'm still thinking, pass."

"You owe me, Jim."

"How many times I got to express my regrets about the dog?"

"I had Pig primed for a main event."

"Tell that to my baller." Jim buckled his seat belt and started the van. "If he aint dead yet from rabies."

❧❧❧

It came to Jim on the short drive back to Junior's. "The Clipper—you can get a good angle with your camera?"

"Other night, he's got this babe on the kitchen table. The view's perfect because the window doesn't even have a shade."

Jim tried to frame it. "Not your usual missionary position."

"And did I mention he's got a bad leg?"

Jim nodded as he drove. "Keep it simple then. Snap your picture, split, send a letter to his casino marked personal. Use a Kinko's processor, gloves. Make sure there are no prints."

"And include a photo."

"Now you're thinking." Jim found the path to the white Victorian, drove over the spot where the bitch hit Pig with both shots. "Tell this Clipper the picture's on the Internet for his wife to see, if he don't pay the price."

"And for his daughter to see."

"See how personal this is?" Jim said as he parked the van. "And how I don't want in?" He could give Shavers a dozen reasons why it sucked.

"Where's the drop?" Junior asked, looking at Jim as if the caper were being developed without his blessing.

"I'm thinking your mail box."

"You fucking nuts?" Junior erased the suggestion with a swing of his hand.

"Think about it. The way it could work."

Junior's haggard face fell into deep thought then he said—like he was in a movie—"What package?" Playing it like he was testifying to the police. "I never seen no package."

"That's how you'll act."

"I been out of town." Junior seemed to be enjoying himself now and went on as if reading a script. "You telling me Clipper put a package of money in my fucking mail box?"

"There you go, but you'll act even more indignant."

"I like it, Jim."

"Now you owe me. Your other plan to go after them both is way too complicated." Jim looked into Junior's terrorist eyes as he got out of the van. "Besides, I'd like to leave the hitter alone. See how far he can go with his streak. He got forty-eight last night in Arizona."

"How about today?"

"They play one more against the Diamondbacks then move on to Denver tomorrow." Jim looked at his former Folsom cell mate. "You got a TV in that old house of yours?"

๛

At six, Jim turned on the ballgame. Nothing but Navo LeJeune, Navo LeJeune, Navo LeJeune. Will he keep it going or will his streak end?

Charlene, not giving one shit, made home-made pizza in a gas stove. The dog-bitten baller finally succumbed to various drugs and shots of Effen vodka. The bitch sat at a table covered with oilcloth, trimming her toenails.

"Leave the tomatoes off mine," she said to Charlene, "and the mushrooms."

"That's what it's made out of, else it aint pizza." Her eyes blazed with crystal meth. Jim wondered about asking Junior to give her time out, the way she kept coming into the living room, swinging it in front of his face.

"I like gravy on mine," he told her. "Aint any shame in my game."

"Looky there!" That came from Junior, sitting on a couch that smelled like Pig.

Jim swung a glance at the TV. "The hitter?"

"Clean single," Junior said. "Number forty-nine, any damn way you look at it."

CHAPTER 28

Dressed for the opener in Denver Thursday night, Navo got word that he'd start in centerfield.

"Give Marvin Riggins a rest," is the way Coach Bushmill put it.

A pang of fear opened an adrenalin gate next to Navo's heart. Centerfield was a monster here at Coors Field. A mute expanse of olive green he'd never roamed. He glanced at Riggins who sat a few stalls away. The stylish outfielder made an okay sign with his long fingers and grinned.

Bushmill caught up with him, first step out of the dugout. His warped forehead indicated he'd read Navo's reaction. "You got the speed."

"Had at one time."

"It's breaking for the ball that counts."

"The break, yeah."

"The angle."

"The angle, yeah."

"Riggins has the best first step in the league," Bushmill gasped as they trotted onto the field. "Take some fly balls out here with him, listen and watch what he tells you about the yard."

"I'll watch and listen."

"You're never too old to learn."

"Never."

"Alleys are humongous."

He and Bushmill, Navo thought. Aging player and a coach. Both hanging on to this season and hoping for at least one more. The ballpark broke cool, green, and deep-fried gold in front of their eyes. "You're right," he said, "Fucking alleys are oceans."

"But you'll play shallow." It was Marvin Riggins's voice, as he glided along on Navo's other side.

"I'll play shallow," Navo repeated like a school boy. But why?

"Air is so thin out here, anything over your head is gone, or you'll end up chasing it anyway."

Coach Bushmill chugged to catch up. His smile slashed his parchment face. "Think of it this way, LeJeune, your turn will come at bat."

"It'll come," Navo said.

"And you'll welcome the thin air."

"With open arms."

Bushmill began to wobble and the two players slowed their pace. "See the Rocky Mountains out there?' the coach asked.

"I see 'em, yeah."

"Aim for those."

"I'll be batting left-handed."

"Then improvise."

"Improvise."

"Hit the motherfucker into that angled pocket along the right field line and you'll run all day."

Riggins laughed into the atmosphere. "Run all day," he repeated.

Later, Navo floated in the mile-high ambience like a newborn, recalling how, when they were kids, Clipper and he would hit balls to each other until the bat handle became sticky from their broken blisters. Grounders for Navo, who seemed born for the infield. Fly balls for Clipper, the natural outfielder. Navo would hit ball after ball into the sky, trying for points beyond Clipper's range. Rarely did he reach one. His brother was too quick to respond to the crack of bat against ball.

☙❧☙

Somewhere in the middle of the game—on a flat out sprint—Navo felt the warning track under his cleats. He gambled for one final search to find the ball against the darkened sky, then collided with the fence. Not his first time, but certainly one of the worst.

He smelled the earth, heard voices. He rolled over and stared at the stars.

Someone mentioned a cart. Navo shook his head. "No, get me up first, I want to test my bones, see if they haven't splintered."

Many hands assisted him. Vitucci trotted out from his position behind the plate. And Josiah Swain must have raced over from right field. Christ, even Toby Mayfield from left field.

"The ball," Navo said to Vitucci.

"In your fucking glove."

"Don't know how you ever caught up to it LeJeune, let alone found it, and put it away," Swain blubbered.

"Might be the greatest catch I ever seen," Mayfield said, turning to trot back to his domain, as if the moment should pass into the archives, as if the game would on forever and the party would never end.

☙❧☙

Navo sat with Domingo Matta at the manager's televised press conference. Half zoned out on a pair of pills given to him by trainer Harry Bloomberg, he listened as his skipper summed up the game. Mirabel Pacal had pitched a gem until the eighth. Wil Campion, and then Weird Al Fletcher had mopped up the damage before it got out of hand.

Giants four. Colorado Rockies three.

"Turning point in the game," Matta said to a cluster of microphones in front of him, "was LeJeune's catch in the sixth inning."

Sixth? Navo slumped in his chair and tried, in a swarm of temporal pain, to recall his times at bat. He remembered being walked in the first.

Shit, he'd walked again in the fourth, hadn't he? He heard his name as every breath in the room formed the word *Navo*. And he thought of *her* name. *Melanie,* another everyday name.

"After walking your first two times at bat, Navo, were you feeling extra pressure?" Many respectful chuckles, some reverent murmurs.

"Who me?"

Laughter. "Your body has been taking a beating."

"You asking which is worst, motorcycles or fences?"

More laughter. "Think you'll be ready tomorrow?"

"That's up to Skipper Matta." Navo wondered if Harry Bloomberg had any more of those pills.

He'd come to bat again in the top half of the sixth. He remembered it now. Yeah, he'd hit a line drive off the fence, right about where he'd crashed a few minutes later.

That had made fifty.

During the remainder of the media conference, he sat in respectful silence as Matta brought everything back to baseball. Back to the Giants as a team.

 భుభుభు

In a marathon fourteen-inning loss to the Rockies Saturday night, Navo managed only one hit in six official trips to the plate. Later, in a sour clubhouse, Coach Bushmill lit into the team as only he could, never singling anyone out, always prescribing ways to lessen mistakes.

In Sunday's day game, Navo pulled the first pitch he saw in the fourth inning down the left field line for a run producing single.

He heard an accusatory sound in his brain that seemed to come from the whole world. Fifty-two games now. Impossible. Couldn't be true. No one would believe this. Or would they?

The sound wouldn't go away. He wanted to apologize. But to whom? Fuck. What if it was true?

With his team ahead by six runs, Matta immediately pulled Navo out of the game and told him to shower and get ready for the flight home.

"With Porterhouse on the mound, we should get out of here quick," Matta said, his face spiritual today. "You'll be sleeping in your own bed tonight."

"Great."

"Your own bed."

Navo nodded. "Got it. My own bed."

ᗧᑎᗧᑎ

After winning this game against the Rockies, the Giants were again tied with the Los Angeles Dodgers for the National League lead. The mood was high as the team got ready for the fight.

Dressed before the others, Navo agreed to a short session with sportswriters outside the visitors' clubhouse. Overall the media's excitement had settled to a slow boil after he'd broken Pete Rose's mark in San Francisco.

Nearing the unreachable number set over a half century ago by Joe DiMaggio now seemed more than just a wild dream.

"It's like you've threatened the goal," *Chronicle* writer Jess Taggart said. "And the goal is fighting back."

This drew a groan from the crowd. Navo cursed himself for agreeing to this. "Give me a break, Jess."

Taggart pressed on. "Haven't you observed the way the earth seems to be standing still?"

He wink-winked at the gathering pool of reporters, as if this interview wouldn't solve world hunger and strife, but Navo's answer might survive the baseball ages.

"Like someone's thickened the gumbo," Navo said, knowing Tamara Bix would love that. He had no problem with Taggart, but the man had never been one to laud him in print.

Taggart chuckled, his wide chest shuddering in mute convulsion. "Like you've shot all the ducks in the pond, and now the gallery is waiting to see what you'll do with the next four."

Navo watched him lick spittle off his upper lip. The others had gone silent. The son of a bitch had mentioned a number, something he knew was taboo.

"DiMaggio's mark," Taggart elaborated, his eyes magnified and amused behind thick glasses.

"I got that, Taggart," Navo said. It was his turn to wink. "Guess you'll have to add 'em one by one."

Taggart pulled open his shirt collar and groaned. "God damn, LeJeune. I've been following you around forever now for a quote like that, and you throw it out here so any short-timer with a note pad and pencil can jump on it."

A rail-thin Denver reporter held up an issue of *Us* Magazine. "Did you see this?"

"Haven't seen that one." Shit, another angle of him with Judi Gillespie in his arms.

Taggart's voice rose again. "You've got bobble head dolls of you waiting in San Francisco."

He amused the constituency by rocking his head side to side. Everyone picked up on that bit of theater, their heads forming a chorus of spasms.

All of them, every last one of them, laughing at the wonder of it all.

CHAPTER 29

Monday morning, Clipper made a special effort to wake up early enough to join Clair and Heather at a table out on the patio.

Clair, in one of her pretty sun outfits made a big deal out of his presence. "To what do we owe the pleasure?"

He thought of saying something about a family eating together stays together but didn't press his luck. Instead he kissed her on the mouth and pulled a butterfly chair over next to her.

He drank some cold orange juice, wiped his mouth with a paper napkin, and looked at his daughter. "Count to fifty-two, Heather."

Clair cut in. "Eat," she told her daughter. Ignoring Clipper she lifted the lid to her clay warming dish. "I made Mexican scramble."

Heather's breakfast suit consisted of a large t-shirt and skimpy gray terry cloth panties, *I'm a Babe* printed in pink across the waist band. She pushed her plate out of her way and began pounding her fist on the redwood table, "One, two three—"

"Okay, that's enough," Clair said. Her voice sounded husky with sleep, maybe her sleeping pills, the three of them together, first time in God knew when.

"Well," Clipper said. "Imagine in your mind counting to fifty-two then."

"I don't get it," Heather said.

"Just listen," Clipper insisted, thinking there ought to be a bounty on females this early in the day. "Hear how long it takes to count that far?" Sunlight through the patio's latticed roof struck both her and her mother's rumpled hair. Clipper lost a breath at the golden sight. "Now count to five," he said.

Clair groaned. "Christ, Clip."

"Come on Heather, count."

Heather shouted, "Onetwothreefourfive."

Clipper smiled at her spirit and gave his wife a triumphant glance. "See how quick and easy the last five were, compared to the first fifty-two?"

Heather answered for her mother. "Navo's at fifty-two, which took him for-freaking-ever." She stretched, yawned. "Now the next five should be a snap is what Daddy is trying to say."

"And puts him over DiMaggio's number," Clipper said.

Heather gave him a high five. "One more than Joe's fifty-six."

"Game's been going on two hundred years, and it's come down to Navo and DiMaggio." Clipper sat in the blue wash of baseball scenarios, mocking birds cawing, as if in applause.

"Where's Navo playing tonight?" Clair asked, never knowing shit.

"Giants don't play today." Clipper enunciated slowly, so it might sink in. "Tomorrow they open a three-game series against the Phils."

"You going?"

"Has a red rooster got four toes and a cock?"

Clair rolled her blue eyes. "What about your mother? She made you stay home from the Giants road trip."

"I took care of business," he said. "I always take care of business."

Clair began to clear the table, allowing a slim leg to escape her robe. "Around here you need to catch up on a few things."

"You said you'd buy me an iPad today," Heather reminded him.

Fourteen and she could bat her eyes with the best of 'em. On her t-shirt a huge blood splatter contained the screaming face of a rocker. Or what they called an alternative punk, as if that was a fucking compliment.

"Eat your mother's breakfast," he told her. "It aint every day you get the chance."

"It's burnt."

"It's supposed to be crisp."

Heather snapped at a plank of toast with perfected teeth and chewed, "Navo was in *Rolling Stone*."

"Hell you say."

"Hell I don't."

"Jesus," Clipper said, "my kid brother made *Rolling Stone*."

Clair shot him that grin he liked from years back, when it had been so easy for her to let it grab her lips. "Before you did."

◈◈◈

An hour later, wife and kid off shopping, Clipper saw the two men on the walk. He opened the front door, stepped out into the smell of damp lawn, heated stone, and tended landscape holding flora he couldn't name.

Play it cool, he told himself.

The two men strolled toward him. Tan suits, ties, shined shoes. Big smiles, like, Aint it a nice day? Two vice dicks out on a morning stroll, their black and white cruiser parked behind their car, two uniforms inside its cab like crash dummies for the entire neighborhood to see.

The lead detective he remembered from high school football, Danny Triplett.

"That you, Danny?"

"It's me, Clipper."

Looked like Triplett had added some jowl below those dead eyes. Other dick was black, tall, kinda familiar. Both men's aftershave rode the mid-morning air. By this time, a blood knowledge had risen within Clipper, likely a heritage from his grand-père.

This was a bust, he reasoned, something of minor ilk he could beat.

He shook Danny Triplett's extended palm. "You boys lost?" He ran a hand along his belt line, stuffed in his golf shirt. "Church was the smaller building you passed down the road."

Triplett attempted a grin. "This here is Detective, Tremain Cray."

Another handshake, this one firmer. "Any relation to Devon Cray, owns the funeral parlor on the West Side?"

"He's my father."

"When I was fifteen, sixteen I used to go out to your daddy's parlor with my grandpa."

Cray didn't seem impressed. "Yeah?"

"Papa Boo Paboolian," Clipper went on, winking at Triplett. "We'd visit with your daddy among those caskets and flowers, soft organ music from somewhere, and your daddy would settle up his hand book with Papa Boo. You know, take care of his lay-off money."

"Long time ago."

"Like history don't count?" Clipper barked a laugh. "Man, I wonder how much action your old man handled out there. Every black ass on the West Side needing a place to sit, knock back a drink, make a bet now and again like everybody else."

Triplett grunted as he shifted his weight.

Clipper smiled at him. "The knee?"

"Ever since my senior year, that game your brother cut me down."

"Kid was a killer free safety."

"That he was." Triplett cupped a hand over his kneecap. "He's not doing too bad here lately, playing baseball."

"Fifty-two in Denver."

"Don't we know it?"

The two uniformed cops had exited the cruiser to stand in the bright sun. The girls would be about half way through their buying run. Had Heather found her iPad? he wondered. Shit, a grand in geek toys, until the next craze came along.

Triplett groaned again, cleared his throat. "Clipper, you're under arrest."

Yeah, yeah. "On what charge?"

Detective Cray recited a Penal Code as if it composed a great psalm.

"Bookmaking, Clipper," Detective Triplett said. "Conspiracy to engage in illegal gambling."

"As opposed to what?" Clipper offered his wrists for Clay's handcuffs. "Legal gambling?"

Triplett said, "You can look at it that way." Those lifeless eyes lifted to his. "We got search warrants."

That blindsided Clipper. "You gonna want in my home?"

"Your home, vehicles, Club Aces, Dingers, anywhere you do business."

"You're lucky," Clipper said. "Damn lucky you cuffed me before telling me that."

"Or you, Mr. LeJeune," Detective Cray said. "It could be you who's lucky. The cuffs are for your protection, not ours."

❧❧❧

Much later Clipper and Marty Fishman were in the vacated Dingers restaurant, musty smell of past transgressions hanging in the dead air. "They mumbled me through the whole bust, Marty," Clipper said. "What the hell they got? Bookmaking? Hell, I own a casino, for Christ's sake. That aint enough action, I got to find more on the streets?"

"Conspiracy." Marty wiped a stool, straddled it. Summer suit, peach-colored shirt, white tie, and the lawyer had spent half of last night seeing to Clipper's bond. "Two or more people discussing an overt act."

"FBI? ABC? IRS?" Clipper asked. Christ, it almost sounded like he was picking the alphabet out of the dormant restaurant's stale air.

"Local vice." Marty cleaned his shades with a bar napkin. "Like the old days. I'm guessing they got an informant."

"Nah."

Marty drank from a bottle of Jade water. "Mercenary or straight-up revenge. Maybe a girlfriend."

"My girlfriends don't wear body wires."

"Put an informant together with an elected official who needs her ego served, and we got trouble."

"Meaning our D.A.?"

"Mercedes Garza," Marty said. "Can you see that?"

Clipper could see it. Mercedes Garza and Gloria LeJeune, legendary foes. His mother told him it went way back to the old days, when their fathers walked the downtown streets, Garza in uniform, Papa Boo in his dark suit and snap-brim fedora.

"Christ," he said. "I've got to call my mother."

"Gloria's fine," Marty said. "I told you she took it in stride."

"She's a Paboolian."

"Through and through. She wants to go downtown, rip some eyes out."

"I should call Clair again; tell her I'll come home when she settles down."

"You want to turn on the evening news, see what they have on it?"

Clipper pulled on his unshaven chin. "Dammit, I was leaving for the game today."

"That's another thing," Marty said.

"What's that?"

"Navo."

"What about Navo?"

Marty raised an eyebrow, a million words in that slight alteration of expression.

"I better call him," Clipper said. "But not now. He's probably sleeping."

"Yes," Marty agreed. "You don't want to get his mind off the game."

"You sound like you got a bet on his streak."

Marty smiled. "Hasn't everybody?"

CHAPTER 30

In Tuesday's first of three against the Philadelphia Phillies, Navo pushed the constant pressure out of his way. It was still there, but in a different brain chamber, one that didn't direct his every thought or every move. At the plate, he made good contact his first time up, hitting a line drive right back to Philadelphia's clever left hander, Rick Leaman. Leaman walked him in the fourth to a chorus of boos.

Then in the seventh frame, Navo drew upon what a Japanese woman once told him was his *Satori,* and hit a liner into center that cleared the fence for his sixth home run of the season. His streak now stood at fifty-three games.

Macon, the freckle-faced rookie, had been called up from Fresno's Triple A team had started the game for the Giants. After tiring in the eighth, the kid from Junction City, Kansas watched from the dugout as Weird Al Fletcher preserved his first major league victory. Navo was left untouched after the game.

In this magical, safety net formed by his own will and his teammates' reverence to the game's line of history, he figured he might live another day.

⌘⌘⌘

"Conspiracy?" Navo said into his cell phone. Not a sound this Wednesday morning in his apartment, except Macon's snoring across the hall.

Clipper's dark voice said, "Marty Fishman thinks they got nothing."

"I don't like conspiracy." Blood rose to his throat, thumped to the beat of his heart. "You say this happened around noon yesterday?"

"I didn't call because you got the game last night."

"I thought you were in the stands. Did you see my home run on TV?"

"Does a fat woman love a foot bath?"

"A Giant's fan gave me the ball."

"El numero fifty-three and he hands it over?"

"Told me to give it to my kid." He left that alone. Left out too, that it was signed, authorized and on its way to Joe Blake.

Clipper cleared his throat. "Makes you happy you belong to the human race."

Navo studied his bare legs, wondered if they'd be capable of lifting him off the edge of the bed. "I don't like the word *conspiracy.*"

"That's just a term goes back to the old days," Clipper said. "To when they wanted to make a neighborhood bust look like they were cleaning up the Mafia."

"What was your bail?"

"Couple hundred grand."

"Christ."

"Don't mean anything."

"Clip—"

"This aint going to touch you, Navo."

"How are Clair and Heather taking it?"

"Clair's a mess. Heather thinks it's cool." A pause, then, "I had to change my plans about coming tonight, but soon as I take care of a few things, I'm heading for San Francisco."

"I understand." Navo saw his mother's face, felt her eyes on him, but didn't mention her.

"The Phils are a tough bunch," Clipper said.

"Always are." Navo's turn to take a breath. "Did the cops shut down Club Aces?"

"Nah."

"Can you go near it?"

"Not until the investigation is over."

"How about a baseball stadium, can you attend a game?"

"Not a problem," Clipper insisted. "Unless they got a window there taking action on the game, then the fuckers will be all over me, yeah."

After the phone conversation, Navo stared at the wall. Again Clipper's exasperating life had overlapped his. And this time, being his golf partner, tag-teaming his barroom scuffles, and singing harmony to his lead baritone might not be enough to stop the bleeding. *Conspiracy to make book.* On what? Lord help him if it involved baseball. Over the years, he'd known players who'd gambled thousands in casinos, sports books, and on the Internet. He'd seen teammates lose a grand on the turn of a card during a rain-out game of stud poker. But on baseball, you stayed away from any side of any bet, and you avoided anyone who did.

He checked the time, and felt a pang of hunger. And a stab of fear. He yearned for Melanie and felt lost again after being so grooved yesterday. Most of all, he was angry at Clipper. Angry at the legacy handed down to the two of them.

"Fuck it," he said aloud. We are what we are. Sins were born in lines of succession.

eↄeↄ

After a session with a photographer up near Nob Hill, Navo had asked Bix to drop him off at McCovey Cove, saying he wanted to walk around the area in hooded sweats, dark glasses, and one of those ski caps he could pull down over his brow. "I'll sneak into the ballpark."

"It's a bit early to be near the park," Bix warned.

He waved goodbye, saying nothing about meeting a Fresno detective who'd called not ten minutes after he'd gotten off the phone with Clipper this morning. Danny Triplett somehow had his very private number. That still had Navo stumped as he spotted Triplett walking along the curb, running his hand atop the waist-high concrete baseball replicas lining the walk. The dick didn't even recognize Navo when he stepped into view.

"Looking for somebody, Danny?"

Triplett removed his sunglasses and returned a smile. He wore a summer suit that appeared to be a tight fit. Beer and weight training, Navo surmised—never a good combination. Triplett shook his outstretched hand then used his big paw to shade his eyes as he looked out at the bigger-than-life sculpted figure of Willie McCovey, the legend poised for history against the sky.

Triplett nodded at the monument." You ever meet him?"

"Had the pleasure couple of times."

"What kind of guy?"

"Maybe the best I've met."

"How about Willie Mays."

"Him too," Navo said. "His statue fronts the stadium."

"Saw it last night going in."

"You watched the game?"

"I did." Triplett swept a hand toward the stadium. "Shall we take a little walk?"

Navo felt board-legged and started slow. Triplett picked this up. "They had you playing for Canderas."

"Those double plays." Navo exaggerated a wince. "The Phillies make you pay. And I used to think shortstop was my position." He studied Triplett's gait. "You look a bit gimpy yourself."

Triplett showed his teeth in an old schoolboy way. "Chasing crime. I been like this since you put that hit on me, must be near eighteen years ago."

Go back in time and it's a Friday night in Fresno's Ratcliff Stadium. The two of them, across the line from one another, ten thousand people watching them play a high school football game. Navo would lose him on a wide-out pattern, pick, him up late, and while Danny stretched for a pass coming to him way too slow, Navo would aim for his planted leg. Helmet to his knee.

And made it the last football game Danny would ever play.

The ballpark loomed ahead, its port walk arcade, the dream-sized four-fingered glove and angled Coke bottle in left center taking some sun. Scoreboard, flags, and massive grandstands stood guard over the hollow bowl where he'd played hours ago to the thunder of forty thousand voices.

Triplett balked at the sight. "I can't imagine how it must be, being part of all this." Another hand motion, this time indicating the mystique of the complete scene. A team of joggers slipped by them on the walkway, their pace in rhythm to their leader's iPod. Navo stopped. "Danny, you didn't come here just to watch some baseball."

"No." The word a shovel against Navo's gut.

"Then let me have it." Navo looked out at the serene water, glinting in spots from the bright sun. "Shit, let's get it over with."

"A warrant is going to being issued for your arrest." Triplett closed his eyes and placed his fist against his forehead. "You want to know how I see it working in the best scenario for you?"

"Yeah." Like he'd been cornered and would listen to anything.

Triplett shut his eyes again, as if watching the bust go down. "Let's say I'm too late to act on the warrant, and you're able to play in the game tonight." He took a moment to pick at the corner of his eye. "Now I see you tomorrow afternoon, visiting your home town, coming in to the Department, surrendering yourself."

"When do you see me coming back?"

"My vision isn't that sharp."

Traffic was building on the Lefty O'Doul Bridge. Over at the structure, two figures walked arm in arm and laughed into the wind. Navo glanced off at the stadium where early fans speckled the grandstands with color. "I got to go to work, Danny."

"Good luck, LeJeune."

"You, too."

As Navo headed for the ballpark, he picked up his pace. He best not tarry. One shout of his name from the milling people and he might not make it.

ↁↃↁ

In the clubhouse, TV images teased Navo's peripheral vision. One screen showed him rounding the bases after last night's home run. Another displayed Clipper, the swagger in his limp undeniable as he was escorted by uniformed officers into the Fresno Police building.

The juxtaposition of player to perp wrenched Navo's gut. He hadn't puked before a game in a long while, but now he headed for the toilets. But he brought up nothing but bile. It left him shaky and weak. Too nauseated for the catered spread of food, he shuffled through the clubhouse. Cyrus growled, "Get 'em, Bossa Navo."

Playful pokes pummeled his frame. A rush of white hot energy overtook him, and he upchucked last night's meal onto the floor near Mayfield's locker.

Mayfield didn't turn to look. "Clean-up on aisle nine."

One of clubhouse manager Moe Whitney's crew, quick with a mop and pail, shouted, "I got it, Navo. Pay it no mind."

When he reached the sun field, he wiped the tears that clouded his vision and spat cotton.

R. L. Bushman found him. "You study the book, watch the videos on the Phils pitcher, what's his name?"

"Man's name is Zapata," Navo answered, "Miguel Zapata." His grin must look pathetic out here in the stadium's clean brightness. "Where you want me today?"

"Not sure yet." Bushmill's grin was no better than his. "Check out the whole fucking yard," he said. "Tell me where you think you'll fit in."

Shortstop, Rudy Canderos, had evidently overheard them. "Play another one for me, Navo. You looked great out there last night."

Navo cocked his brow at the shortstop. Canderos wasn't one to want another day out of the line-up. "You mean that?"

Canderos flashed him a smile. "Besides, I'm like one for seventeen against this Viva Zapata."

"I'm not much better."

Canderos pressed a finger on Navo's wrist and made a sizzling sound through his teeth. "But you're hot, amigo, too hot to cool down."

Alone with the coach, Navo took several deep breaths. "How do I look?"

"Terrible."

"You don't look so good yourself."

"Did you meet that detective, what's his name? Triplett?"

"So that's how he got my number."

"You leaving tonight?"

"Yes."

The coach hitched his belt tighter, took off his cap, and ran his gnarled fingers across his lined brow. "You're taking me with you."

This baffled Navo. How could the club let this valuable mentor go away during this tight pennant race? "Thanks for the support, Coach, but I'll be fine."

Bushmill spat from his twisted mouth. "Hell, I aint worried about you, LeJeune. It's me I'm looking out for."

CHAPTER 31

When Junior Shavers left the house, Charlene was still in bed, though half the day was gone. Starting his pickup, he thought how useless it was to include anyone in your life. To hell with Charlene. To hell with Jim Caruba and the outfit he brought to town with him, especially the dude who'd tried to kick Pig. Jim's ho blew away the dog like it was target practice.

Then Jim had the audacity to give him the five-shooter piece, saying it was an equal trade for the champeen fighting bull.

Hell with 'em all.

In no time, he reached the rough strip of land just north of the Paboolian place. These five acres, still shamelessly wild, had been his sanctuary for years, the only place or thing he'd missed during his three-year stint in prison. He'd described it with such passion in a piece he'd turned in to Ms. Lovegreen that she'd read it aloud to the creative writing class at Lompoc.

Birdlike woman said he had a *voice*. Other cons snickered at that and passed signs among themselves like monkeys in a zoo.

Outside the pickup, he walked the untamed terrain bordering the razed vineyard. With black walnut trees at his back, he felt shaded and protected. Looking up, he made out a few worn boards, remnants from a tree house he and Clipper LeJeune worked on together over twenty-five years ago.

Maybe he should bring his Geiger sweep out here, give the area another going over.

From where he stood it was nothing to reach the tool shed undetected. Then the old tractor. Then the house. Look at it, quiet in the unbearable sun.

He wished it would rain, turn the soil dark and bring back the smell of grapes. Nearby, a small crop of marijuana he'd planted was vulnerable and dry now that the vineyard was gone. His work boots turned up dust, and he pulled his red bandana up over his nose. Desperado waiting for a stagecoach.

In dust at his feet an old shoe surfaced. Wingtip. Same style his father used to wear.

When he was a boy he thought his father was the most handsome man alive. Dave the Shave. Blue jaw slick with Old Spice. Black hair perfect as a tango dancer's. Cordovan shoes spit shined.

He'd tell Junior, "I run bets for Papa Boo my whole entire life."

Junior came to know what that meant.

He could still hear his father say, "The man telling me all the way along how he's going to take care of me. I devote myself to him. He's like the father I never had. When your mother died, he paid for her funeral. That's how close we were. I learned his every move, so when he stepped down, I'm ready."

Junior would listen, fascinated.

"The man croaks and leaves me dick, Junior. I'm stuck with his book, but I got no working capital. I figure at least I'll get the farmhouse and the vineyard he don't give a shit about. Something I worked years for, son, so one day it could be yours."

Junior would let that sink in.

"And believe me, Junior, there's got to be stash out there somewhere. Half a century of it. The way the LeJeune woman came in to raise those two kids by herself, found the time to drive that old Dodge Dart all over the valley selling cardboard houses—you know she didn't do it on insurance premiums."

Junior asked, "Did Papa Boo ever use a bank?"

"Shit, Junior, the man *was* his own bank."

"How come nobody, like, you know, made the ultimate withdrawal?"

"Because he had me to protect him," his father said. "And times were softer then than now." Dave the Shave, before he passed on, recognizing how times were getting harder every day.

ᏯᎦᏯᎦ

That afternoon back at the house, Junior checked on his lab out in the shed to make sure Charlene hadn't burned it down. Cooking crystal was dangerous. The best he got out of it and left the top for others to mess with. The high was more devilish than weed, but just the fumes could bake your liver.

When he came back into the kitchen, Charlene evidently read his disenchantment. She pointed out to the shed. "Your friend Jim liked the operation. 'Course he has more balls than you."

"Bullshit."

"Well, he does." Charlene was half naked and sailing in amphetamine winds. "He don't fear the law like you."

"Yeah, like walking right down the road to do a hand-to-hand dope deal with these niggas that run that outdoor auto-body on their front lawn. He don't have no fear of that, long as he's splitting' back to L.A."

Charlene was boiling hotdog wieners, fixing up buns. "I wish he would've stayed."

"You would."

"I bet he can dance." She initiated an outrageous hoedown, studying him intently while she moved. "You're jealous."

"Of you?"

"Of him." She whipped her head, lank hair flying. "Remembering a *Brokeback Mountain* moment with him, your time in stir."

He said nothing to her while eating his hotdog. Nor did he speak later when they fucked. It was when he was putting his boots back on that he spoke. "Get me that digital camera with the flash, and that .32 Jim gave me."

"It's only got three bullets."

"Just get it."

"Farmhouse watch again tonight?"

"Yep."

"The ballplayer's brother?" Charlene flicked her hand as if to dismiss a notion. "He's in so much trouble he's probably hiding out."

"The streak hitter might be coming into town." He gave her time to wrap her mind around that. "He gets number fifty-four on Tuesday." Junior lit a joint. "Last night he gets two walks, a sacrifice bunt and a sacrifice fly ball, so his streak is still alive at fifty-four., Can you believe it?"

Charlene had that dumb look like she has no fucking idea what he was talking about.

"I said, his streak is still going. The whole world is watching." He tried to make her see it. "You can't go anywhere without a radio or TV blasting his name."

"But you said he's in trouble with the law."

"And that just makes it more huge."

Charlene grinned. "We need to pick up somethin' to drink, some sunflower seeds."

"If you're planning to join me," he said to her, pawing his thick beard, "you walk home the first fucking complaint out of your mouth."

"When we going?"

"Not 'til it starts getting dark."

"What do we do 'til then?"

"Hell, I don't know," he said. "We got stoned, ate our lunch, fucked, and Pig ain't around to groom for a fight."

Charlene shook her head left to right in that cute way of hers. "Well, we could start all over again, the part where we get stoned."

CHAPTER 32

R L. Bushmill studied Navo's hands on the wheel and the sure way he handled the car coming down to the flatlands off Pacheco Pass. "Isn't this an odd way to go to the Central Valley?"

"This is the old way," Navo said, glancing in the rear-view mirror.

Unbelievable, the way Navo could handle all this stress. "This rental isn't a bad ride."

"If it isn't, I got a Merc minivan in Fresno my brother bought for me we can use coming back."

One game shy of DiMaggio's mark, and now Navo had to face this shit with his brother. "I wouldn't be advertising that fact." Bushmill leaned back in his seat, to ease a pain that kept jabbing at his chest. He glanced at Navo again, feeling a burn of guilt. Damn, he was adding to the player's problems. "Any chance for a pit stop?"

"Ahead in Los Baños." Navo turned, gave him an inspecting glance. "You okay?"

"Don't I look it?" Bushmill thought of how slick they'd escaped all the commotion last night at the ballpark. "Your agent—she comes in handy. Not a dry eye, the way she convinced all those reporters that your family needed you."

Navo nodded, as if he was tired of everything and was ready to surrender.

"That, God willing, you'd return to San Francisco right away in quest of your goal."

"Not bad, eh?"

"Telling them you was going home."

Navo looked at him. "Not good?"

"In a way saying you'd be lucky if you get to come back." Bushmill sucked his teeth. Had the pain moved to his jaw? "Like you're going back to *conspire* with your brother."

"Ah, c'mon, Coach."

"Leaving the head office to wonder."

"That why you're here?"

"Pull off at the first café you see."

The pain was everywhere. Chest. Arm. Jaw. Navo had spotted a café and pulled into a lot. Getting out of the car, Bushmill felt his legs buckle.

"Watch that first step, Coach."

Bushmill cursed the mid-morning heat, the way it spun in his face, mixed with a spoiled fruit smell and the reek of bacon fat from the truck stop. "From here to Salinas," he said with a touch of dram. "Steinbeck country."

"*Grapes of Wrath*," Navo chipped in as they walked. "Tom Joad."

"Right." This LeJeune was a strange one, he thought. Most players held to a world where the past was irrelevant, strife and conflict too complicated. War was merely images on a screen, all calamity desensitized by instant replay. "Jesus, a player who reads."

"Henry Fonda in the movie."

"You could be him, only with a nose."

"I'll pass that by Vince Vitucci," Navo said. "He's the movie critic."

ℰↃℰↄ

Once settled inside, they ordered coffee and cold water. Above their table a miniature train circled the room's perimeter. Its engine's lonesome wail brought to Bushmill a sound as far away as his childhood.

Their young waitress appeared fresh—no heavy makeup, sunny disposition. "Want pie with this coffee?"

"One piece of apple pie," Bushmill said. "A la mode with two forks." He watched her walk away. "Country girl."

"Not many left." Navo sounded old-timey, sitting there, his face in blue shadow, his eyes way too old for his years.

Bushmill made no secret about spiking both their coffees from a flask out of his windbreaker. Generous pour into his own mug, dash for the driver's. "In case you're wondering the club didn't suggest I tag along."

"What are they saying about my situation?"

"Nothing. They're sitting on it."

Navo sipped his coffee, shuddered. "As we speak, a warrant's being put out on me." He cleared his throat, pawed his face. "I'm not sure what all's going to happen, Coach."

"I know that."

"I want you to know I'm clean."

"Never doubted it."

Navo's eyes shone like a cat burglar's. "Really?"

"Yes." Bushmill drank his brew, slipped a breath under the pain in his sternum. "Same with Domingo Matta, and there's not a better man to have in your corner."

The server brought the pie. They dueled at it with their forks and chuckled. The young girl returned, grinning shyly at Navo.

"Busboy thinks," she began, "that you look like that baseball guy on the hitting streak."

Bushmill rose with a grunt to leave money for their bill. "Tell the busboy to keep it quiet 'til we make a break for it."

Outside, getting into the Pontiac, Navo said to him, "I saw that bill you left for the girl."

Bushmill winced as he slid in next to the ballplayer. "Like you said, LeJeune, there ain't many left like her."

"Well that C-note should cover her 4H Club dues for quite a spell."

Bushmill buckled up. "You'd know about that, LeJeune. Now let's get the fuck out of here."

☙☙☙

God almighty, Bushmill thought. They must have slipped him a sedative when he came into the emergency room, the way he was bouncing between memory and dreams. This new room kept changing. One minute he was in the hospital, his thoughts coming to him rationally. The next he was with Lil Alston in the apartment near Comiskey Park on South Parnell, a breeze coming through the bedroom's window and cooling the golden beads of sweat on her body's dark swells.

A big blond nurse moved alongside his bed to take his blood pressure. "You get tired carrying that big ring around on your finger?"

"It's a World Series ring," he said, trying to grab a piece of the present. "You'd be surprised how light it is."

"One seventy over fifty," she said, unwrapping his arm. "I hear you're a coach with the San Francisco Giants."

He took in the space, seeing it clearly for the first time. It must be late. The guy in the next bed was snoring. The hall outside was dim and quiet. "You heard right."

"The streak hitter..."

"Navo LeJeune."

"Yeah." She'd moved close enough he could smell her neck. "Does he use steroids?"

"Never." She looked disappointed, so he added, "Why do you want to know?"

"I got a girlfriend who lifts." Big blonde pressed an imaginary weight over her head. "She juices, and it doubled the size of her clitoris."

"Yeah?" Jesus these broads today.

"But guys, they juice and it shrinks their penises." She lowered her voice so as not to disturb his roommate. "Or is it just the testicles?"

"I aint your expert on that." This is what it was coming to, for fuck's sake? Answering questions about dicks and balls?

"You ever use 'em?"

"Steroids? Do I look it?"

"Not down there." She showed her teeth. "If you did, there's no negative effect."

"You sure you're a nurse?"

She chuckled like he'd hit on an inside joke. "This Navo LeJeune, how'd he get on this rampage he's on?"

"That's this game," he said, seeing it all of a sudden, a piece of the puzzle finding its place. "Baseball is an act upon the nature of life. It's constant. Always the same and always different."

Shit, for a moment he had the answer tight in his fist. Then it was gone as fast as it had come, back into the clouded mystery.

∞∞∞

Bushmill woke groggily. At his bedside stood Dr. Franks. Same guy who'd treated him that time before, when he'd managed the Grizzlies, their inaugural year, when they played out at the college's park. Before the stadium downtown was built. Dr. Franks was rail thin with black spidery hands. He wished he'd kept in touch with the man, sent him some Giants tickets these past few years.

Bushmill tried a grin that sent molten lead down both his upper arms. "You came."

"I did."

"You still my cardiologist?"

"Evidently."

"Great."

The doctor faded in and out. "Why don't you tell me what's going on."

He looked for the big blonde, but she wasn't around. "I could use a bunch of the little pills you gave me last time."

The doctor consulted a chart. "Last time was about five, six years ago, Mr. Bushmill."

"Well, they sure did the trick."

"We'll know more tomorrow after your catheterization."

"My what?"

"Angiogram."

Fear slammed like an axe blade into Bushmill's spinal cord. "What's that entail?"

"Get some rest," the doctor said. "I'll bring you up to date in the morning."

"I got to make some calls."

"To Navo LeJeune?"

"Among others."

"I heard that LeJeune is out on bail already. He's been asking about you." He hovered above, smiling with the sweet sorrow of a man who'd traveled extra miles with little hurrah. "Celebrity must be served."

"He aint a celebrity."

"Yeah," the doctor said. "And you've been taking good care of yourself, few little pills and you're back in the game."

Dr. Frank strolled away, free hand swinging behind his open smock. The big blonde out there in the hall gave him a look as he sauntered by. The doc was probably a chucker when he was a kid by the look of his gait. Maybe a natural split fastball with those long fingers. When he wasn't playing fucking basketball.

CHAPTER 33

When Ara Paboolian dropped dead in front of his room at the Victoria Hotel in Fresno's old downtown, Navo, who'd just followed his brother Clipper into high school, grieved for many days and nights. First his father, now Papa Boo.

Then one day after Papa Boo's funeral, two men came out to the farmhouse. Navo watched them from behind the screen door as they approached his mother on the front porch.

"No need to show your badges," she said, stopping them on the steps with a fierce look. "I know who you are and what you want."

Both men were handsome in their pressed suits, but something about them chilled Navo's young bones.

His mother raised an arm. "You needn't fear me continuing Papa's business," she told them. "In fact the whole operation is yours—lock, stock and barrel."

She seemed to be watching the men take that in silence. "There's a saying back in the Louisiana shit towns I've been in." She dropped her hand as if to fire from the hip. "Watch out for the person who knows where you smoke your sausage."

Navo would learn in the years to come that the two men were plain-clothed cops. Dean Richenrader and his younger brother Freddie, both born beyond the railroad tracks where German and Italian families worked hard, paid their mortgages, swept their dirt sidewalks, and raised tough kids. Freddie, the younger brother, had played minor league ball, all field and no hit. Dean had starred for years in the local semi-pro leagues.

At the time they'd come out to see Gloria LeJeune, both were veteran cops. On the side, they ran a bookie operation in a Chinese restaurant on Blackstone Avenue. Through the years, before they retired as high-ranking officers, they'd done a few favors for Gloria LeJeune.

eɔeɔ

Friday morning, Navo gave the media a quick interview outside his mother's home on Van Ness extension.

Minutes later, Luke drove him north, moneyed people's houses passing left and right in the glaring sun.

"Now you can relax," Luke said, his eyes and sideburns silver in the light. "I told you when I brought you to her, your mom would be okay."

Last place Navo wanted to go after being released was to his mother's. "I didn't believe you," he said. "Did she sleep at all?" He'd awakened during the night to sense her near presence.

"Paced in front of your door all night."

Navo let that sink in.

"It was something in her eyes when she saw you on TV, being hauled in to the police station," Luke went on, obviously proud of his keenness. "I had the feeling she'd take care of you." He chuckled. "Besides, where could we go? The bars were all closed after I bailed you out."

She'd touched his face this morning, thumbed his temples like a sculptor might smooth clay. "Right." It had taken him back many years, the warmth of her touch. "Right," he said again.

They'd reached Herndon Avenue, the big artery that was no longer the town's extreme northern border. Luke checked the rear view. "Amazing," he said. "Not a soul behind us." He tilted his head skyward. "Unless it's the helicopter above us we got to lose."

"You never know."

"Where we headed?"

"St. Agnes Hospital. Coach Bushmill called, said he didn't stay in a motel last night after I gave him the car keys."

"That can't be good."

"No." Navo felt himself sinking. "He never said a word, but all the while I knew something was wrong." Luke turned right and grabbed a lane that had been added since Navo was here last. "Man," he said, "this town never stops sprawling."

After his mother touched his face, she'd woven her fingers into his long hair and drawn his head downward into her bosom, told him everything would work out and not to worry. "I'll be thirty-six next week," he said to Luke. "And I've never worked a day in my life."

"What's that mean?"

"That I'm grateful."

"Working isn't all it's built up to be," Luke said, as they headed west. "I hope you never have to learn that."

❧❧❧

This new addition to St. Agnes was unfamiliar. Not the halls Navo remembered, where Clipper endured all those surgeries and endless therapy that would leave him spent and racked with pain.

R.L. Bushmill's room was a double. The coach was in the window bed, his face angled to the door as if he'd been waiting for Navo to walk in. His neighbor snored behind a tracked curtain.

"LeJeune." The coach's voice sounded helium-filled. Inhaling through little plastic horns inserted in his nostrils that dispensed oxygen, he thumbed a button that sat him upright.

"Coach." Navo creped in closer to observe the intravenous hookup on Bushmill's hand, wondering how they found a big enough vein among the scatter of freckles.

He placed a *Chronicle* on the swing-out table, pushed it so it fit above the coach's lap.

Bushmill shoved it away. "My eyes are gone," he said. "Read me yesterday's box scores."

Navo opened the paper, slipped out the sports section. "Giants win big."

"Go on."

"Guy named LeJeune sneaks off with Coach Bushmill right after it's over."

Bushmill released a chortle. "We still a half game behind the Padres?"

"And tied with the Dodgers."

"You see that big blonde when you came in?"

"Must've missed her."

"Maybe I've been dreaming," Bushmill folded his hands on his chest. "I know I dreamed about you."

"Nightmare?"

"Somebody told me you got out on bail. I should have stayed with you."

"You're where you should be."

"This morning they threaded this tube into my groin, up all the way to my heart. Told me I might feel funny while they released a dye that spread through my main circuit. To see if it detected any trouble."

"That doesn't sound like a walk in the park."

"Made me think I was a kid again."

"Up on the double Ferris wheel?" Navo remembered Lil Alston, the night in Chicago.

"Top of the world."

"What's the doctor think?"

"Don't matter what he says." Bushmill leveled a look at him, his eyes the color of oxblood. "You and me are driving back to San Francisco. We open against the Dodgers tonight."

The odds that wouldn't happen were immense, but still he said, "I hear that."

"Then go out there and find a doctor, looks kinda like Willie McCovey, and give him the news. Both of us have to get back, if the Giants are going to make it to the World Series."

"Right."

"That all you got to say? 'Right?'" The coach levitated, inches off the bed. "You ever play in a World Series?"

"You know I was in Japan the year you won it."

"It's like walking into America."

"Yeah?"

"Like walking straight into your country's heart." The coach sank back into the white bed. "Remember that, LeJeune. God dammit, remember that."

☙☙☙

It took a while, but Navo rounded up Doctor Franks. A tall, angular man, the whites of his eyes huge and moist against his dark skin.

"Results aren't good," he informed Navo. "But we expected that. The man's five main arteries show severe blockage." Franks ducked his head, brought it back up. "Five," he said again, spreading his hand wide in the air.

Navo straight-armed a wall for balance. "What does it look like?"

"Surgery, but he won't buy it."

"He'll want to finish the season first," Navo said. "Can he do it?"

"Not in the shape he's in." The doctor watched uniformed figures move about in the corridors. "He stays here, we operate. He recovers the way I think he will, he'll be with you for the playoffs, the World Series if you get that far."

"He might buy that."

"Yes." The doctor's eyes pinned him against the wall. "How are you making it?"

"I'm good."

"You look beat up and then beat down."

"So do you," Navo said, trying on a smile.

"You go on now," the doctor ordered, holding charts to his abdomen as if they comforted him. "Talk your coach into sticking with us."

After taking a long stride down the hall, he turned and placed one hand above the other as if grasping a baseball bat.

"Good luck, Mr. LeJeune." He moved his hands through a smooth swing. "Nice and easy."

❧❧❧

"Drive me over to the main building," Navo told Luke, getting into the car next to him. "The rental is somewhere near the emergency entrance where Bushmill left it."

"How is he?"

"He'll have to stay a few days." Navo swallowed hard. "Surgery, recovery time—with luck he can be back in uniform for post season."

"How'd he take it?"

"Like Neil Young if you take away his guitar."

Luke seemed to be weighing something on his mind. "It's not too bad," he said "I had a triple bypass, couple years ago."

"No."

"During the summer. You were on a long road trip. I never got around to telling you."

"I'm sorry." About what? About never caring? About never checking up on a friend as true as Luke, a man that had been like a father? "I wish you'd told me, Luke."

"No big deal."

Nobody had told him. Didn't want to bad-news Navo while he was busy playing ball. Shit, that might disrupt him.

"Well, where to now?" Luke smiled at him. "You said something about meeting Clipper and his lawyer."

"Clipper's probably playing golf."

Luke laughed at that.

"I think I'll drive over to Dingers."

"It's closed up tight."

"I got a key. I got a ton of calls to make."

"I bet."

"My agent."

"Sure."

"Team publicist."

"Right."

"Maybe Domingo Matta or someone in management."

"Maybe," Luke said, "the Commissioner of Baseball."

"Or maybe not," Navo said. "Maybe just call my artist lady, ask her if she's on the road yet."

He felt a churn of excitement in his belly. "She is coming to see me."

Jesus, Luke must be amused at this, judging by the smile at the corner of his mouth.

"You could do that."

"Maybe call a couple reporters that are shadowing me," Navo said. "Get it over with."

CHAPTER 34

Melanie purposely got into the elevator before her attorney caught up with them. Neil stood opposite her, his face gray in the closed space. She almost asked if he was okay, but thought better of it. When the elevator doors opened, she stepped out to view what used to be the ground floor of the Pacific Gas and Electric Company.

Now it resembled a vacant ballroom. Outside the line of windows, downtown Fresno had begun to wake up a bit. Nothing like the old-timers would remember it, she was sure, but still maintaining a heartbeat since the town's migration north years ago.

Neil matched her pace. "I told you I would be the perfect gentleman. And I didn't bring an attorney along to get this matter cleared up."

She gave him a long look. His suit was one she remembered from a dozen years ago. Aware of how hard he'd been hit by the failing economy, she sadly looked back at how he'd always been able to maintain an air of success, an air she'd never been fooled by, but one she'd often admired as pleasant. For just a split second there she remembered how damned *nice* he could be.

"And some of it was embarrassing," he said.

"You were *embarrassed* because I was concerned about my health?" She walked out onto the sidewalk, glanced across Fulton Street at the grand old Warnor's Theatre. "I remember how worried you used to get if I caught a cold." Careful, she warned herself. Don't give him an inch. He'd proven he didn't deserve it.

"I think," he said to her above the light traffic, "we made good progress though, don't you?"

"That remains to be seen." The rules had been set. She was sure of that. "We'll evaluate things in a month or two."

"Meanwhile," he said, "I don't get to see Joe. Can't we negotiate that?"

A glance north told her the Wilson Theatre had been converted into a church. "Don't push it, Neil."

"Where you headed?" His smile appeared strained. "Out to the ringleader's hideout?"

She watched his smile fade. Had he landed on Navo's arrest in a desperate attempt to stall her? She mentally sketched his features. They didn't match the face he'd brought to her attorney's office. "You go there, Neil, and you may never see Joe again."

"By the way where is Joe?"

"I told you he's at my home. The Murrietas are staying over, and so is one of his friends."

"Keyes Haythorne? Jeez, Mel, You think that surfer is the right influence?"

They'd reached her pickup. She unlocked the door and got in. Without rolling her window down, she mouthed "Goodbye." Looking into her rearview mirror, she saw him standing like part of a photograph, a man alone, the rest of the picture ripped away.

She'd agreed to meet Navo at his mother's home. God, she'd have consented to anything he'd asked. His voice on the phone earlier this morning had been so full of emotion, She suspected a family affair awaited her and would give anything right now to be alone with the ballplayer. Given the circumstances of what he went through last night, she was sure his choice would be a place where they could meet secretly. They'd have that later.

"Some time together," he'd promised.

❧❧❧

Melanie located the residence, no problem. This area along here, other than occasional rebuilding, was as she remembered it. Huge homes, spacious lots, some new money replacing old. A few minutes early, she parked on an abundant asphalt strip that fronted a four-car garage with a structure above it that looked perfect for a studio. Nicely landscaped yard, dramatic entry, big door with glue-chipped glass.

She pushed a button, heard the chime, and counted to ten. The door opened and, though she'd been preparing herself for this moment on the half-hour drive from downtown, she buckled a bit at the woman's dark beauty.

"You're early," Gloria LeJeune said. No smile. A take charge woman in her comfort zone.

"Should I wait in the car?" Take that; see what you do with it. "That's a joke."

Half grin. "I hate jokes."

Melanie smiled. "I do, too."

"Come in, anyway." The woman's graceful hands directed her deeper into the home. "Navo is still out but should be along soon."

Melanie followed her gestures and sat in an informal area that viewed an open-style kitchen. Bold colors, textures, spicy aromas. Why, she asked herself, hadn't she driven around, called Navo's cell, made sure he was here. But then she shook the question off. Meeting this woman one-on-one might prove valuable. It might tell her more about the ballplayer whose haunting TV images were still in her head, the phantom-like nearness of him she couldn't shake.

"I've been doing some cooking," Gloria said, moving into the kitchen's sunlight. Her coarse black hair and dark eyes glinted, as her creamy skin contrasted the earth-toned outfit she wore in diaphanous layers. Silver jewelry adorning her clinked softly. "Navo said you'd have your boy with you."

"No." Keep it simple.

"I've met his father."

Shit. "Oh, really?"

"Navo says you're an artist."

"Yes."

"What do you paint?"

"Navo didn't say?"

"Come to think about it, he did."

"Great."

Gloria busied herself behind a counter for a moment, then those piercing eyes speared her again. "I like your top. What's that hanging on your belt?"

"A fob made from a chunk of lava."

"From your home?"

"My mother's actually."

"Bora Bora?"

"Close. Pago Pago."

Gloria stood motionless, the house silent, spaces left and right masterfully designed. "Is everyone from there as gorgeous as you?" There, for a second, was the woman's warmth. Her smile was painfully rare, Melanie was sure, on her wide, scarlet mouth. "I've fixed some things," she said. "How about helping me set the table out on the pergola?"

Outside, the heat was tainted by the chemical smells of chlorine off the glistening pool and pesticides from fields to the west. Gloria offered a running commentary about the food as they brought it out to a redwood table.

"Armenian string cheese," she said, ripping a piece loose from a small bundle for Melanie to try. "The kind with sesame seeds." She tipped her chin at the table. "Pickled okra, Texas style, just to piss off my brother, Haig. He likes it softer." She flicked her finger in a bowl of hummus, licked it dry. "Nothing to this, if you have a Cuisinart, canned garbanzos, garlic, some lemon juice." As she spoke, she seemed alert to every sound, as if she were listening for the arrival of her family.

"Yalanchi." She placed a tray of rolled grape leaves on the table and stood back. "Secret is tender grape leaves and Cal Rose rice—because it doesn't grow when cooked like long-grain does. Tomato paste and pomegranate molasses to tighten things when you roll them." She looked at Melanie sternly. "You are now the only non-Armenian alive to know about the pomegranate molasses."

"I'll guard it with my life," Melanie said, holding a grin until a change came to Gloria's eyes. It was the same look Navo would get when he'd allow his mind a moment of freedom. But then a storm stirred her irises again, and she turned back to her chore.

಄ఌ಄

When Navo arrived, he stood for a time in the opening to the patio. Melanie was standing on the pool decking, an island of man-sized rocks and Japanese maples almost hiding her. She stepped into clear view and, when their eyes met, waited not only for his reaction, but for her own feelings to rise.

My God, were they going to charge across the spaces to clash together like two cymbals right in front of Gloria?

Yep.

Their mouths chewing, tongues digging. Swallowing air as if to ease an ache or fan a fire.

"Oh Christ," he finally gasped.

"Yep," she said, laughing at the both of them "I know, Navo. I feel it too."

He held her to his chest, the heat dampening his polo shirt. "Where's Joe?"

"Keyes Haythorne is driving him to the game tomorrow."

The sound of others arriving, coming through the kitchen, stepping out onto the patio, came to her and she held on to him tight.

"How was your trip?" he asked.

"Not bad," she said. "At least I didn't have to check in with the jailhouse soon as I got here." She pulled away to give him a look. "That was a joke, Navo. Geez, what's with you people?" Big grin as wide as she could offer it.

That change in his eyes as his muscles relaxed. She liked that.

෪෪෪

Clipper and Uncle Haig barbecued Andouille sausage and marinated lamb Clipper had brought to the party in an ice chest. The smell of the smoke worked to stimulate conversation, much of it combative among Uncle Haig's wife Roxie, Clipper's wife Clair, and Gloria.

Soon Gloria had enlisted them in a common rally against the city's shakers and movers, state assemblymen and officials, and law enforcement officers within one hundred miles.

Clair's daughter Heather, catching Melanie alone as Navo fetched drinks for the cooking team, asked if she used a tanning studio? Told no, she said, "And no waxing?"

"Nope."

The teen-aged girl expressed show-stopping astonishment. "Oh, that's right," she said loud enough to draw attention. "You don't have any Fresno Indian blood in you." She cupped her mouth, whispered in a rasp that easily carried across the patio, "Like I gotta, you know, bleach my freaking eyebrows."

Before the meat was ready. Luke Kaminski took her on a tour of the house. Navo had talked of the man and she immediately saw what Navo liked about him. She could tell, as they strolled, that the finely designed spaces were mostly his doing.

"I've seen your work in *Art Forum*," Luke told her. "Can't wait to see a full exhibit. Navo said you show in Santa Monica."

"Bergamot Station." Then after thinking Why not? she added, "And in New York later this month."

"Where in New York?"

"Gallery called Nedia's on Twenty-second."

"Man," Luke said. "You tell Navo?"

"Not yet."

"The Giants have a series with the Mets coming up. It's fifteen, maybe twenty minutes over the Queensboro Bridge and he's in Manhattan." He paused, a tall man not quite meeting her eyes, like he was giving her time. "That is," he went on, "if you need someone in your corner."

"Is he good at that?" She looked off into a room of somber quietude. "Being in your corner?"

"Terrible," Luke said. "But he's getting better, and converts make for fanatic changes in behavior."

Walking back outside, she turned to him. "It's Navo that needs the boost right now."

"How are you at that?"

"Terrible," she said. "But like you say, Luke, we're all capable of change."

e/se/s

Night finally began to fall and brought with it the smell of an August rain. They feasted under a fan that whirred above on the pergola's wood-beamed ceiling. A misting system spun rainbows in the night lights.

Melanie, who'd snacked on the appetizers, found herself eating the sausage and lamb off the barbecue like a ravaged animal.

With juices warm on their tongues, she and Navo talked so close they could be kissing. When she pulled back from him, both would laugh at how foolish they must look. Then they'd bend to one another again as if grazing off each other's existence.

Gloria had evidently invited a news team assembled out front to come around back and join the action. Clipper produced an accordion, and Gloria began to pry Navo away from Melanie.

"Give the TV crew a song with your brother," she said to him while her eyes caught Melanie's. "Let them know how tough we all are."

CHAPTER 35

By ten thirty, Clipper, burping shish kebab, beer, and wine had picked up Tatum Dearborn in front of Club Aces and was walking her into her apartment, a typical two-bedroom unit not far from Dingers. He took a seat on the sofa while she moved into the kitchen, a nice little sway to her bottom.

"Care for a drink." That look she could get, trying to be tough.

"I won't say no."

"You never do." At her kitchen counter, she began fixing vodka over ice.

"I was surprised," he said, "when you said okay to me picking you up after work."

"Why?" She handed him his drink and took a seat across from him, her hostess dress so summery he could blow it off with a sneeze. "Since my DUI I'm not too choosy how I get around." She crossed her legs. Loose-cannon chick, slapped with a recent drunk driving charge, in her little apartment, already turning bitter. "Besides, it's not the first time you've driven me home, pun intended."

"First time with you wearing a wire." See how that suited her.

Confusion. "What?"

"A wire," he repeated. "Are you wearing a wire?" This stopped her drink inches from her mouth. "If you're not recording me, prove it."

She stood, reached down, grabbed her dress's hem and pulled it up to her chin. "You got the wrong person, Clipper. It wasn't me who turned you in."

"You were pissed," he said, watching her let the fabric fall back down over those curves. "At me. At Navo. At the way your life's been going."

"Right on all three." She got up and went back to her kitchen counter to build her drink up. "But I'm not a spy."

He measured her, the way she kept her chin up, brushed her lustrous auburn hair from her eyes. Hard luck girl, he thought, but always a loyal employee.

"Maybe I jumped to a wrong conclusion."

"Look," she said. "You got your enemies. It could be any number of people."

"You have to pick somebody, who do you pick?"

"Chad."

"Chad Van Arsdyle?"

"He hates you."

"He's my chef."

"Was your chef."

"He's gay, for Christ's sake." He stood, finished his drink. "Gays don't spy on people. Shit, it's the other way around."

"He liked to make bets."

"Bets? You call that betting? He picks a team, says he wants a hundred on it. End of the week we settle up. If he's down, I cover, say it's a bonus. If he's ahead, I pay him, he calls it winning."

"You always talked gambling around him."

"I talk gambling around everybody," he said. "It's what I do." He took his wallet out. "You need to fix this place up. Nothing in here looks like you."

"What do I look like?"

"Still in your twenties—which you aint. Pretty face and an ass that Joshua couldn't bring down if he blew his horn all night long."

"Thanks for the compliment."

"Anytime." He left half the bills in his stash, maybe five, six hundred on the counter near the vodka bottle.

She looked away from the money, away from his eyes. "How's Navo doing?"

"Kid's on a roll."

"Can he catch DiMaggio?"

He stood up. "I got him two-to-one." He waited until she looked at him. "You want a piece of it you got to go against him." He grinned. "That's the only way I'll take it."

"You'll never change."

"Never."

"Neither will Navo."

"You're wrong about that, Tatum." He kissed her brow and headed for the door. "Navo's found the glory road, and he aint ever coming back."

∽∾∽

The route out to the farmhouse went quick in the thin, silent rain. Clipper parked in the wooded area where he and Navo played as kids. He got out of his SUV and peered at the house. Its windows were dark. Maybe Navo and his artist lady had left the party late, and his brother had sense enough to duck the press corps.

Hell, maybe he and Melanie had decided to get a motel. At any rate Clipper wanted to check out the area for signs of Junior Shavers and his spaced-out girlfriend. Yeah, there was a small hobo fire, still warm, the two of them evidently playing Tarzan and Jane out here recently. He unzipped his fly and helped the rain douse the few live embers.

The showers had cooled the air. Sky above was a vast spread of heavy dark clouds, not visible unless you blinked at the rain and stared.

He caught sight of the old tree house up there in the eucalyptus, part of the rope ladder still attached after all these years. More of it and he'd climb up there, sleep until dreams brought him his knee back.

About to return to his Escalade, he heard a vehicle, saw its lights swing this way. From behind the iron smoothness of the tree's barkless trunk, he waited.

The car pulled in not thirty yards away and went silent. A moment later he saw the driver, walking like a night-alley drunkard among the black tangle of vines and Junior Shavers's old marijuana crop.

The figure stopped when he came to a spot where his eye must have caught the SUV. Yeah, you could tell, the way he stiffened, swung his head left, right.

Clipper, thought Why not? and stepped in the man's direct line. "Can I help you with something?" And scared the shit out of the guy. He was wearing a windbreaker, hunched like he'd been birdshot in the brambles. Clipper didn't give him time to breathe. "What's that in your hand?"

"Flashlight," said a high pitched voice.

"Turn it on and show me your face."

The man held the light under his chin. Shit, he looked like a goblin. "Back off so I can see you better."

The light held at arm's length showed the man's features.

"Damn," Clipper said, "don't I know you?"

The light went out. The man didn't move. "I'm Neil Blake."

The structural engineer, out here to check on what, the fucking tree house? "What you doing out here?"

"I was hoping to find out if my son is okay."

A mixture of intuition and sure knowledge began to ignite Clipper's mind. "You're talking about Joe," he said, closing space between them. "I spent time with him in Dodger Stadium, drove him home from L.A. to his mother's place after the game."

"For your information, I've not seen him much since." Blake's voice sounded formal in the huge, rustic night,

Another step and Clipper clasped Blake's shoulder. "I'm going to assume a few things here," he said. "That okay with you, Neil?" Adding hunches to his thinking, he went on. "Looks to me like you're looking for something you aint going to find."

Blake said nothing. Clipper squeezed the ball of his deltoid until Blake's knees buckled.

"Your best bet," Clipper told him. "Is to call it a night, get back in your car, and go on home." Then he added, "Joe isn't here, but you knew that."

"I'm not sure." Blake turned his flashlight on, shined it back at the path he'd taken out here from his car. "Please don't let this affect our working together," he said. "I'd hate to lose you as a client."

"We'll be needing you." Clipper softened his tone. "All that redevelopment stuff downtown."

"I want to keep up the college fund I've set up for Joe."

"Got a daughter the same age," Clipper said. "I know where you're coming from." Giving Blake what Marty Fishman would call a *mitzvah*, a gift.

Moments later, after he'd watched Blake's departure, Clipper put a number on how many times the engineer had asked him to bet Giants games for him recently.

Clipper had figured him a harmless amateur, the kind of guy who thought making a sport wager might grow him a muscle.

Shit. Now he wished he had him back here. He'd of checked the fucker for a wire.

CHAPTER 36

"D idn't know you could sing."

Melanie's teasing glance thrilled Navo as he drove her pickup away from his mother's house. He'd traded an on-camera interview in front of the Action News van for the opportunity to drive off without being further pursued. "My brother is the one who sings."

She fingered the short, dark hair at the nape of her neck. "*Jolie Blon*, eh?"

"Cajun national anthem."

"I liked the one, *Joe Pitre*."

"Traditional song. Joe had himself two women, Rose and Rosa."

"Ah."

"*Et moi j'en ai pas.*"

"That means?"

"I don't get none of neither."

"Poor old Joe."

They chuckled in unison. In the distance a roll of thunder mimicked them.

She said, "Where you taking me?"

"Is your bag in back?" He'd noticed that she'd removed the customized racks.

"I got a toothbrush back there somewhere."

"I'll give you a choice," he said, "farmhouse out in the country or a motel."

"Both sound sexy."

"Then it's the farmhouse."

"Your hideout?"

The way she said it made him wince. "Something wrong?"

"Nothing."

He turned the truck east toward a sky dark as slate. "I owe you an explanation on this stuff about gambling."

She touched his knee. "Thanks."

"I think it comes from someone in Dingers, the restaurant Clipper just shut down. Somebody could have wired us talking about betting, maybe tapped Clipper's phone, heard him calling action to Vegas."

"You made bets with Clipper?"

"*Talked* about bets. Other than nine ball, darts or golf, I don't bet. Never have. It's like Clip caught the family bug, and it missed me."

"What do you think will happen?"

"Ten-to-one," he said. "Nothing."

"Thought you didn't bet."

"Knowing the line, the point spread—I guess that part is in my blood."

"Are you scared?" Hand on his knee again.

"Yeah."

"But you didn't do anything."

"Neither did Shoeless Joe Jackson. But when the Commissioner's office got done with him, he was selling booze in a roadside liquor store, his baseball days past, and his future taken from him."

"That was a long time ago. Times have changed."

"Baseball hasn't," he said. "And that's what worries me."

ɔɔ

Rain pelted their arms and faces as they darted across dappled ground toward the house. The night was deep, wet and black. Rain and wind chattered above in the yard's tall cottonwood tree.

Air smelled of the ravaged vineyard cooling. He lifted her onto the haggard lines of the porch, opened the screen door then unlocked the windowed front door. Inside he switched on a lamp. Facing her he felt foolish. The house bore his fantasies but had nothing to do with her.

"Christ, Baby, I don't know what I was thinking."

"Hey, it's a hideout. What more do we need?"

That word *hideout* again. "It's not my hideout. It's just a place from when I was a kid."

She dropped her carrying bag, looked at the second floor's landing. "It's got its charm."

"Clipper's used the place," he said. "Is that going to be a problem?"

"It's not a selling point."

"You need to be sold?"

"Nope. I asked for it."

"We can go to a motel."

"Or walk outside in the rain."

"Wash the slate clean?"

"Start all over again."

At the door she halted him with a palm to his heart. "Let's do it naked."

"Naked it is."

They stripped as if there was a buzzer to beat.

"Like our time on the mesa," she said.

"I can hear the surf."

Holding hands, they walked outside and crossed the porch. Rain fell like golden beads in the doorway's light. He embraced her, rested his chin on her shoulder. Her scent was aromatic, flowery as he turned her waltzing. In the scant light her eyes closed, and rain drops sparkled on her lashes. She kissed his throat, her voice guttural, lost against his neck. He'd ask her to repeat her words, but he was afraid to break the spell. Afraid he'd lose her, even for a second.

He held her, the two of them deep in a lover's swoon. "You wet enough, we can go back inside?"

"You mean try it on a bed?"

With that she broke from him, bounded away, girlish fanny firm then pillowy as her bare feet made for the porch, sure as a ballet dancer's.

⸕⸕⸕

Clipper had told him he'd find the place in order. "Clean sheets, remodeled bathroom, champagne in the fridge," was what he said.

He was right.

They made love in the downstairs bedroom like lovers inventing the game. Only *yeses* from her as he initiated a maneuver, never a *wait a minute* from him when she took charge. At the point when he feared both its ending and its continuing, she cried out. He rushed to join her, their voices ringing in the close room.

For Navo it was as if something living had entered his body, thrashed about next to his soul before flying out.

He murmured gibberish.

So did she.

They lay in exhaustion, night air moving through two windows—one facing the lost vineyard, the other his boyhood's cottonwood, the wind in its branches causing the old tree to groan. On hands and knees, he backed off the bed. In the soft glow from the light outside the room, he watched her malty contours move against the white bedding.

He found Clipper's music setup in the closet. From a favorite CD of his own, he selected the track he wanted. Zachary Richard's haunting Louisiana French lyrics played into the room.

Melanie turned to watch him. "My God, that's gorgeous."

"*Cap Enragé.*" He interpreted the song as it drifted past him. *"The wind is whipping his face, freezing the soul of his boat."* He knelt to kiss her damp thighs. "It's about the enraged cape at the edge of the sea that faces all of us."

Feeling the music, he walked from the bed, through the doorway, and past the lamp, touching an old chair and familiar surfaces as he went. In the kitchen he switched on the evaporative cooler, found the champagne, uncorked it, and poured two glasses.

She came off the bed and followed his every step.

"Look what I've found," he said, handing her a glass.

She smiled. "Just happened to have it handy?"

They drank like desert nomads. He refilled their glasses and ushered her to the stairway. The lamp projected their ascent, reminding him of how he'd fantasized her presence last time he was here.

On the landing they paused to look below. Richard's voice blended with sax and accordion reeds in a Cajun dancehall song.

Melanie swayed to the strains, her arm sweeping out. "This your old bedroom?"

"Yeah."

"Is it off limits?"

"Not tonight."

"Good." Her gliding hand landed on his face, then dropped, touching him tenderly as it fell.

"I'd make a joke about being a pull toy," he said, "but it would be in poor taste."

"Thanks," she said, firming her grip on him. "I'm like your mother; I don't much appreciate jokes, especially at a time like this."

CHAPTER 37

Navo and Melanie showered in the newly tiled bathroom downstairs. With their flesh still damp and fragrant, they got on his mother's old bed, propped pillows against the iron headboard, and finished off the champagne. They whispered stories drawn from their lives to each other.

"I could tell you anything," he said. "I feel so close to you."

As if in tune with his innermost thoughts, she nodded. "Tell me about Clipper's knee."

His words came up in a rush from a hidden place. "It happened the summer he'd signed with the Yankees." He was so near to her he felt her eyelashes on his lips. "I'd just finished my junior year in high school. Clip had opted for the baseball draft after his first year at USC."

Her hands were in his hair, her breath in his mouth. "And?"

"We'd played golf at The Fort. Clipper knew the bartender and was getting him to slip us some booze in our paper cups. By the time we headed back in Clip's El Dorado, we were both drunk." He felt her muscles tense. "Shit, you know what's next."

She kissed his eyes, one, then the other, soft and tender. "Tell me."

"We missed a hairpin turn." He had to go deep for the rest. "No seat belts. Clip lost part of his knee."

"And you?"

"Bumped my head. Knocked me out." His lips caught her ear lobe and he took it into his mouth. "We both went out the passenger door. The driver's door was locked." He began to tremble. Her hands moved along his torso and arms, over his back muscles. Fast, then slow, until her rhythmical caresses began to calm him. "I couldn't remember a thing afterwards, never have been able to."

"Your brother?"

"The same."

"Never a word."

"Never." He knew what she wanted. It was what they all wanted—one of them to admit guilt after the accident.

"Twenty years?"

Before he could answer her finger touched his lips. "That's enough," she said, "That's plenty for now."

When she slipped down to stretch out into sleep, he turned off the bed lamp and positioned himself next to her, close enough he felt her pulse linked to his.

She took his hand and manipulated his finger along the area between her brow and temple "My scar—proud flesh from a reef I encountered too far out in the ocean, and wasn't sure I wanted to come back."

He kissed the spot, afraid to breathe, afraid to distract her from the story.

"My father worked high steel," she said. "He was a blond and bronzed man from Tulsa, Oklahoma who walked the beams. All the new high rises in Australia and New Zealand. One day when I was fourteen he cried out, "Fire in the hole," and stepped off onto a twenty-story fall."

"Lord."

"Yeah, Lord," she said. "Every time I swim, I promise myself that I will know when to turn back." She was quiet for a moment then she moved his hand to her breast. "I promise myself I'll have a reason not to go out to far."

"Your art."

"And Joe."

ℭℛℭℛ

Navo lay awake, one part of his mind refusing to let his thoughts drift from Melanie. In mid-breath, he listened to the night. Nothing but the sound of the whirring cooler fan in the kitchen, the dripping of rain water off the house's eaves. The scent of her had perfumed the room. Scant light played across the bed from the bathroom where he'd left the light on and the door ajar.

Was that a movement in the window on her side of the bed? He waited; saw it again in that section not covered by the shade. He remembered being fooled by shadows and fabricated visions in this house. But still...

He slid away from Melanie's warmth and eased himself out of bed. Naked and chilled, he crept to where he'd piled his clothes near the front door. As he reached for them, he heard the soft groan of weathered wood.

Someone had been at the window and was still on the porch.

Trying not to make a sound, he picked up his pants and shoes and made his way, blind as a burglar, through the living room and kitchen. At the kitchen door he pulled on his pants and laced up his shoes with trembling fingers.

He wondered, should he go back to Melanie? No. Too dangerous. First, he'd go out this back route, see what's really going on out there. And yes, he remembered locking both the screen and front doors when they'd come in from the rain.

He opened the back door as careful as if it might fuse a bomb. The night was moonless, but at least it had stopped raining.

Navo stole his way along the side of the house, his shoes silent on the Bermuda grass and puncture vines. Melanie's pickup was right over there, the empty field behind it barely visible. He ducked under a ray of light from the bathroom window and proceeded to where he could peek at the porch from the corner of the house.

How many times had he committed this same act in ditch 'em games with Clipper?

On the porch, a dark figure danced in place as if controlled by an unseen puppeteer. His outlandish action and grotesque silhouette suggested a collective dementia that Navo had seen before.

"Well, I'll be damned," he said. "What the hell are you doing here, Junior?"

⁊ᔆᔆᔆ

Clipper had slept in the Escalade. Long enough, he felt fine for the trip home. Still bothered by hunches about the engineer, he looked into the darkness to chart his own gains and losses. This self-examination bore upon him like a huge weight.

Christ, maybe he wasn't shaped for this life of partnering Indian gaming. The tribes recently rejected the term *non-tribal land*. They were claiming now that any sites they chose for their gaming purposes were *ancestral lands*. He remembered how Papa Boo would preach discipline in his world. "How you handle your winnings is what counts at the end of the meet," he used to say. "Try for too much action and you'll end up getting snake bit."

Thinking he better take a leak before he left, Clipper got out of his vehicle, made his way through the tall, wild growth to Junior's camp fire. Christ, it looked like Shavers and his girlfriend had been here. That fucking wine bottle and empty Doritos bag wasn't there before. He pictured the two dopers sitting there, not even knowing he was parked, not that far away.

After he urinated, he decided to linger, give his life some thought. Gazing into the darkness he figured, shit, maybe he'd attend the next County Board of Supervisors' meeting. Tell 'em he would quit pushing for another casino in the Sierra hillsides if they'd quit taking campaign contributions from the Indians. See how they'd like that.

The rain had stopped. Time he got his ass in gear and headed back to Clair. Man, he could do a little work in that department too. Yeah, take her and Heather with him to San Francisco soon. This brought him to cast a glance back at the farmhouse. Looked like Navo had settled in with no problems. Yeah, there was faint light in the downstairs' bedroom, the artist lady's pickup next to the house. Shit, was that something else in the grainy darkness?

Two figures ran from the house, coming this way. Instinctively, Clipper moved to intercept them. Yeah, he was a faulty machine, he'd admit, with one useless wheel. But he traversed the rough terrain handily, his old wound biting at him like a hound.

It was like racing to catch a fly ball hit directly at you, the worst kind. You had to determine many things as you ran. Will you dive for it? Slide to meet it with your glove outstretched? Trap it if you're a split second too late?

Main thing was, you didn't—no matter what—let the damned thing get by you.

Then, of course, he fell. Ass over eyebrows into the dampened soil—a real tumble. He lay on his back staring into blackness as drops of rain started to come down again. Rain in August was always a blessing if it came early. Too late and the raisins would be vulnerable with the fruit spread on trays between the rows drying in the relentless San Joaquin Valley sun.

"Get up," he commanded himself. *Get the fuck up, and this time watch your step. You ain't the outfielder you once were. But you still got the instincts. So move your muscles. They still contain the cognition, that old natural-born knowledge. It don't ever go away.* "Get up, goddammit."

⸙⸙⸙

The raggedy man fled from Navo, arms flaying the dark. Something flew from his hand.

Navo caught him easily. Grabbing his shirt under his long, shaggy hair, he forced him to the earth, nearly tripping himself in the process. He gripped the man's shoulder and spun him around so he could see his face. Angered by the absurdity of the chase, he jerked the man to his feet.

"It is you," he said, "isn't it, Junior?"

The man confirmed nothing.

Navo shook him until he heard his teeth click under his beard. "God damn, man, I chased you enough times when we were kids to know it's you."

"Why am I the one always being chased?" Junior's voice came from years back, that same old questioning tone.

"You tell me."

"'Cause you sonsabitches think it's your purpose in life, I guess."

Navo released him. Vague sounds from the field drifted in the night. From back in the house's direction, his name—clearly Melanie's call from the porch—caused him to turn. There she was, buttoning her blouse over her breasts, her legs bare in the doorway's faint yellow light.

"It's okay," he told her, "I'll be back in a minute." Then to Junior, "What in Christ's name brings you out here this time of night?"

"I watch the house now and then."

"Do you? Under whose orders?"

"My old man's."

"What old man?"

"My father."

"Dave the Shave?" Navo recalled his mother telling him Junior's daddy looked just like the old movie star Victor Mature, that he was quite the ladies' man when he ran bets for Papa Boo. "Your daddy giving you orders from the grave?"

"Doesn't yours?"

A laugh rose in Navo's throat, ran through his tired limbs. Junior stepped back. His sour scent spread through the air as he moved, the whites of his eyes vivid in the dark.

"You never told me what that was you were carrying," Navo said.

A ghost-like figure stepped from the shed, no more than ten yards away. "What Junior carries is his own business." The voice was female, raw, and breathless. "And what I got in my hand, Mister Clipper, is my business."

"There, there, sugar," Junior sounded like he was soothing a child.

Navo saw her now. And he saw the weapon in her hand. Good Christ, wasn't it just minutes ago he was in bed with Melanie? The world, under the soft beat of night, had been as safe and unthreatened as he'd ever known it.

He lifted his palms in front of him. "No wait."

The first shot snapped at his right ear, same time as the pistol's percussion slammed the night. He swayed as if struck with a sudden, hard wind. There was the woman, so close to him he could smell her. She appeared ethereal, blondish, pale-skinned against the rust-black tool shed.

Taking aim again.

"Charlene!" Junior's voice was a wail.

"Navo!" Melanie screamed from behind him.

The second shot hit Junior as he stepped into her sightline. It sent his hair flying, his arm straight up as if in a salute. A shower of blood joined the rain that was coming down again.

Charlene screamed.

"No, Charlene. Honeybunch, no," Junior pleaded from the grass on Navo's left. His right arm stuck out in front of him, clawing at the inky night. Ruined at the elbow, it flopped like a broken wing.

Charlene was close enough, Navo read her madness. He saw the white knuckles of her shooting hand, the dark tip of her trigger finger.

"See?" Her words rushed out as the rain beat the tin structure behind her. "See what you've done, Clipper?" She was taking a bead on Navo once more, smacking her lips at the rain falling from the black sky. Her stringy hair was nearly as white as her one open eye.

Navo heard someone approach came from the leveled vineyard. The awkward cadence sounded familiar.

The voice was unmistakable. "Give us a look over here, Charlene. The man you're trying to gun down ain't Clipper."

Navo pivoted to see his brother. The cocky grin, the arrogant stance that challenged every God damned thing surrounding him.

"I'm Clipper," his brother said, "I'm the one you want."

Charlene got the shot off before Navo could reach her. In his peripheral vision, he saw Clipper go down.

∽∾∽

In the following minutes, Navo was aware of extracting the gun from Charlene's fingers, shoving it into her belly, and pulling the trigger. He heard no sound, other than a huff from her as she collapsed to her knees.

He cried out, his voice a raw screech as he stumbled toward Clipper's prone body. He lifted his brother's face from the soupy soil, saw his fluttering eyelids, and felt the warm blood gush onto his hands from the wound in Clipper's neck.

Navo's throat locked up as he tried to call Clipper's name, then he cradled the heavy head in his lap, bending over to umbrella the rain.

⌘⌘⌘

Clipper tried to speak to the conjured faces of his momma, of Clair, of Heather as they came into sharp focus. But he couldn't. Seeing the bleakness in his brother's eyes, he tried for words again but failed. What he wanted to say to Navo was, *"Now we're even."*

A little LeJeune humor that Navo wouldn't have laughed at. So maybe it was best it went unsaid. In a quick, surreal beat of time, Clipper felt François LeJeune's beard stubble, smelled his cologne as the man lifted him to snuggle faces. Heard his words. "Your younger brother's too much like your mother—not exactly a barrel of laughs."

One more thought came to him. This involved the closeness he felt to his father again, and his daddy's body appeared in a bright flash, his face flat against an oyster-shell road in the dead of a Louisiana night.

Clipper tried for a smile at Navo. Then he turned his own face into the dirt, thinking this was his chance to bring something else back to even.

He put his ear to the wet earth, and listened for the music to rise. Yeah, yeah.

e/ɔe/ɔ

Clipper's head slipped from Navo's hands and off his lap. He quickly lifted it and brought it close to his chest again as he searched for life in Clipper's half-opened eyes, those eyelashes black and wet in the pale oval of his face. Then Navo felt him shudder violently and his head once more lolled toward the very mud that had cooled their bare toes long ago in the irrigated rows.

Way back in those lazy summertimes, when the smell of grateful vines rode in the warm valley air.

CHAPTER 38

Navo had risen full of wrath from the place with Clipper, the spot where his brother's life had seeped away much like the place that had accepted their father's final heartbeat. For a moment, Navo had felt their father's presence, the wayward rambler right with them amid the rain, the blood, the senselessness of what seemed the trinity's destiny. So, yeah, he rose with fury and rage.

But soon after making sure no more death would ride the night, he went to Melanie. He went to her so desperately, with so much wanting that he feared he'd overwhelmed her. He didn't remember their exact words.

Had he told her he loved her, or had he asked that she save him? He'd watched as Melanie separated him from the police, demanded that he be allowed private time. Time alone with her.

Now, in a surreal zone that seemed to be much later, he felt the heated shower water pelt his shoulders and back, Melanie's fingers pressing points along his taunt muscles. When she finally shut off the current, they stood glistening in the bathroom window's light.

Her flesh sparkled much like it had that day at Montaña de Oro, when she and Joe had pulled him from the sea.

He placed his fingertips on her nipples. "All-star break."

Her eyes were huge, each orb reflecting his memory.

"So long ago on one hand," he said. "Like it never ended on the other."

"It never has."

"You understand?"

"Navo, I remember thinking that day how something had started, something I'd never be able to put an ending to." Her hair parted by the water showed a perfect line of scalp, lighter than her flesh color. Her hands landed again on his shoulders. "Come now, with me."

She led him into the bedroom, painted yellowish by sunlight. They began to dress. She'd found enough of Clipper's spare gear for him, and for her, a Club Aces shirt she'd turned up, and her pants, still damp and soiled.

In the kitchen Luke Kaminski had made them instant coffee. He'd also brought a bottle of Jim Beam down from the cupboard. They sat at a chrome and Formica dinette set, Navo thinking back when a Fresno furniture store had sent a truck out to repossess it, and Gloria LeJeune had run them off, the only weapon her black eyes.

Luke poured three shots of whiskey into glasses. They all downed it like it was prescribed medicine. Taking seats, they sat speechless with their coffee cups in front of them. In the window above the sink, the sun had broken through great cumulus clouds to turn the fields a glorious sienna.

At the other window, the swamp cooler chugged out musky air.

Luke raised his hand in a limp gesture toward Navo's face. "Looks like the bullet left its mark."

Navo nodded. "Shaved off my sideburn."

"Police have blocked every way in," Luke said, his voice soft in the stillness. "Even up there near that stand of black walnut trees." He puckered his mouth after a swallow of coffee. "Couple of them are still out there."

"Danny Triplett?"

"He's taken off."

Navo shuddered. "I thought for a while I'd killed the woman."

"No." Melanie said. "There were only three bullets in the gun."

"Junior?"

"Shot in the arm. Remember fixing the tourniquet?"

"Yes." He waited, not wanting his voice to break like glass. "I don't think Clipper suffered."

Her hand covered his on the table. "No. Paramedics assured us of that."

"I could tell he wanted to say something." He couldn't bring the words up, the message that Clipper might have been forgiving him. He wanted to say it aloud but could not.

Luke didn't give him the chance. "You two need to make any calls?"

"I've called Joe," Melanie said. "He and Keyes Haythorne are at my home in Nipomo."

"It happened too late for this morning's paper," Luke said. "But I'm sure it's on radio, TV, the Internet."

Navo had turned off his cell phone last night and couldn't remember now where the damn thing was. Thinking, Cyrus, Coach Bushmill, Tamara Bix, he knew he'd have to make the calls soon. "What time is it?"

"Nearing nine." Luke swung a glance around the room. "I've not seen a clock."

"Clipper never cared about time." Navo stood. "I've got to go now and tell my mother he didn't suffer. She needs to know that."

ↄ৩ↄ৩

Half the yard was blocked with crime-scene tape all the way up to the tool shed. Sun rays caught the shed's roof and parts of the old tractor that rested nearby. The ground where Clipper had fallen shone as if it has been washed. Navo got into the passenger side of Melanie's pickup, remembering something about last night.

"What did Junior throw away?"

"A camera." She buckled her belt and started the engine.

"That son of a bitch."

"Yes." She began to follow Luke, who was alone in his faded Cadillac. "The both of them, he and the girl, were out of their skulls on drugs."

They passed through a gauntlet of vehicles. A news team on foot followed them with cameras. On his side, close enough to touch, stood Margo Dalton, the beat writer from Sacramento, her fist in her teeth, her eyes hidden behind dark glasses. The sun ignited her red hair.

Melanie's cell phone rang. She checked the caller, placed it next to her.

He said, "Not Joe?"

"No." She turned onto Valley View, still following Luke. "If you want me too, I can stay until tomorrow."

"I do want that."

She turned to look him full in the face. "Then I'll have to get back to Joe."

"Sure."

"Maybe..." she hesitated.

"Maybe in San Francisco," he said "If you can work it." Thinking of returning to the team was like a tonic, a balm to his exhausted mind and body. "The minute after the funeral, I'm leaving."

She looked back at the road. Clouds had covered the sun. "Yes, that's probably the best thing you can do."

He wondered if it was raining in San Francisco. He wondered, looking at her, if she was closer to him or farther away since last night. "Pull over," he said. "Stop the car for a minute."

She slowed and stopped. It was warm in the cab, though the windows were down. The air coming in carried the smell of a fallow field on one side, an orchard the other. Blackbirds had found the scalding black top ahead. A squadron of white butterflies teased the windshield. He leaned across and tasted her lips. They both unbuckled and embraced, their panting in the profound silence combustive. Their scent grew heavy and thick, as sweet as opened fruit.

When they broke apart, she snapped on her belt, turned the air conditioner on full blast, and eased the truck off the road's shoulder. The blackbirds shooting above them weren't threatened—not a care—while he felt like he'd slid off the face of the world.

಼಼಼

In the apartment-like quarters above the garage, Navo watched Marty Fishman below, as he addressed the milling crowd of media people out in front of the house.

Behind Navo, his mother sprayed air freshener about the room. She'd changed into a nightgown and had wiped her face clean of cosmetics. She swooshed over to the other window that looked down at the pergola and pool area where earlier they'd assembled again, same as last evening. Minus Clipper.

"I had Luke fix this space up for himself," she said, casting a proud gaze over the furnishings. "Then the asshole doesn't move in." She paused. "Except to raid my kitchen and make a mess of my bedroom."

"Maybe he needs time to fully commit," Navo said lightly, hoping she'd smile.

"It's too late. I couldn't take him full time." Her face changed as if alarmed by a thought and she moved away. From behind, she appeared diminished, the set of her shoulders broken, her proud carriage devastated.

"Momma." Navo reached for her and placed a hand on her upper arm.

She yanked his hand across her bosom so that it cupped a breast, plush under the thin gown. She held his hand as if daring him to challenge her propriety. "Neither one of us should use this time to be confessing to each other."

He started to speak, thinking it would be easier now that she'd opened the moment for him.

"No," she said, squeezing his hand so that he felt his veins beating in her grip. "Please, Navo, I said no." Finally she relaxed her grasp and moved his hand to her neck, under her scented hair. "He outlived his father by five years," she said in a tight whisper. "But he couldn't find a better way to die."

"He took the bullet for me. I don't think I could die doing something like that."

She spun to face him, eyes wet, fathomed by times she'd shaken him in anger or soothed him when her mood was light. Then, with her back to him again, she peeked out of the window facing the street below.

"How do they carry those damn cameras around for hours like that?"

"It's what they do."

She snorted at his answer. Or was it a sob? "I won't see him until tomorrow," she said, still gazing out the window. "As I remember, he was clean shaven."

"Yes, he was."

"I hope so. Your father looked like he'd boycotted Gillette by the time they let me look at him." She adjusted the blinds so the window became opaque. When she turned around, her face astonished him, as if an artist had worked for hours to capture every nuance of her statuesque beauty. "Will you be okay?" she asked, one eyebrow high-arched, waiting for the truth.

"I'm okay."

"You're not going to let them break you?"

"No. Some of them are on our side."

At the door she gave the room a sweeping glance, then nibbled on a fingernail. "You know what he predicted?"

Navo put his hands in his pockets, lifted his shoulders, and waited.

"That Indian gaming and Internet gambling will spread like wildfire."

"It already has."

"That it's liable to burn us all alive was how he put it."

"He had a way of putting things."

"How much did he owe you?"

"What's that?"

"Don't play dumb," she snapped. "Dingers, how much?"

"What difference does it make now?"

"It's business."

"Not anymore."

"You're almost as tough as he was."

"Almost."

She sighed. "I'll tell Melanie that the room's ready."

"Thanks."

"A reporter gave Luke a copy of *Sports Illustrated*, said it was going to hit the newsstands tomorrow."

"Yeah?"

"A pretty redheaded reporter."

"Margo Dalton."

"She told me that you will be on the cover, swinging your bat."

"That's what I do," he said. "It just took me awhile to get it going."

୧୬୧୬

Melanie slept in spurts, popping awake at intervals to see Navo across the bed, transfixed in the blue gloom of muted TV images, the screen flickering endless highlights of the day's baseball games. She moved a leg so that her foot landed on his thigh. "This is the one where the guy throws the ball away at first base, and two runners score." She kicked him hard enough to rouse him. "This is the fifth time you've watched it that I know of."

"Sorry." A click and darkness snuffed the screen.

"The Giants lost, no matter how many times they replay it," she said.

"You're right."

The strange room presented shadows that she made into defined shapes, some of them human, but non-threatening. She counted his breaths in the manner she'd often measured waves, her own body afloat, adrift beyond the break. Feeling the swells lift her, then drop her just before the rescinding roar.

She thought of how earlier today Neil's voice mail had threatened her. "I'll contact the authorities," his voice had warned. "This unsavory mess you're putting my son through must end."

She hadn't mentioned this to Navo. And wouldn't now. She'd contact Walker Gustine for help. She couldn't risk losing Joe over all this. Joe. She mentally drew his face on the gray ceiling. She had to get back to him. Staying here longer wouldn't help Navo. She could tell. He'd become silent, withdrawn into a place apart from her.

"I've got to leave in the morning."

His tone startled her. "I understand."

She turned onto her side. "You want me to get closer?"

"That's okay."

God, what was on his mind? Was he spooling scenes of his brother and him? Repeated images much like those he'd been watching on the TV screen? Endless scenarios that played like flame from a thousand memories? After some time she felt him thrash, twist in the bed, his breath on her face. She wrapped a hand over his shoulder, patted his flesh.

"No," he said.

She withdrew her hand.

"Not like that." His voice sounded blood-filled, almost like a growl. "I want you to touch me like a lover, if you will."

"I will."

"Like a lover."

"Yes, Navo," she said, "Like a lover."

CHAPTER 39

On the drive to San Francisco Monday morning, Navo was jerked out of deep thought by Tamara Bix's harsh voice. "I said, hitter, that it was big of the Fresno Police Department to drop all charges against you and your brother."

"Real fucking big."

"You ready if Domingo Matta puts you in the line-up tomorrow night?"

He dug a hand into the small ice chest between his feet, grabbed his third bottled water since leaving Fresno, and looked at Bix's pigtail and Margo Dalton's soft reddish hair. "You mean there's a fucking chance he might not?"

Bix drove on, looking unperturbed. She'd been taking charge of him since yesterday's quick services for Clipper. His mother, while uncharacteristically gracious, had refused to treat the affair as a celebration of her firstborn son's life.

She'd accepted respectful condolences and that was all. No funny stories, no maudlin reminiscing, and please, no tears. Navo had quickly concluded she wanted the real grieving to belong to her alone.

The jag swerved, and then smoothed out. "Fucking cowboy," Bix growled at the driver ahead of them. "Can't handle a ten-foot trailer."

Margo swiveled to send him a smile. "Okay back there?"

He guzzled water. "Still some noise in my right ear."

Wasn't much of a wound where the bullet had grazed him, but a sound much like you'd hear putting a shell to your ear wouldn't go away. Jesus, he'd been thirsty since Melanie had left yesterday morning. Hungry too. And hearing a roar in his head since she'd driven away in her red pickup.

Nearing the Bay Bridge, he felt uneasy. Here he was again. Right back in the eye of the storm, the pass they'd given him for a couple of days no longer in effect. Maybe he should have followed Bix's advice and not read any papers, not turned on the radio or watched TV.

He said to her, "I thought Taggart was a friend of yours."

Her shoulders squared as she stared straight ahead. "Now what?"

"Taggart's piece in this morning's *Chronicle*."

"In Taggart's defense, he had to mention it. Doesn't mean he invented it."

"I haven't enough troubles, now I'm on the juice? What was the stimulant he mentioned?"

"Modafil. If you'd read it carefully, you'd know Taggart gave little credence to it."

"Guess I missed that part."

"Easy."

"Fuck you, easy." Jesus, would this bridge ever end? There's Alcatraz out there, the island sunny today. He put on Ray Bans to hide his eyes. "Unnamed sources," he said. "What kind of shit is that?"

Margo gave him a look, her green eyes sympathetic. "He's keeping up with the others, but his slant is skeptical. He's in your corner, Navo."

'He made it sound like I got the stuff in June when they sent me down. To increase my bat speed."

"He said there was no credible evidence."

"But still it's out there. Fucking lie, but it's out there." Thinking of Clipper, he felt a swift pain deep in his gut, deeper, like it was in his soul. "My brother isn't dead forty-eight hours and the bastard has him juicing me up on steroids nobody has even heard of."

Tamara Bix's profile brightened as she admired the San Francisco skyline. "Look there, Navo. Isn't coming home grand?"

"Fucking lies," he repeated. Margo Dalton looked over her shoulder at him. He challenged her eyes. "Always heavier in print than the truth."

"Well, don't be getting your honker out of shape again," Bix ordered. "We'll need it for endorsements."

While she fought the traffic, he tried to clear his mind. But he couldn't push away his grief. It was deep and cold, causing that old tremor to find his hands again. And Melanie—those swooning thoughts of her came like the sensation of falling.

"Tell me again what Bushmill told you," Bix said.

"That he'd decided to have surgery." Navo remembered how the coach had paced his hospital room this morning, more upset with Clipper's murder than his own medical problems. "He wanted to put off surgery but his doctor said no."

"More reason we win this upcoming series with the Dodgers."

"Shit, that who we're playing?"

Bix burst out with her merry laugh. "Now don't you go taking that as extra pressure."

"Oh hell no," he said, trying for a grin and missing it. "I won't do that."

ᘒᗡᘒᗡ

"Nine ball, corner pocket." Navo chalked his cue stick, leaned across the felt, set his bridge, and stroked. Missed the shot and cursed.

"Nine ball in the side." Vince Vitucci knocked it dead in the side pocket, grinned, and began to rack 'em up. "Who else wants a piece of me?"

Cyrus took the stick from Navo, slid it back and forth through his thick fingers. "Challenger breaks."

"Winner breaks," Vince said, and bam! The balls scattered.

Navo joined Luke Kaminski at the kitchen's counter and fingered Asian food into his mouth from an array of open cardboard containers.

"Thanks for coming, Luke."

"You couldn't keep me away."

"You got tickets for tomorrow?"

"Got 'em."

Not a word about Gloria, except to say she was coping. Doing her best with Clair and Heather to get through the days, suffer the nights since Clipper's death. Navo watched Bix struggle with a coffeemaker. He was bone-tired.

Time he turned in, but he feared what his dreams might bring. He joined Margo, who had said little to him since the drive from Fresno. Hunched over her laptop at the small table off the kitchen, she looked up.

"You about ready to run most of us out of your apartment?" she asked.

"Nah." He knew everyone was there to support him, keep him occupied 'til nightfall. Cyrus and Luke had already put their gear in the other two bedrooms. He nodded at Margo's laptop. "You ever get tired of this stuff?" He moved a hand above her work. "The daily struggle?"

"Not when it's like this." She took off her glasses, pinched her nose, and regarded her screen. "I'll print out some stuff you should look at later." She smiled. "And Tamara says your in-basket's full of mail."

He looked for Bix, saw her at the pool table where she'd evidently talked her way into the game. Yeah, she handled her stick like she was a natural.

"The world has latched onto you," Margo said. "You have no idea of the magnitude."

She put her glasses back on, made a fuss about her vision bothering her. He was astounded to see that tears had streaked her cheeks. A pool ball slammed a pocket. Bix cheered. Vitucci moaned. Playing a game to lighten the moment for him, he knew, while tomorrow's contest gnawed at the evening like a living beast.

He asked Margo, "Can you put any of this into words?"

"Why don't you try and help me?"

"We're just kids playing a game," he said. "Tell 'em that."

"Nobody will believe it. To most people you're both mythical and mystical. Even those who don't follow the game. Take it away? Close the ballparks? People will feel violated. At least in this country."

"Other places too. Trust me, I've been to a lot of them."

"See?" She blew her nose into a tissue. "You agree with me." Her green eyes glistened with moisture. "I look at your world and marvel how simple it is."

"Like I said, we're just a bunch of kids."

"You measure all the cities you're fortunate to visit by how much cyber and video equipment is available in your hotel suites." She took a deep breath. "And the women you invite into your rooms."

He waited, knowing there was more. Hell, he could write the script.

"The half of you who bother to register, vote Republican. And you cheer pre-emptive war and invasions, yet none of you have fought for your country and never will."

"But we're both mythical and mystical."

"And you're multi-millionaires on top of it."

"Not all of us."

She gasped as if hit in the stomach. "Oh, my god." She reached for his hand. "You don't need this right now."

"And we're pampered."

Her fingers squeezed his. "Spoiled as hell."

His apartment phone rang on the kitchen's counter. Bix answered, listened, and said to Cyrus, "A Ms. Golumbewski is down in the lobby."

"A who?"

"A Ms. Maxine Golumbewski." Bix's canted eye found Navo. "Says she has a raincoat to deliver."

"That be Maxine the suit lady," Cyrus grinned. "Send her on up."

"Damn," Navo said, "I was starting to believe my fog cutter was never going to make it."

CHAPTER 40

Navo saw batting Coach Blair Farraday and Manager Domingo Matta studying him through the screen as he took batting practice. Behind them, the entire home plate area had been roped off to contain the bulging press and television membership and their many species of cameras.

It took time, but Navo began to get his eye back. Then his stroke smoothed out, and the ball soon began to fly off his bat and soar deep into the afternoon haze.

He asked for more.

Matta agreed.

Navo crossed over to the other batter's box. Swinging right-handed, he showed equal power. Early arriving fans cheered as one of his drives struck the fence in left field. When another carried into the blue seats beyond left-center's 382 mark, the crowd behind the ropes danced about in a kind of wild hoedown.

He hit another over the fence then strode from the cage. The mob parted for him, their faces as rapt in the sun as his.

Man, they'd probably think his bat was a weapon the way he carried it with him, wringing its handle in his gloved hands, waving its barrel back and forth as he marched. Would they wonder if he could be on—what's the shit called—Modafil? Yeah, like he was juiced to the fucking gills. He found himself grinning. Somebody better get a piss sample, the way he felt right now.

He stopped, faced the cameras.

Waited for someone, anyone, to mention that his streak, since it had been interrupted, shouldn't count. Rulebook said his streak was alive until he failed to hit in a game where he had at least one official turn at bat. Yeah, he'd heard of streaks that had spanned seasons. The way the grandstands were filling up, the way they'd began to rock as he started to jog, he'd give odds most people agreed with him.

❧❧❧

Navo glanced up. Cyrus, who'd been charting pitches with Coach Littlejohn near the phones, strolled the length of the dugout to sit next to him. The Giants, down two to one, hadn't gotten to the Dodgers pitcher Dennis Holcomb, and it was getting late.

Navo hadn't touched Holcomb his first two times at bat. And he was due up third this inning. They watched Josiah Swain step into the box as a pinch hitter.

"Holcomb's having his way," Cyrus said, his voice soft and soothing. "But he's tipping' his slider." His eyes narrowed to slits as he studied the opposing pitcher. "There. You see him giving his Roger Clemens impression, lookin' over his glove at Swain? Now watch, see if he goes into his windup, or if he wait and look into his glove a second."

Navo looked out to the mound. Holcomb stared at Swain. Went into his windup.

"Fastball," Cyrus said before Holcomb's release.

Cyrus was right. Fastball, high and tight, Swain leaned back and watched it zip under his nose. Holcomb stared in again, this time dipping his head a bit. Shit, there it was. A pause to look into his glove. Maybe just to blink. *Maybe to change his grip on the ball.*

"Here come his slider," Cyrus said.

He was right again.

Swain swung, missed.

Another pitch. Cyrus called it. "Fast ball."

Swain let it come in at ninety five on the inside corner for strike two.

Holcomb's third pitch was another fast ball. Swain caught up to it and slammed it into centerfield for a single.

"Holcomb's burned," Cyrus said, with an amused chuckle. "He'll be using that slider more, you can bet."

"Yeah?" Navo rose from the bench. "I'm on deck."

"Then grab yo' bat."

"I intend to."

"And watch that mothafucka's eyes, see if he don't try and slip a fastball by you, his first pitch."

৩৩৩

After Thoroughgood popped up, Navo made his way toward the plate. The crowd's roar swept down from all the decks like a cyclone. The sky had turned indigo. The lights, blazing now, gave the field a bright, surreal blush. In the left-handed batter's box, he dug in, watching

Holcomb's eyes all the time. Yeah, he could see the right-hander's irises, fiery as a madman's.

The Dodgers pitcher never once averting his gaze from the catcher's target, dropped his glove away from his face and began his leg stride.

Fastball.

The stubborn son of a bitch was throwing a first-pitch fastball to a man on a fifty-five-game hitting streak.

Make that fifty-six.

Navo took off as the ball found that seam between the outfielders in left centerfield. He made the turn at first base, just like Clipper had taught him when they were kids. He never slowed, for the choice to stretch the hit into a double must be made at full speed.

Yeah. Two more seconds of full-out sprint, and he hit the dirt. With one smooth motion, he completed his stand-up slide, beating the tag by that measure of time designed just for this game.

This perfect game. Every perfect inch of it.

CHAPTER 41

On the edge of sleep, Navo fell into a dream.

He was running down Magazine Street with Clipper. They confronted a funeral march, old black men in their Sunday clothes, women twirling umbrellas to the beat of a brass band.

The dream flickered, and they were dodging a bright green cable car, tooling along St. Charles Street, all the way down to the Carrollton District, where endless trees shaded them from the sun.

Clipper waved, yelled for him to catch up. "Daddy's burning barbecue and squeezing music down by the levee."

Navo ran as fast as he could. Breezes filled with fragrances of magnolia and oak trees blew tender against his face. His heart was bursting. He had never been this happy.

သသ

He awakened to lay motionless, not fully trusting the coming day, and listened for the sound of his protectors. He heard the unique tread of Cyrus's bare feet in the hall. Navo got up, stretched, and headed down the hallway. Stopped to check on Luke, who was still asleep, his long frame crossways on the bed. He greeted Cyrus in the kitchen, the smell of Asian carry-out food still in the close air. Dawn brightened the windows' rectangles,

Navo smiled. "Nice boxer shorts."

"Big and Tall." Cyrus had found the remains of a smoothie he'd concocted last night. He held the chilled glass forth to Navo.

"Pass," Navo said. "But thanks for the offer." He watched Cyrus drain the drink. "How's the arm?" He checked the right-hander's eyes for anxiety. Today was his turn to pitch.

Cyrus's eyes appeared ghostly but calm. "Tolerable."

"Numbness in your hand?"

Cyrus flexed his fist. "Not bad."

"Must be time for one of Bix's toe-jobs."

Cyrus sat on a barstool, three hundred pounds of deep burgundy muscle. "They asked me yesterday, do I want some Kanye West on the clubhouse music today."

"You tell 'em they do and Shawn Temple will have their ass?"

"They asked me what you'd like."

"You tell 'em?"

"Told 'em you weren't pitching, wasn't your call, the music we play."

"That's true."

"Told 'em you could find your own music somewheres else."

"Is that so?"

"They picked up my Corey Harris CD before I could stop 'em. Said we'd have to listen to that today."

"We can make that work."

"Say we will."

Sunlight slanted into the apartment, illuminated the many e-mails and printouts on the pool table's felt surface. Navo stared at the clutter, the strewn messages that spoke of his worth.

"You okay, Bossa?" Cyrus asked.

"I'm coming around."

"I've noticed."

"Don't mean I'm about to start going to church."

"Lord no," Cyrus said. "It don't mean that."

🙙🙛🙙

Bix arrived with a huge bag and prepared coffee, making a production out of the task, mumbling how she had blended the beans, ground them herself. "So know when you drink this brew some time has gone into it, hitter."

Luke pulled up a stool and joined him at the counter. "Your mother called again," he said, buttoning up his striped dress shirt. "She said not to bother you this time. I guess Clair and Heather need her a lot right now."

Navo nodded. He and Luke had always been able to communicate with few words. "I'll call her." After the game, yeah. He'd call.

Margo was next to show up, slipping through the apartment's door like she was one step ahead of a posse. In minutes, she was keying more of Navo's life into her laptop's keyboard. At his side, Bix slid documents under his elbow, and demanded he sign them with a ballpoint pen she stuck between his fingers. After a quick glance at the copy in the documents, he scrawled his signature on the pages. There was talk of Twitter, and Navo waved the subject away. Shit, Even Bix with Margo's help had trouble keeping up with Facebook.

Again Bix needed his signature. Again his pen scratched a contract. "I didn't spell my name right," he said. "In case you screwed me."

Her odd eyes winked wickedly. "You just earned a million dollars, you sweet son of a bitch." She cackled. "And I didn't do too bad myself."

Navo tried to resist the feeling that he'd committed a crime. "That easy, eh?"

"You'll have to shave in front of a camera."

He rubbed his stubble. "Maybe after tonight's game."

For a moment it was if everything had halted. Luke, Bix, Margo, and Cyrus, who'd just come down the hallway, became a still picture with Navo LeJeune. Why? Because what he'd said about the oncoming game was the first inference anyone had made to his streak in days. Sure it was a weak one. Something mentioned that you had to be turning your ear to understand its meaning.

"Fucking streak," he said.

Bix jumped up and down, evangelistically, her face rabid with mad joy. "Streak on, streak on you streaking motherfucker."

Margo had closed her eyes, a million secrets behind her lids, pale against her deep blush. "Streak," she whispered.

Cyrus danced around the pool table with the weightless agility of a taxi dancer. "Talkin' about some streak here," he sang in a voice so heavy with soulful timbre, Navo reckoned Manheim the security guard in the lobby far below could feel the vibrations. "We talkin' some streak now, children."

Luke turned his head up and howled, "Streak!" He sprang off his stool and joined Bix in a cool version of some long lost jitterbug, paying no mind to his tin knee and jump-started heart.

Maxine Golumbewski walked in on them soon after they'd settled into quieter, more reserved moods. She, like the other two women, possessed a kind of conspiratorial glow, though all three were dressed down and were wearing minimal makeup.

Maxine handed Navo a page she'd evidently torn from a magazine. "Is this the suit you said was so sharp?"

Navo examined the tear sheet. He read from the page. "*Esquire's* five-thousand-dollar wardrobe."

"You still like it?"

"Sure I do."

"It's the Versace one, with the faint taupe pinstripes on steel gray."

"By God, it sure is."

"I ordered the whole outfit." Maxine rose up on her toes, settled back down. "Told my Hong Kong tailor to copy it all thread by thread. It doesn't show it in the ad, but I'm having shoes made to match, some Cesare Etros. Size eleven, right?"

"Right."

"And don't worry about the cost," Maxine said. Pretty golf-cart-girl standing proud. "Just tell 'em where you got it."

"I can't let you do this."

Bix interceded, waving her arms like a referee calling time out. "Get used to it, hitter," she said. "Take it while you can, 'cuz nothing lasts forever."

The group was silent, as if time had again halted its march. Then Cyrus took a long step to stand facing him. "You ready, cousin?"

"Is it about that time?"

"It's getting there."

Still half-dressed, they embraced in the center of the room. It came to Navo, while in the hug of his friend, that this moment right here was what he should have experienced years ago, before the years had taken the shine off everything.

Maybe it wasn't too late.

He didn't let go of Cyrus's huge shoulders immediately but stretched the moment and basked in it as if it was his only connection to the human race.

CHAPTER 42

The clubhouse rocked to Corey Harris's blues beat as Navo prepared for the field. Thoroughgood, from a few lockers away, danced in the aisle with a subtle L.A. street corner bop step. Vince Vitucci moonwalked past him in trade for a grin. Marvin Riggins shuffled some Detroit city jive. Cruzamonte and Canderos flashed their mambo, Shawn Temple his Texas two-step, and Suzuki Ogata his kabuki.

Navo tuned into the beat.

His own dance contained a mix of rapture and fury. Homage, he was sure, to his father and to Clipper, it lasted no longer than a collective held breath here among these many spectators. Coming to a stop, he accepted his teammates' cheers, knowing his dance, though influenced by family legacy, had contained a certain one-of-a-kind quality.

For sure it had. Cyrus gave him a look that confirmed it.

❧❧❧

Melanie followed Joe to the section above third base, her mind still swimming from the turmoil the two of them had experienced since arriving this morning in San Francisco. Joe had said it best when he'd opened his arms wide the moment they made their way out of the hotel this morning.

"The Day of the Bat. The Day of LeJeune."

It had been the week of LeJeune, his figure six-stories high greeting them on the side of a building their first moment in the city. A city she loved had become a hive, buzzing about her lover. Navo's name had caused a steady whir in the wind, everybody moving to it in a kind of ecstatic dream.

Finally in their seats, she allowed the vast stadium to posses her. God, she thought, it was more than a theater, it was an empire filled with fanatics. Shocked by both its feeling of community and its serene vastness, she sat silent, almost reverent as she tried to find Navo somewhere in the brightness.

"Tell me when you see him, Joe," she said, trying to pitch her voice above the crowd.

A roar rose at that moment. Jesus, she thought, all hell had broken loose. The world had slipped off its axis, and she had to stand against its rocking She turned to see her boy, taller than she now, but still a boy. His face was flushed, eyes sparkling in the combustion of sun and electric light.

He was telling her without speaking, for voices now were impossible to discern against the thunder, that she would find Navo easily enough. He'd be the one separated from the others.

The one, on this particular day, at this particular time, who would be playing for the dreams of millions of people, even people like her who'd never seen a game in person before. Extend his streak or not, break DiMaggio's mark or not, this moment had taken everything her lover had to give in order to make it this far.

Art could do that, she'd realized early on. It could take and take and take. It could hurt, it could wound, it could leave you empty. But if you loved it enough, loved the idea of it, the performing of it, the combativeness of it, you might find a way to kick its ass, put your name on it forever.

God, there he was, running out on to the field, one more time for the challenge, his hat off for a beat or two as he raised it to the stands, his hair flowing in the unreal turbulence, where the roar was strangely lost to the blood rush in her ears, giving Melanie a bit of time with him alone, just the two of them for a second together in a space apart from all else.

∾⋘∾

Navo had caught Melanie's eye in the first inning when he'd come to the plate under thunderous applause and lined a drive that Dodgers centerfielder Hap Zenimura had caught. He'd found her again during the game, her brilliant features repeated on Joe's face next to her.

The sight of them, their singularity, in that moment had mesmerized him. His artist lady, her first Major League ball game. Her son cupping his hand to his mouth, explaining the game into her ear.

Once, when the action on the field had lapsed, he'd played a little movie in his head about the future, where, arm in arm with Melanie, he pointed out to Joe a plaque on the Giants History Walk where his name had been immortalized in next year's opening day's lineup.

Melanie faced the sea, where pelicans dove at glints of sun on the water, the scene mirrored in her eyes. R.L. Bushmill, striding with them, squinted at the tall palms guarding the Ferry Terminal ahead.

As they paraded the airy promenade, Navo teased the coach about a World Series just played, kidding that they might need another to equate a remembered carnival ride he'd made with Lil Alston.

Navo shook away the feeling of panic that could come after slipping into that solitary moment of escape needed before facing the red hot reality of the game. He'd swung the bat well all afternoon but was yet to find a hole in the Dodgers defense. Cyrus was pitching a masterpiece tonight, so it looked as though this at bat in the eighth would be his last chance to extend his streak.

Waiting to be announced as the batter, he watched as another quick series of images spooled in front of his mind's eye. It was early in September. The team was in New York for three with the Mets, and he'd made it to the gallery in Manhattan where Melanie was exhibiting.

In the center of the gallery, her paintings looming behind them on the walls, they embraced. She told him how she'd been hoping he'd make it.

He asked her if she liked his suit, not admitting right off that it was a fake Versace.

✿❀✿

Wind off the Bay blew through the stadium with its odd swirl out in right field. Clouds formed over the park, but the combination of sun and electric lights was brilliant on the batters' box as Navo stepped up to bat right-handed.

The crowd greeted his appearance at the plate with such a roar he quickly muted it by sheer will so he could find his stance.

A peacefulness had found him earlier today. Landing on his tight shoulders, it felt far different than the awful weight of loneliness. Basking in it now, he pointed his bat at the Dodgers left-hander and then cocked it behind his right ear.

Everything was suddenly windless, soundless, just the breathing of catcher and umpire behind him.

Navo's breath was silent in his chest, but as perfect as the season's calendar, one game following the other, and it by yet another—all in mystical clarity that matched, he'd give you odds, the endless stars, the deep tides, the very spinning of the earth.

THE END

About the Author

Larry Hill is a writer and artist. He was the winner of New York University's 2010 Goldenberg Award for Fiction (final judge, Gail Godwin), and his short story collection was shortlisted for the William Saroyan International Prize for Fiction. His stories, two of which have been nominated for Pushcart Prizes, have appeared in numerous literary journals. He is based in California's Central Valley, and his work tends to focus on the hardscrabble characters of that neglected landscape.